REALMS OF EMOTIONS

By
N.L. Beam

PublishAmerica
Baltimore

Softcover 9781629071749
PUBLISHED BY PUBLISHAMERICA, LLLP
www.publishamerica.com
Baltimore

Printed in the United States of America

CHAPTER ONE

JANUARY 11, 1992

"Okay Carol, get me a suture kit, and give Mr. Nichols twenty milligrams of Demerol, and why haven't you checked Mr. Nichols' vital signs yet? That's not like you to forget such a routine thing." Doctor Kelly brazenly scolded Carol, which was totally out of his character.

Carol's lip quivered and her eyes filled with tears. Her bottled up emotions were starting to come to the surface, like a dam about to burst.

"Are you all right Carol? I'm sorry for snapping at you like I did, I realize that you're having personal problems, but you're going to have to keep your mind on your job."

"I'm sorry Doctor Kelly." Carol replied. She knew that she had been neglecting her duties, but her job was the least of her worries, and besides, no one at the hospital seemed to care about what she was going through.

"Okay! Mr. Nichols we're going to get you all fixed up for you can be on your way."

The night was an extremely busy one in the emergency ward. Carol had been too busy for her to be mulling over her problems in her melancholy life.

With only ten minutes left to go in her seven to seven shift, she was completely exhausted, mentally as well as physically.

The hospital was a haven for her. She just didn't know what kind of horror that would be waiting for her at home.

Carol walked out of the room and almost walked right into Nancy from the maternity ward. They were very close friends.

"Girl, you look like death warmed over." Nancy blurted out.

"I feel like death warmed over." Carol replied.

"Do you want to talk about it, kiddo?" Nancy asked sympathetically.

"Thanks Nancy, it's nice to see that someone cares around here." Carol said, trying to keep her emotions in check.

"Well I care kiddo. What are we waiting around here for? Our shift is over ... come on, I'll walk you to your car."

"So, did you leave that son-of-a bitch yet? I tell ya, if he were my husband, I would have killed the bastard." Carol didn't even give her an answer. She had enough violence in her life and the last thing she wanted to hear was talk about killing someone. Carol just gave her a hollow smile then turned away and walked toward her car.

She unlocked her brand new Mustang and sat in the sequestered front seat. Carol relished the tranquility.

Driving down Lake shore Road with the morning sun warming her jaded face, she reached over and turned the radio on. The forty-five minute drive to her Cedar Rapids, North Carolina home was the only serene time that she had experienced lately.

As she pulled into her Collins Avenue driveway, her pulse quickened,and she began to tremble. She closed the car door so delicate as not to even arouse a tiny sparrow that was perched on a tree not more than ten feet away. She walked up the stairs, stuck the key into the lock, and entered the house. She removed her shoes then peeked into the master bedroom.

She seen that her husband Lloyd was sound asleep. She gently closed the bedroom door, and breathed a sigh of relief. She slipped off her nurses dress, white stockings, her bra and panties. She sauntered to the bathroom to take her daily rejuvenating shower.

The warm water trickled down her body and soothed the tension on her one hundred and two pound frame,which made her feel almost human again.

Suddenly she heard the squeak of the bathroom door opening. Fright took over her once placid mind. A hand violently broke through the shower curtain and took a strangle hold of her by the throat. He dragged her out of the shower in a fit of rage.

"What the fuck are you doing in the shower when you know I have to get my sleep? You know I work late! That phone rang off the fucking hook, waking me up, while your lazy fucking ass was in the shower!" Carol shook profusely. Trying to calm him down, she said, "I'm sorry sweetheart, I wasn't thinking. It won't happen again ... I promise."

"That's not good enough bitch!" Lloyd yelled out.

He walked toward the bedroom, then turned around and walked back to Carol. He gave a viscous punch right between her eyes, knocking her to the floor.

As she laid there dazed, he gave her a swift vicious kick in the ribs. She moaned in pain, curled up defenseless on the floor.

"Now, I don't want to even hear a peep. Do you hear me, bitch?" Carol wasn't able to respond. The kick had knocked the wind out of her. Lloyd stepped over her and went storming back into the bedroom, slamming the door.

CHAPTER TWO

JUNE 1991

Carol Crawford was on her knees, in the weed infested garden. Her portable CD player was playing "Blowin' in the Wind," by Bob Dylan. The begonias, marigolds and roses were fully in bloom. Their beauty, camouflaged by the overbearing and unsightly weeds.

Carol, was an easy going young woman at twenty five. She had a real zest for life. She was very strong willed, but too passive, and a little too naive.

Carol was diagnosed of having bipolar, a mood disorder, in which she refused to believe it.

She was just over six feet tall, with a hour glass figure, Her silky blond hair was just past her shoulder. She was single; and very attractive. She would make any man's head turn as she walked by.

Carol had graduated at the top of the class at Dorothy Winston's School of Nursing. She worked as an ER nurse at the Westwood General Hospital.. She worked there for over five years.

She lived with her parents, Jason and Jean Crawford, who were in their mid-sixties. They could not even remember the last time that they had any kind of quarrel or conflict with their daughter. She was a parent's dream.

"Is that how you're going to spend your day off, honey?" Her mom was carrying a tray of sandwiches and a pitcher of lemonade. Carol got to her feet from weeding the garden, and said, "Oh Mom, you're timing is great. I sure could use a break."

They sat on the front porch talking to each other as they ate their lunch, not in a manner of mother and daughter, but as two best friends would. They were a very close knit family.

"I'm meeting Garry after his shift. He's taking me out to dinner and a movie."

"Well that's nice, dear." Her mom said with a smile.

Carol jubilantly jumped up as soon as she seen her dad's station wagon turn into the driveway.

"Hey dad, how did you do today?" She yelled out as he got out of the car.

"Hi pumpkin," he said, gleefully. "It was sure hot out there today I tell ya, but I did pretty good. I shot a couple of birdies, but that wasn't good enough to beat Cliff." He was grinning from ear to ear. He was always a happy go-lucky man, always smiling.

"Awe Dad, I think you just let him win."

"No pumpkin, I just let him keep score." He jokingly replied. They had a good laugh.

Jason walked up to the porch and gave his wife a kiss on her cheek, and gave Carol an affectionate caress on her shoulder.

"Going to take a shower, girls." He said as he opened the front door of the house.

No sooner did the screen door snap shut, Carol stood up from her chair and she briskly walked to the station wagon and removed her dad's golf clubs from the back seat.

The clubs weighed in excess of twenty pounds. Carol in her hundred-and-twenty-pound frame, barely managed to haul them up the stairs and into the house.

"Carol you are so thoughtful, what would we ever do without you?" Her mother praised her.

Carol took a shower and got ready to meet her best friend Garry at the restaurant.

Carol and Garry sat at a corner table in the Cassadora Restaurant, chatting as they looked over the menus.

Garry, a twenty-five year old energetic man, who was also a nurse, on the opposite shift of Carol's. He stood six-five. He was a very handsome man, with a great sense of humor.

He was a homosexual. That really bothered Carol, not from him being gay, but he was a man of her dreams. She would marry him in a minute.

He volunteered a couple days a week for the Westwood Crisis and Suicide Intervention Center. He manned the phone and befriended anyone who needed someone with a good ear to listen to all their dilemmas that life had cast upon them. Some were just lonely and needed a link to the outside world. Some were suicidal.

Garry and Carol had been best friends since high school.

He was her savior. He was the one who Carol could turn to when she was feeling blue. Garry could make anyone laugh no matter what their frame of mind was. He had a quirky sense of humor.

"How was your day in the ER, sweetie?" Garry asked.

"Don't ask, it was brutal, it was like a mad house the whole shift. Two D.O.A.'s from a car accident and as usual, Betty was her usual bitchy self. Okay ... let's not talk shop anymore, okay honey?"

"Okay, sweetie."

"Have you decided what you're going to order yet?" Garry asked.

"Yes, I think I'll have the fish and chips special. with a diet coke."

Garry's eyes sparkled, and with a big smile, he said, "I think I'll have the same, except for the diet coke. You know, Carol, you need that diet coke like I need two heads."

Carol's face was beaming from what Garry had said.

The waiter was a tall slim man with a long pony tail.

"May I take your order?" He asked, arrogantly, he was very obnoxious.

"Yes, I'll have the fish and chips special with a die... a regular coke"

"I'll have the same sunshine." Garry mocked the obnoxious waiter, which made Carol's face turn red as a beet.

"Excuse me?" The waiter asked, with a stern look on his face.

"I'll have the same, please". Garry repeated.

When the waiter took the order, he walked away with his nose to the air, Carol bursted out in laughter.

Carol's eyes were fixed on Garry. She was completely tuned out in deep thought. She was thinking of how he would be a wonderful husband. He was so kind and loving, and was such an uplifting person to be with, and so good looking too. But if only, if only ... she thought to herself.

"Carol ... You-hoo" She snapped out of her trance.

"Where were you? You were way off in 'Disney Land'. What were you thinking about?"

"Oh sorry, nothing ... really.." She could feel herself blushing.

"Do you want anything for dessert, honey?" She asked, changing the subject.

"No, thanks sweetie, lets hit the road."

Jason and Jean, Carol's parents were sitting at the kitchen table having a cup of tea when Carol walked in.

"Hi hon, how was your evening?" Jean asked.

"Oh it was just great ... we had a wonderful time."

"That's nice, dear." Her mom, said with a big smile.

"How's Garry doing, pumpkin? We haven't seen him in a while." Her dad asked.

"He's fine, Dad, you should have heard him in the restaurant. He was so funny. He had me laughing so hard that I almost wet myself." Carol's face was beaming with merriment as she explained about Garry's antics.

"He's quite the character pumpkin. You two have been together for a long time now."

"Yes, we've been friends for a long time, dad." Carol replied.

"Well, don't you think that it's about time that you guys made a commitment? Garry would make a fine husband and a great son-in-law too."

Carol knew that her parents would bring this up sooner or later. She only wished that she would have explained things to them sooner about her and Garry's relationship.

Her parents always loved Garry.

Carol pulled out the chair and sat down. "Mom, Dad, you know I love Garry very much, and you're absolutely right, Garry would make a perfect husband. There isn't any other man in the world that I would want to marry, but I don't think there's any chance of us ever marrying. I'm sorry I didn't tell you sooner, I figured you knew that Garry and I were just good friends ... and ..." Carol paused. "Garry's gay."

Jason and Jean sat there expressionless. Carol squirmed in her seat.

"Oh. I see." Jason said. He went quiet for a moment, scratched the back of his head, then said. "Well, that explains a lot. I hope that you weren't afraid to tell us that, thinking that we would feel any different toward him." Carol could feel her face turning red and felt a little guilty.

"Oh no, not at all. I just didn't think it would make any difference, that's all."

Jason stood up and put his arms around her and said, "Well it doesn't change any of our feelings toward Garry, right Jean?" Jean just smiled and nodded, giving Carol some support.

"That's right we still love him just as much as we always did. Don't worry dear, nothing could ever change our feelings about Garry; you know he's a big part of this family and will be for a long time to come."

The tension in Carol's shoulders released, and the guilt escaped her mind.

"You are the best parents anyone could have ... thanks for understanding." Carol was so proud that she had such accepting parents.

She never told anyone else that Garry was gay.

CHAPTER THREE

"You idiot!" Carol yelled out at the unyielding driver as he sped through the stop sign, narrowly missing her.

"That's just great, he goes through the stop sign, almost hits me, and gives me the finger!" She held her fist up in disgust and yelled out.

Carol was on her way to her brother Matthew's house to have a coffee with Matthew, and his wife Cathy, and their fifteen year-old son David. It was something Carol wasn't looking forward to. Her brother and sister in-law were heavy drinkers, and every time Carol dropped by for a visit, Matthew and Cathy would usually be drunk, and fighting about some minute thing. It sickened Carol to see what they were doing to their son David.

Carol and David had always been very close. They had spent a lot of time together, going to baseball games, movies, or just going out for a drive to talk things over on what was going on in David's life. They always had so much fun together, but once David became a teenager, their closeness diminished, David had other interests, and wasn't interested in spending time with Carol anymore.

Carol missed the times that they use to share together, especially now, when she was going through such a lonely and sad stage in her life. No one had the slightest notion about the way that she really felt inside. Carol always held her feelings in, bottling her emotions. She could always put up a front when she was feeling blue, and always put the feelings of others ahead of her own. Everyone thought that she was a happy go lucky woman, but in reality, she was a very sad, and a lonely woman. She yearned for some intimacy in her lonely life, someone to hold and cuddle her and make her feel like she was somebody. She had such a low self image of her-self. In her eyes she thought of herself as unattractive; just another 'plain-Jane', even though she was very attractive.

In the past few months there had been more lows than highs. If it wasn't for the closeness that she had with Garry and her parents, and all the jesting around at the hospital with her friend Wanda, she wouldn't be able to cope at all.

Carol turned into her brother's driveway. She sat in the car, with the engine still running, she thought to herself why she had come there in the first place. She thought about changing her mind, but decided to stay, since her shift didn't start for another hour and a-half.

A tear rolled down her cheek, she was about to break down.

She wiped away the tear nonchalantly, 'Come on Carol, be strong,' she thought to herself.

She got out of the car, and walked up the front steps.

She wiped the tears out her eyes, took a deep breath to calm herself before knocking on the door.

"Hi David, how are you? Carol asked with a make believe smile."

"Hi aunt Carol. I'm alright, I guess. If you're here to see my mom and dad, they went out to dinner and they left me fuck all to eat."

Carol could see in David's eyes and by the way he talked that he was stoned. She didn't feel comfortable in the least being around David. 'If only you were the sweet little nephew you once were.' She thought to herself as she looked deeply into his eyes.

David had started hanging around with the wrong crowd.

Even he and his father's closeness had diminished. Along with his new friends came his newfangled attitude.

"And how are things with you David?" Carol asked, feeling a little intimidated.

"Okay ... I guess, but it would be a lot better if there was something to eat around this dump," He grumbled. to Carol, it was more like a whine.

"How about if I give you ten dollars and drop you off at King Burger?"

"Yea, I'll take the ten bucks, but I'll walk." David said with an attitude. Carol handed him the money even though she felt like reneging on her offer. He crudely snatched it out of her hand, and without even a thank you, he turned away and walked into his bedroom.

Carol was glad to get out of the house. It hurt her to see David this way, and gave her another reason to feel depressed. She could still smell the stench of marijuana that was so strong in the house, and her eyes were still burning.

Carol pulled into the hospital parking lot forty minutes before her shift started. She anticipated a hectic night in the E.R as she looked up and seen the full moon which was beginning to show its presence as dusk began to settle in.

As she entered the E.R., she could see that the waiting room was about half full, which was the norm for this time of night. The hectic time would be when the bars close.

"Carol, what are you doing here so early, your shift doesn't start for over half an hour?" Betty snarly asked.

Betty Newton was the day shift supervisor, who everyone at the hospital referred to her as 'Bitchy Betty'. She seemed to be always so miserable. She was loathed by just about everyone that she came in contact with.

"Hello Mrs. Newton, I thought I'd come in a little earlier and see if you needed an extra hand."

"No Carol, we don't need any extra hands now! Too bad you weren't here a couple hours ago, it would have been a different story. Go get a coffee or something ... don't just be standing around here!" Betty bellowed at Carol. .

Carol just turned and walked away with tears in her eyes

"Now I missed my chance to talk to Garry ... damn you Betty!" She murmured to herself in disgust.

Carol went to the hospital's cafeteria for a coffee and to put some time in and to cool off after her confrontation with 'bitchy Betty.'

"Wake up in here, don't you know who I am? I'm Captain John Snipes of the fourteenth regiment! I want the military police in here right now and arrest this corporal for insubordination!"

Carol rushed to the registration booth to see what all the commotion was all about.

"What's going on Linda?" She asked.

"This man thinks I'm his corporal and says he's Captain John Snipes." Linda said, obviously shaken up from the Captain's torrent.

"It's okay Linda." Carol said calmly. "Give psych a call and tell them that we have a patient for them .... Okay Captain Snipes, our commander is going to come and see you." Carol cleverly rationalized with the patient for not to get him too excited. She new from experience that psych patients were totally unpredictable and that she had to keep him calm and occupied.

"Well let's get it in gear here!" The captain bellowed out, drawing more attention to himself.

"Don't you know there's a war going on? You have a lot of my soldiers in here and it's time for them to get their asses back out in the battle field. Now are you going to get them or do I have to kick some ass and get them myself"

"Linda, call for a code black please." Carol requested a Code black, which was a call for all available orderlies to report to the appointed area, stat.

It took less than a minute when the announcement came over the hospitals

P.A. "Code black to ER … code black to ER".

The captain was a big man, and Carol knew if he became violent, that it would take at least three orderlies to get him under control.

Two orderlies arrived, which made the Captain a little more hostile.

"Easy now, we're going to take good care of you sir." Bruce Stern, a six-foot-six, husky orderly said, persuasively.

"If you leave with these two fine gentlemen I'm sure it will be worth your while." Carol said in her best flirtatious way, with a little up and down motion with her eyebrows, which made everyone that was standing around observing at what was going on, they were snickering.

"I'll see you later darlin', don't forget now." The Captain yelled out excitedly as he was being led away.

"Good work Carol, you handled that really well, and it looks like you have a date with the Captain." Night shift supervisor Wanda Jenkins heckled Carol.

"Oh yea, we're going to paint the town red!" Carol jested.

Wanda and Carol were very close. No one would believe that Wanda was Carol's supervisor by the way the two of them always carried on. They got along so well together, and shared the same kind of sense of humor.

"Carol can you check on the man in room four?" Wanda asked. "He says he needs a shot of Morphine for his sore back. I remember him coming in here last week complaining about pains in his stomach. He's a junkie, looking for a fix."

"Okay Wanda, I'll give him a shot, but I don't think it will be Morphine. Maybe one on the side of his head." Wanda just turned around and walked away, laughing and shaking her head from what Carol had said.

Carol opened the door to room four and walked in, catching Mr. Smith off guard. He was scurrying through the medicine cabinet, obviously looking for drugs.

"Okay Mr. Smith, what seems to be the problem tonight?" Carol asked in a firm and confident manner, which was totally out of her character. She had always been accused of being too passive with patients like this.

"Oh you got to help me nurse ... this pain in my stomach is killing me," Mr. Smith complained. He was bent over and sounded as if he were dying. But Carol was a lot smarter than he thought.

"You say it's your stomach Mr. Smith?" She asked.

"Oh yea, it hurts real bad, I think I need a shot of Morphine... that's what they gave me last time."

Carol starred sternly into Mr. Smith's eyes.

"Well Mr. Smith, how come it says on your chart that you came in complaining of a sore back? What is it your back or your stomach?" Carol could see right through his act, and she wasn't going to let him pull any wool over her eyes.

"It's my back ... it's my stomach ... oh just give me some Morphine damn it!" He demanded.

"What does a person have to do around here before he gets anything, die?" Mr. Smith pleaded, but he could see that he hadn't convinced Carol about his fabricated sickness.

"How about if I give you a laxative, Mr. Smith?"

"Don't you fuck with me bitch! Give me some Morphine now, and I mean right now!" He screamed out as he smashed his fist on the medicine cabinet, making Carol more than a little nervous.

"I'll meet you out side at the end of your shift, then we'll see whose fucking with who!"

Carol felt totally terrified from Mr. Smith's threat. She slowly backed herself away from him and edged her way towards the door.

"Okay Mr. Smith ... if you will sit down, I'll have a doctor come in and take a look at you." Carol said in a shaky voice.

"That's more like it ... you nurses think you know everything. The damn doctor better give me my Morphine, or there's going to be hell to raise!"

Carol walked out of the room, and explained to Wanda how Mr. Smith had threatened her. Wanda went right to the phone, and asked for another 'code black'.

It took less than a minute when the same two orderlies that escorted the 'captain' to the psych ward walked in to the ER, with a look of frustration on their faces.

Wanda explained the situation to them, and they quickly went into room four.

"I'll kill you bitch, you're ass is mine ... you fucked with the wrong guy .... " Mr. Smith hollered out as the two orderlies struggled to get him out of the ER area and restrain him until the police arrived.

"You okay, Carol?" Wanda asked.

"Yea, I'm alright." Carol said, but Wanda knew different.

It was obvious that Mr. Smith had really put a good scare into Carol.

"You go get yourself a coffee and take it easy for awhile sweetie. I'm sorry that he put you through that, I should have handled that idiot myself."

"Thanks Wanda." Carol's hands were trembling. She was really shaken up as she walked down the hall towards the cafeteria.

As she looked in to the cafeteria, she could see a couple of doctors talking over a cup of coffee. Carol turned away before they noticed her. She went in to the ladies washroom, where she went in to one of the stalls, sat on the toilet where she had a long hard cry.

CHAPTER FOUR

Carol pulled out of the hospital parking lot right behind Wanda. They both turned on to Lake shore Road. Wanda pulled into the doughnut shop, Carol just kept on driving. Carol usually stopped in after her shift to have a coffee and a muffin with Wanda along with a few other nurses. It gave them a chance to unwind before going home. Carol was just too depressed to stop in, and her eyes were so red and puffy from crying. Mr. Smith had really shaken her up, but it wasn't just he who had made her cry, she just couldn't shake the feeling of dejection that she had been feeling for so long.

Carol felt relieved to finally get home. She walked into the house, everything was quiet, her parents were still asleep. She went directly into her bedroom and laid down on her bed.

After a few minutes of starring at the ceiling in deep thought, she broke down and cried. She missed the intimacy of a man. She was so lonely.

"Oh Garry ... why did you have to be gay?" She whimpered to herself. Her love for him was so deep that it hurt. She wished that she could tell Garry her true feelings and maybe somehow he would see her in a different way, and maybe fall in love with her too. She loved the thought, but she knew that it was just a fantasy. She had felt this way about him for as long as she could remember, and knew that her feelings would never change.

After a long hard cry, she dragged herself out of bed, stripped out of her nurses uniform and climbed into the shower. The hot water splashing onto her languished body helped to bring calm to her emotions. She leaned against the wall and started laughing, "I'm probably the only woman that could fall in love with a man who is gay ... oh Garry if you only knew. "

She stepped out of the shower, and was still laughing as she dried herself. She slipped on her over sized night shirt with Winnie the pooh on it and went back to bed.

As she laid there, she went into a deep thought about her past and her future.

"Damn it!" She said to herself, "There is no reason why I can't find a decent man ... and just as good as Garry!"

She knew it in her heart that there was no other man that could ever compare to Garry. Her mind was racing through all the different scenarios.

After a few minutes of fantasizing, she fell into a deep sleep.

Carol awoke feeling rested and in better spirits.

"Good afternoon, mom!" She said as she walked into the kitchen.

"Hi honey, do you want me to cook you up something to eat?"

"No thanks mom, I'll just have a coffee. Where's dad?"

"He's out in the back yard digging up the garden."

"I don't know why he doesn't ask Ken for his rototiller. He knows damn well he's not suppose to be doing anything strenuous with his heart condition." Her dad had open heart surgery a year ago and was told by the doctors, not to do anything strenuous. He was a very stubborn man.

"Don't worry mom, I'll go out and give him a hand."

"You're so thoughtful, thanks honey.".

Carol made a couple of cups of coffee and walked out to the back yard. She could see her dad was struggling, but had the garden just about all dug up.

"Hi pumpkin. How did work go last night?"

"Hi dad, I had good night, it wasn't too busy at all."

Carol explained to her dad about the incident with Captain John Snipes the psychiatric patient.

Jason smiled, then his expression changed and said, "Well I hope that he doesn't really think that he has a date with you."

"Oh no dad ... " Carol laughed. "At least I hope not anyway."

"What's so funny over there?" Ken hollered out.

"Oh brother, here we go." Carol murmured to her dad.

Ken had been their neighbor for the past ten years.

"Why didn't you ask me for my rototiller? I would have let you use it! It would have saved you a lot of work." Ken said with a smirk on his face.

"Why would I want to use your rototiller? Do you think I want to become a lazy ass like you?" Jason shouted back. Jason and Ken had been carrying on like this for years. To anyone else, it would seem as if they didn't get along with the bantering that they did, but it was quite the opposite. It was like a ritual to them whenever they would see each other out in their yards.

Ken laughed, then turned around and went back into his house.

"Way to go dad, you put him right in his place."

"No, he's a great guy, pumpkin ... he means well. You can't take him too seriously. You should hear us the way that we carry on. You should always remember pumpkin; things aren't always what they seem to be."

Carol thought for a moment on what her dad had said, then quickly got off the subject.

"How about taking me out for something to eat, dad?"

"Sure pumpkin, just as long as you're buying."

"Sounds good to me," Carol said.

"Carol and I are going out for something to eat dear, did you want to come?" Jason asked his wife.

"No thanks dear, you guys just go yourselves, I'm really not that hungry." Jean felt that it was good for Carol and her dad to go out by themselves once in awhile, and this gave her a chance to spend some time by herself as well.

They pulled into the Denny's parking lot. A group of teenagers were congregated in front of the restaurant, doing no harm but making patrons feel a little uncomfortable as they went in and out of the restaurant.

"Excuse us guys." Jason politely asked. The group of teens stepped aside as not to intimidate them, or impede their path.

Carol and her dad managed to get a table close to a window.

"Good afternoon and how are you today?" The waitress pleasantly asked.

"Just fine thanks dear." Jason said with a smile.

"Are you ready to order?"

"Yes, I'll have a western sandwich with coffee please."

"And I'll have the same too please," Carol said.

Carol took a quick survey of all the people in the restaurant, concentrating on the men that were sitting alone. Trying not to look too intrusive, she could see that there was a few good looking men, but not any that would be of interest to her, "As if I can be picky" she thought to herself'.

"Are you looking for someone pumpkin?" Jason curiously asked.

"No ... not really dad, just looking around."

"Hey you old son of a gun, don't tell me Jean finally kicked you out of the house."

"Hey how the heck are ya Cliff? Don't tell me you're splurging for once in your life."

"Hell no. Mary's picking up the check, you wouldn't want me to ruin my reputation now would you?" Cliff quipped.

"Where are you sitting Cliff, we didn't see you when we came in?" Jason asked while looking around to see if he could spot Mary, Cliff's wife.

"Well you must be blind old man."

"See Mary sitting over there in the corner?"

"Oh my gosh, how in the heck did we miss seeing you guys?"

Jason became flustered, and felt a little embarrassed from not noticing Cliff and his wife. Jason turned around and waved at Mary. She smiled and waved back.

"And how are you Carol"?

"Hi Mr. Penny. I'm fine, you certainly look just as spiffy as always."

"Well thank you darlin'. You guys take care, I got to get back to Mary. She's going to think I abandoned her. Say hi to Jean for me and don't forget our game Sunday."

"I'll be there Cliff don't you worry about that." Jason proudly replied.

"Now there's a character," Jason remarked.

"Yea he's quite the character dad and so are you." Carol smirked.

Cliff and Mary waved as they walked out of the restaurant, Carol watched her father's face light up as he waved back. It made her feel good to see her father so content.

The waitress placed the bill on the table, Jason picked it up and seen that it said 'paid in full'.

"Excuse me miss." He said to the waitress. "Why does our bill say paid in full"?

"The man and his wife that was sitting in the far corner table paid your bill." The waitress answered.

Jason thanked the waitress and handed her a two dollar tip.

"Well how do you like that?" Jason was in awe. "That is definitely a first."

"That was nice of him dad."

"Yes, it sure was pumpkin ... it sure was." Jason's face was beaming with pride.

The traffic was backed up and almost at a standstill as Carol drove down Drummond Road on her way to work. She could see flashers up ahead, as she got closer, she could see a police officer directing traffic. It was obvious that there had been some kind of a car accident. Then she saw a horrifying sight of a child's bicycle that was completely crumpled up like a pretzel. She held her hand over her mouth in shock, thinking of the poor child that got struck.

"What happened officer?" She asked the stocky cop.

"Just keep it moving please." The officer sternly replied.

"I'm a nurse, officer."

"I don't care who you are, now move it!" He yelled out.

Carol wasn't expecting such a tantrum from the cop, but felt empathy for the officer, realizing what he had to go through from such a dreadful scene.

The ambulance sped off with sirens blaring and going straight through the red light. Carol knew that it would be very intense once she entered the E.R.

She parked her car and walked briskly to the hospital's rear entrance.

Carol opened the door to the trauma room a crack and could see the lifeless mangled body of a young child laying on the gurney. It was evident that the little boy's life had just ended by the dejected look on Doctor Kelley's and the nurse's face. The wires and tubes were still attached onto his lifeless body and the horrid sound of the alarm was still sounding on the monitor.

A man and a woman rushed in through the emergency entrance in a frenzy. It was obvious that they were the parents of the little boy by the traumatic look on their faces. Carol closed the trauma room door and walked towards them.

"Nurse, we are Mr. and Mrs. Thomas ... we were told that our son was brought in from an accident."

The mother cried out in desperation.

"They told us that he was brought in by ambulance!"

"Mr. and Mrs. Thomas, can you come with me please?" Carol asked, then led them in to the room that was just for parents and relatives who were going through such a crisis as this.

"Mr. and Mrs. Thomas, the doctor is with your son now, I'll go and find out whatever I can for you."

"Thank you, nurse." Mrs. Thomas replied with a quiver in her voice.

Carol dreaded the thought of going back into the trauma room. This was part of her job that was the hardest for her.

"Betty, the parents are here ... what do you want me to say to them?"

"Just tell them that the doctor will be in to see them in a moment ... and no more!"

Carol walked out of the room and wiped the tears from her eyes before going back in to talk to the parents.

Mr. and Mrs. Thomas could tell by the look of despair on Carol's face that their worst fear was about to happen.

"Is our son okay?" The father asked as he held onto his crying wife. Carol placed her hand on Mr. Thomas' shoulder compassionately and said, "The doctor will be in to see you any minute now ... is there anyone that you would like us to call?" Carol asked, trying to keep her emotions under control.

"No ... no thank you ... we just want to see our son." The anguished Mr. Thomas said.

Doctor Kelley entered the room, Carol quietly walked out, and went to the nurses station, where she sat down and cried. Betty compassionately placed her hand onto Carol's shoulder. Carol took a hold of Betty's hand and their eyes met. Looking into Betty's eyes made Carol see another side of Betty, which made her feel a certain closeness towards her, something that she had never felt before towards her. She could see that Betty was feeling the same way as she was. Betty's eyes began to tear up. She quickly let go of Carol's hand, turned then walked away.

"Okay Carol," Wanda said. "Nancy is in room two with a patient, and if you would check the patient in room four, that would be great."

The night was a long one for Carol and unless there was some big catastrophe in the city, she would be out of there after this one last patient.

"What do I have waiting for me in room four?" Carol asked, hoping that it would be something minor.

"Well I guess you'll just have to wait until you get there ... unless you want to take over for Nancy, she's doing an enema" Carol knew that Wanda was toying with her by the smirk on her face.

"No thanks," Carol said. "I'll take my chances in room four, thank you."

"Good luck." Wanda said, trying to keep a straight face.

Carol took the patient's chart from the door, took a deep breath, then entered room four.

Carol felt her face flush the moment she seen Lloyd Smith sitting on the bed. He was holding an ice pack on his hand, which Carol could see that it was very swollen.

Lloyd Smith was a very handsome twenty-five year-old, who could easily pass as Muhammad Ali's twin.

"Hello Mitter Mith," Carol stammered, "Oh I'm so sorry Mr. Smith... it's been a long night." Carol said, red faced.

"No need to apologize," he replied. "I know what it's like working in a hospital, you nurses do all the work and the doctors gets all the credit. Am I right?"

"Yes, you're absolutely right. You must have worked at a hospital before Mr. Smith."

"No, I never worked at a hospital before, let's just say I've had my share of hospitals in my life. Please call me Lloyd."

"Okay Lloyd, my name is Carol."

Lloyd reached out his hand and said, "It's very nice to meet you Carol." They shook hands. Carol was surprised at how gentle he was, for such a big man.

"What happen to your hand, Lloyd?" Carol asked, as she gently took his swollen hand into hers.

"Oh I just slammed it in a car door, its fine. I'd really rather talk about you, Carol."

"Oh ... you wouldn't want to hear too much about me, I don't have much of a life outside of this hospital." Carol said, coyly.

They talked together as if they had known each other for a long time. Carol didn't realize how long they were talking until Betty walked in to the room, catching Carol off guard.

"Why are you still here Carol? It's eight o'clock, you should have been out of here an hour ago!" Betty, said snarly. Carol was still holding onto Lloyd's hand. Her back was turned towards Betty. She wished that Betty would just go away. She turned around and gave a vindictive look at Betty and said, "It's okay Betty, I'm just about finished with Mr. Smith. He's going to need to go down to x-ray."

"Oh I see, so you're playing doctor now. Well you can leave now and we'll let Doctor Peters see if Mr. Smith needs to go for an x-ray!"

Lloyd could see the hurt in Carol's eyes. "It was very nice to meet you Carol,

I hope that we can see each other again some time."

"It was very nice meeting ... " "Okay Carol," Betty interrupted. "Enough is enough ... now let's go!"

Carol was infuriated, and was so disappointed. She was on the verge of tears. She stormed past Betty and out of the room. Betty grinned at Lloyd from Carol's escapades, and said, "I'm very sorry Mr. Smith, another nurse will be in, in just a moment." Lloyd felt the same as Carol did, that Betty had ruined a good thing. But he knew that it wouldn't be the last time that he would see Carol.

Carol sat in her car and brooded, thinking about what Betty had done to her. "My one chance I get to meet mister right, and she ruins it for me. Well the war ain't over yet sister, believe me." She thought to herself.

Wanda walked up to the side of the car, and she could see that Carol was upset about something.

"What's wrong Carol?" She asked.

"Wanda, what a hunk. Wasn't he gorgeous? He was about to ask me out when that damn bitchy Betty barged into the room and ruined everything."

"Gorgeous, and what a personality. Now I'll probably never see him again, thanks to that bitch. She makes me so mad!"

"Bitchy Betty strikes again. Don't worry sweetie, I'm sure you will see him again."

"I hope so Wanda, this guy was definitely mister right."

"Well there had to be something wrong with him." Wanda said.

"What do you mean there must be something wrong with him?" Carol got worked up, from what Wanda had said.

"Easy girl ... calm down," Wanda laughed out. "There had to be something wrong with romeo or he wouldn't have come to the hospital in the first place."

"His name is Lloyd!" Carol raised her voice. Wanda just stared at Carol, grinning. Then Carol realized what Wanda had meant. "Well I guess so you dumb cluck!" They both roared with laughter. "But the only thing that was wrong with him was his broken hand. He was mister perfect!"

"I'm sure he was sweetie. I'll tell you one thing Carol, I'm coming in a half-an-hour earlier tomorrow and I'll put that bitch in her place."

"Thanks Wanda, you are just about the greatest ... well next to romeo anyway."

"Let's get out of here kiddo and go for a coffee."

"Sounds good, Wanda. Maybe we'll see mister right there."

"You never know, kiddo, I'm sure you'll see him again."

CHAPTER FIVE

Carol stood at the kitchen window, watching her neighbor Dorothy Robins across the street as she struggled to cut the grass. Her mind was on other things.

The phone rang for the third time, Carol came out of her trance and heard the fourth.

"Hello." Carol answered the phone in a hoarse morning voice.

"Hello ma'am, this is 'rotter rooter'. Would you like me to come over and clean your pipes?"

"Oh Garry you're such a card." Carol laughed, but was in no mood for such giddiness. She went along with him anyways, for not to hurt his feelings.

"What's bothering you sweetie?" Garry asked. He could always tell when something was bothering Carol.

"I just can't put anything past you, can I?" Carol said.

"No you can't sweetie, I can read you like a book. Now tell me what's bothering you." He asked, sympathetically.

"Oh it's really nothing hon, I just had a bad night at the hospital. I'll get over it."

"Well it's sounds like you need some cheering up there lard-ass."

"Lard-ass ? Who you calling lard-ass?" Carol was now laughing.

"You just get that caboose in gear and get perked up there kiddo, you're too beautiful to be feeling so blue. I have to go, someone's at my door, I'll phone you right back."

Carol just shook her head and laughed to herself as she hung the phone up.

"Lard-ass ... what a character."

She knew that Garry was just kidding around. He had always teased her for having such a bony butt.

Carol put a couple of Eggo's into the toaster. She hoped that Garry would call back soon. He had put a smile on her face, she could feel her mood starting to plummet again.

"Come on Garry, hurry-up and phone back." She murmured to herself.

The door bell rang. Carol looked out the window and was thrilled to see Garry's car parked in the driveway.

"Why you sneaky son of a gun!" Carol excitedly said as she sprinted to the door.

"You must have been driving ninety miles an-hour to get here so fast!" Carol was elated.

"No, just eighty." Garry replied.

"Come here numskull." Carol gave him a big hug.

"Good old' Garry to the rescue again, thanks hon."

"So tell me what's wrong, sweetie?" Garry asked.

"Nothing really ... just a little depressed that's all."

If it were anyone else other than Garry, she would have explained about Lloyd Smith, her mister right that came in to the hospital. Carol just couldn't bring herself to talk about him to Garry, fearing that it would somehow hurt their relationship.

"Well how about coming to the carnival with me?"

"I have to work tonight."

"So why don't you just play hooky? Come on ... just think of all the fun we could have?" Garry asked, jubilantly.

The thought of playing hooky was enticing to Carol. She wasn't looking forward to going in to work. She feared that something was going to hit the fan when Wanda was going to have a war of words with bitchy Betty, and Carol knew that she would end up with the brunt of the storm. The last thing Carol wanted was another confrontation with Betty.

Garry could see that Carol was really thinking about his offer.

"Oh dear, you look terrible," he said. "I think you should call work and tell them that you're deathly sick."

Now Carol was sitting on the fence, not knowing what to do.

'What would Wanda think? She wouldn't know that I wasn't really sick. She thought to herself.

"Okay ... let's do it." Carol said, hesitantly.

"All right Carol!" Garry was astounded. He never thought that he would be able to talk Carol into skipping out of work.

The hardest thing for Carol to do now was to phone the hospital, and make them believe that she was really ill.

Carol went to the phone and rehearsed in her mind what she was going to say before she dialed.

"Okay ... here I go ..." Carol's nerves were starting to get the best of her. She nervously chewed on her fingernail as she waited for someone to answer.

"Hello Westwood General, Judy speaking. How may I help you?"

"Hello Judy," Carol said, with a quiver in her voice.

"Could you put me through to the nurses station in the ER please?"

Garry could see that Carol was very nervous and felt guilty for putting her through this.

"Hello, Betty Newton speaking." Carol froze when she heard Betty's voice, then furiously slammed the phone down.

"Carol, what's wrong?" Garry calmly asked.

"Of all the people to answer the phone, it would have to be her." Carol could barely get the words out, she was so infuriated, and disappointed. Not disappointed because Betty answered the phone, but disappointed in herself for not having the back bone to speak up to Betty.

"What was that all about?"

"I just about had all that I can take of that damn bitch Betty. She's the one who answered the phone.

Boy if I had some back bone .... "

"Easy now sweetie, don't get yourself all worked up over her, she's not worth it."

Garry reached out to embraced Carol. She accepted his open arms and laid her head on to his shoulder. She hastily pulled away and said in a domineering voice, "No more will I let that witch get the best of me! She's going to see a different side of me from now on!"

"You have to watch yourself sugar, you could get yourself fired you know."

"That would give her a lot of satisfaction .... Let's go for a drive, I need to get out of here and unwind."

"You sure do ... let's go."

"How about stopping at a store, I got to get something for this sore throat?" Garry asked.

Carol pulled the car in to Bevan's Variety parking lot, narrowly missing a boy, who was preoccupied studying his baseball cards. Garry didn't say anything, but was starting to get more than a little worried about Carol.

The store was filled with the typical crowd of customers, buying lottery tickets, cigarettes, and little kid eyeballing all the candy, trying to calculate how much candy they could get with half a buck.

"Do you need anything Carol?" Garry asked.

"Yea, get me a couple of those scratch and wins, the way my week is going, I think I deserve to win a couple million."

"Okay, but fifty-fifty if you win." Garry said with a smirk on his face.

"Who's that guy over there staring at you, Carol?" Garry asked inquisitively.

Carol casually turned around, her face turned red and she became antsy as soon as she seen who it was.

"Let's get out of here Garry ... come on let's go." Carol anxiously said.

Garry wasn't as enthusiastic in leaving as Carol was. He was curious to see who this man was that was starring at her.

"Who is he, Carol?"

"Just never mind let's just get the heck out of here." Carol commandingly said. They were causing quite a scene, drawing attention to themselves.

By the time Garry and Carol finished their boisterous carrying on, the six foot four man was standing right in front of them.

"Hello there darlin' ,you look awful familiar. Do I know you?" He asked, Garry and Carol took a step back. He was very intimidating and his breath reeked with alcohol.

"No I don't believe we have ever met sir." Carol said, but she knew exactly who he was, but she wasn't going to let him know it.

"Okay miss, if you say so." He said, then walked out of the store with his pack of Lucky Sevens. Carol could see the dumb founded expression on his face.

Garry was more than a little curious to find out who that man was.

"That guy was Captain John Snipes." Carol told Garry.

He was a psychiatric patient at the hospital. I guess he never forgot my homely face."

Garry, looked at Carol expressionless. He placed three quarters on the counter and tucked a pack of Halls into his shirt pocket. They both casually walked out of the store, while the attentive cashier watched them leave.

"What did you mean in there, the captain must of remembered your homely face?" Garry never liked it when Carol cut herself down like she did.

"You are a beautiful woman Carol, and don't you ever think that you're not." He said, sternly. Carol opened the car door, got in, and didn't say a word.

While driving down route 55, Carol was preoccupied with the black Cadillac that she could see in the rear view mirror. She had seen the same car parked across the street from Bevan's Variety, when she and Garry drove off, the Cadillac seemed to be following them.

"Garry, I think someone is following us."

"Carol, why would someone want to follow us, come-on don't start getting paranoid on me now."

"Garry ... I'm serious, look for yourself, but don't make it look obvious." Carol turned the rear view mirror towards Garry. "Yea I see the car but I can't see the driver. Slow down a little and let it get closer for I can see who's driving it."

Carol slowed down, then the Cadillac slowed down. She sped up, then the offending car sped up.

"Who the heck is this guy? Slow down, then take the next left really fast and don't use your turn signal." Now Garry was convinced that the Cadillac was indeed following them. As Carol came to the next side street, she sped up and turned left. Garry seen the Cadillac slow down and turn left. they lost sight of it when Carol turned onto another street.

CHAPTER SIX

Carol sat in her car in the hospital parking lot, in deep thought, trying to get up enough courage to go inside.

She could see Wanda's blue Mazda parked two rows over.

Carol hoped that the war of words between Wanda and Betty would already be over. The last thing she wanted to do was to walk in to the E R, and find herself right in the middle of a fracas.

"Okay, lets get it done and over with." Carol muttered to herself. She got out of the car and made her way towards the back entrance. She was in such a state that she clumsily tripped over her own feet, landing on her hands and knees, badly skinning her left knee, and ruining her new pair of white nurses stockings. She stayed on the ground in a daze, not knowing if she was going to laugh or cry.

She looked around to see if anyone had seen her fall, and once she realized that there was no one in sight, she quickly got back on to her feet, and continued to walk towards the rear entrance.

Trying to compose herself, Carol entered the emergency ward. Walking briskly and with her head down, she walked right into Betty, almost knocking her to the floor, Betty's papers flew out of her hand, landing on the floor in disarrangement.

"Oh dear ... 1'm sorry Carol ... are you okay? Did I hurt you?" Carol was stunned, she just stood there expressionless, and starred at Betty.

"What did you do to your knee, dear? Are you okay?"

"Yes, 1'm okay ... 1 just slipped in the parking lot, that's all."

Carol was limping, favoring her left leg.

"Well let's get that knee fixed up, it looks awfully painful." Betty led Carol into room four.

Carol just didn't know what to make out of it. Betty seemed like a totally different person. She even had a smile on her face, and called her dear.

Wanda peeked in to the room, and could see Betty crouched down, tending to Carol's knee. She gave Carol a wink and a fervent grin, then ducked out of the way before Betty got a chance to see her. Betty's intuition caused her to turn around and look towards the doorway, but was too late, Wanda had already gone.

"Thanks Betty," Carol timorously said.

"You're welcome dear. Now if you don't feel that you can work with that knee don't you worry, you go home and I'll stay here for half of your shift and I'm sure someone else will cover for the rest."

"Thank you so much Betty ... I'll be okay."

Carol had mixed emotions. Betty stood up and hugged her and said, "I'm sorry for being so hard on you Carol, I hope that we can start all over again and be good friends."

Carol kissed Betty on the cheek. "I'd like that very much Betty."

Carol was at a loss for words, and felt awkward as well as a little guilty. She knew that she was just as hard on Betty as she was with her.

"Well dear, I'm going to go home and I hope that you have a good shift." Betty graciously said.

"Thanks Betty, you have a good night too, and I'll see you tomorrow."

Carol felt as if a hundred pound weight had just been lifted off of her shoulders. The contempt that she had felt towards Betty for so long was now gone.

Wanda must have had a good talk with Betty, for the drastic change in Betty. Carol thought to herself.

"Hey Smitty, are you going to pour me another drink, or do I have to climb over the bar and get it myself?" Bill Barnes shouted out in a drunken stupor.

"I think you should get the fuck out of here before I throw your drunken ass out." Twenty three year old bartender Lloyd Smith snapped back. He despised drunks, especially guys like Bill Barnes, who would sit at the bar all day and half the night, paying no regard to his family at home.

"What in the hell did you do to your hand there Lloyd?"

Willie Carter asked as he stepped up to the bar.

"Hey, how ya doing you old sow? I kind of broke it in a car door." Lloyd said facetiously, hinting around that it had been something other than a car door.

"You don't expect me to believe that, do you? I bet the guy that fucked with you, won't be fucking around with you again." Willie spoke with a guarded tongue. He feared Lloyd immensely, but was grateful that Lloyd was on his side now, and he wanted to keep it that way.

Willie had both of his knees shattered by Lloyd, for no apparent reason. Lloyd never acknowledged that it ever happened and said that he had no recollection of doing so.

Willie's fear of Lloyd, helped boost Lloyd's self confidence, something that he had very little of, and guys like Willie were easy prey.

"No, that guy isn't going to fuck with anybody for a while, Willie." Lloyd boasted.

"You should have seen the nurse I met at the hospital, man oh man, a real goddess. One who would make a man behave like a gentleman."

Willie's mouth was wide open, eager not to miss any detail.

"Well, did you get lucky?" Willie asked, then drank his shot of scotch down in one fast gulp, then slid his glass towards Lloyd in anticipation.

"Well what do ya think? Sure I got lucky. three times!" Lloyd boasted.

Willie smiled sheepishly, whipped down his second shot, then stood up with a cane in each hand, he labored every step towards the exit.

"Don't be a stranger there Willie..." Lloyd yelled out.

"Yea sure Lloyd .... Fuck you too asshole." Willie said under his breath as the door from Peepers strip club closed behind him.

Carol pulled into her brother Matthew's drive way. She got out of the car and had to step over a heap of trash from a once filled garbage bag. Rubbish was scattered throughout the front yard. The stench made it hard for Carol to draw in any untainted air. The yard had always looked neglected. Her brother was far from ambitious. Carol's brother; Matthew Crawford, served six months in the Gulf War, and came back a changed man.

He was once a compassionate and loving man, but when he returned, he was the total opposite. Matthew started to drink excessively and neglected his family. His relationship with his wife Cathy had deteriorated almost to the point of divorce. Cathy had turned to alcohol to cope with every thing that was going on.

They lived on Matthew's small disability pension, which was barely enough to live off of.

As Carol walked up to the front door she could see Matthew through the tattered curtains sitting at the kitchen, drinking a beer. A collection of a half dozen empty beer bottles lay across the table.

Carol dreaded the thought of this visit but felt guilty that she hadn't seen her brother and his wife Cathy for a few months.

"Come on in, don't be shy." Matthew hollered out.

Carol walked in and gagged at the putrid stench of the house.

"Why don't you open up some windows in here?" Carol pleaded as she opened the window on the aluminum door.

"Well look at what the cat dragged in. How ya doing sis? Long time no see. How have you been?" Her brother said in a load voice, slurring his words.

"I'm doing pretty good. I was here last week and you guys weren't home."

"Yea, I know ... David told me." Matthew had to stop to think what his own son's name was.

Carol's sister in law came out of the bedroom and was caught off guard when she seen Carol.

"Hi Carol," Cathy said in a forlorn voice, also slurring her words.

Carol was stunned at the site of her. She was thirty two, but looked more like a woman of sixty, almost unrecognizable. Her left eye was completely swollen shut and she had a fat lip. It was obvious what had happened to her. Carol pretended not to notice.

"Sit down Carol, and I'll fix us a cup of tea" Cathy could hardly talk with her swollen lip. Carol could see the pain on Cathy's face with each step that she took.

"No thanks Cathy, I just dropped by to say hello and see how you guys were doing. Maybe I'll take David out on the weekend ... if that's okay with you."

Matthew raised his head and said "Never mind the weekend, you can have the little bastard!" Carol didn't even acknowledge that she heard her brother. She was completely disgusted with him.

Carol made her way to the door, she gave Cathy a sympathetic glance, then walked up to Cathy, and embraced her. "If you want to talk, or need anything at all, phone me ... okay sweetheart?"

"Well aren't you going to give your brother a kiss before you go?" Matthew hollered out to Carol. Carol just gave him a stern look, then walked out the door. Matthew jumped out of his chair and bolted to the door. "Fuck you too Carol .... " He yelled out. Carol didn't even turn around. She just got in her car and sped off.

Carol knew that she couldn't keep this a secret, but it would be too upsetting for her mom and dad.

On her way home from work, Carol spotted a black Cadillac in her rear view mirror which looked like the same car that had followed her and Garry before. A surge of terror rushed through her body. The traffic light was red as she pulled up to the intersection. The Cadillac stayed about two car lengths back, not close enough for her to get a good look at the driver. Carol panicked and pressed the accelerator to the floor and sped up, running the red light, narrowly missing the tail end of a transport truck.

Carol pulled erratically into her driveway, she looked around, the black Cadillac was nowhere in sight.

She prayed that it would be gone.

Carol shook like a leaf as she fumbled to open the house door, a black car suddenly came flying around the corner. Carol was sure that it was the same offending Cadillac.

Whoever it was, now knew exactly where she lived. Now Carol was scared.

"What's wrong what's wrong?" Carol's dad hollered out in a panic as she rushed in to the house.

Dad, someone has been following me, her voice quivered.

"Do you have any idea who it might be, hon?

"Dad, I don't have a clue."

"Did you get a license plate, or get a look at his face?" Jason anxiously asked.

"No, I couldn't even tell if it was a male or female.

This isn't the first time either, the same car followed Garry and I the other day."

"Okay pumpkin we're going to put a stop to this right now ... I'm going to call the police and get this son-of-a bitch."

Jason was so worked up that his hands were shaking, which worried Carol, and made her feel a sense of guilt.

Within fifteen minutes, a police cruiser pulled into the driveway. Sargent

Bruce Johnson, a fifteen year veteran with the Westwood Police Department walked up the front steps, and knocked on the door.

"Hello officer." Carol greeted him.

"Hello ma'am, I'm Sargent Bruce Johnson, I understand that you are having a problem about someone following you home. Can you tell me about the incident you had this morning?" The officer asked as he opened his black book.

Carol gave the officer all the details, while her dad sat in silence, and listened to every detail.

"Okay Miss Crawford, I'll take a drive around to see if I can spot the culprit, but there isn't much that I can do if I do catch him, except give him a warning and see if he is wanted for anything."

Jason bolted out of his chair and raised his voice at the Sargent. "What are you just going to let this sick son-of-a bitch keep doing this? Come on you got to do better than that for God sake!" Jason yelled out in disgust.

"I'm sorry sir, there's only so much we can do. I'll go out and drive around the area and see if he's still in the vicinity. If I do spot him, I'll let you know." The sympathetic cop handed Carol his card with his cell number on the back of it.

"I'll be in contact with you mam, but if you see this car following you again, don't hesitate, you phone us immediately."

"I will, thanks officer." Carol said, appreciatively.

The officer walked back to his cruiser then sped off down the street.

Jason was red faced and shook up. Carol placed her hand onto her dad's shoulder, trying to calm him down.

"Don't worry dad, they'll find him, please calm down."

"Is everything all right dear?" Carol's mom asked as she came out of the bedroom..

Jason gave Carol a stare, sending her a signal not to mention anything about the incident to her mother. Carol obliged and handled her mother's apprehensive feelings with kid gloves.

"Here mom, sit down and I'll pour you a cup of coffee."

"Oh you are so kind dear"

Carol placed the half a mug of coffee in front of her mom.

Jean's arthritis had gotten so bad that she could barely hold on to the half filled mug.

A knock came at the door. Carol sprinted to the door, expecting it to be Sargent Johnson. Carol's enthusiasm turned to apathy once she seen that it was Ken.

"What the heck went on here this morning? I seen the cruiser here ... is everything okay?" Ken eagerly asked.

"Yes, everything is all right Mr. Walsh, dad will tell you all about it when he is more up to it. Okay?" Carol was a little sarcastic with Ken, which didn't sit too well with Jason. "I'll talk to you all about it a little later there pal. Right now I don't even know if my ass is punched or bored." Jason said, as he nervously rubbed the back of his neck. Ken could see that Jason was upset.

"Okay Jason, I understand ... I'll talk to you later." Ken walked passed Carol, and went out the door, without saying another word.

"You're awfully quiet today mom? Is everything okay?" Carol asked, feeling worried.

"Oh don't you worry about me, dear, I'm fine." Jean replied, but Carol could see different. She had noticed a big change in her mother in the past month. She just wasn't herself, and seemed to be depressed and a little confused. It was starting to worry Carol.

"How would you like it if I fixed your hair all up nice, and do your nails this afternoon?"

"Oh dear, that would be so nice of you if you did that for me. But isn't there something else you'd rather do today?" Carol's mom asked.

Carol walked over to her mom and gave her a kiss on her cheek, "No mom," Carol said, compassionately. "There's no one else that I would rather spend the day with. I love spending time with you, mom"

Jean's face lit right up from the attention that Carol was giving her.

"Okay, who feels like some blueberry pancakes?" Carol asked, jubilantly.

Jason eagerly stood up, rubbing his stomach, and said, "I sure could go for a couple of those right now!"

"Well that's too bad, we're all out." Carol just stood there straight faced.

"Well, why in the damn hell did you ask us for then?" Jason shot out.

"Well how about some French toast?" Carol was seeing how far she could take this. She knew how to put some spark in to their normally quiescent home.

"No way, now I've got a craving for blueberry pancakes and that's exactly what I'm going to eat. Come on girls lets go get us some blueberry pancakes!" Jason was raring to go.

"No, you guys just go and I'll stay here." Jean timidly said.

"Nonsense mom, if you don't go, then we're not going either. "

"Come on dear, it will be good for you to get out of the house," Jason eagerly said.

Carol and Jason was pleasantly surprised when Jean decided to go.

The three of them walked out of the house with smiles on their faces, forgetting all about what had happened earlier.

As Carol entered the emergency ward, she looked for Garry.

She wanted to talk to him about what had happened to her sister in-law Cathy. She was hoping that maybe Garry could give her some advice.

Carol knew what had to be done, that she had to report such a brutal assault, there was no excuse for what her brother had done. Carol had seen so many cases of battered woman come in to the hospital, and every case sickened her. Carol would have never thought that it would ever happen in her own family. There had always been harmony in her family, never the slightest amount of discontent. Carol now felt that it was a black eye against her family, and felt ashamed. She believed that no man had the right to abuse a woman physical or mentally, and Carol could see it in Cathy's eyes that she had endured both.

Carol thought about it for a moment, then went in to Betty's office to use the phone to call the Westwood Police Department.

Betty was sitting at her desk, which caught Carol off guard. She still felt a little uneasy with her.

"Hello Betty ... how are you doing today?" Carol asked, nervously.

Betty looked up at Carol, and smiled contently, and said, "Oh hi Carol, please sit down. How is your knee?"

"Oh it's much better now, thanks." Carol said with a half hearted smile.

"Is there something bothering you Carol, you look like you're worried about something, is everything okay?"

Carol was a little hesitant, then opened up to Betty.

"Betty, my brother Matthew is battering my sister in law. I went to their house this afternoon and Cathy's face was a mess." Carol explained, with tears in her eyes.

"That's absolutely heartbreaking Carol. I'm so sorry. Is there anything that I can do?"

"No, but thanks for asking I have to handle this myself. I have to report this to the police. There was no excuse for what my brother did."

Carol pulled out Sargent Bruce Johnson's card, and reached for the phone. Betty made her way toward the door, gave Carol a sympathetic glance then walked out of the room, giving Carol some privacy.

"Hello I would like to talk to Sargent Bruce Johnson please." Carol waited nervously for a reply from desk Sergeant Lucas Watson.

"No I'm sorry mam, he's out on patrol right now. Can I help you with anything?"

"My name is Carol Crawford and I need to talk to the Sargent about an urgent matter."

"Okay mam, I will contact Sargent Johnson right away and tell him you called.

"I am a nurse in the emergency ward at Westwood General, and I'll be here until seven tomorrow morning."

Carol gave the very caring desk Sargent the details at how to contact her.

"Okay Miss. Crawford, I'll give him the message and Sargent Johnson will contact you as soon as he can."

Carol hung the phone up, and hoped that the officer would come before long, if not, it was going to be a long night for her, having this playing on her mind.

"Mr. Williams you're going to have to sit still for I can clean your cut. If you would stop chasing all those woman around, things like this wouldn't happen." Carol was cleaning the wound of seventy-two year old, feisty, Jacob Williams, who came in with a laceration to his scalp from a fall in his bathroom. Carol was amused about Mr. Williams' antics, he was so flirtatious and comical. He had a good size gash on his scalp, but he wasn't the least concerned.

Wanda entered the room and motioned to Carol. "Carol, there is a police officer waiting for you at the nurses station. I don't know what you did but I'll do the same thing if that cop comes to bust me." Wanda said in her usual perky way. But Carol was in no mood for giddiness now, she knew that this was going to be a tough thing to deal with and for what was about to unfold.

Wanda saw the serious look on Carol's face, "I'm sorry honey," in a more serious way, then said, "go ahead and I'll take over for you."

Mr. Williams grinned from ear to ear and said, " Gee I'm doing pretty good tonight, two for the price of one!"

Carol beamed with a genuine smile at Mr. Williams. "You take it easy now Mr. Williams, and try to keep your feet on the ground." Carol blew him a kiss, then proceeded to the nurses station, where the Sargent was waiting.

Carol was at the nurses station talking to the officer. He apologized for not being able to locate the offending black Cadillac that had been following her. The Cadillac was the least of Carol's worries now. The only thing that was on her mind was her sister in law Cathy.

Carol explained to the officer about her sister in law's battered face, and about her brother Matthew.

"My brother has never been the same since he served time in the gulf war . I would have never thought that he would have done anything like this ... it just makes me sick."

"Okay Miss Crawford, I'm very sorry. I'll go and have a talk with your brother and sister in-law. I'll be in touch with you as soon as I can to let you know what's going on. From what you are telling me, Miss Crawford, I will be arresting your brother"

Carol was grateful to the empathetic cop. She knew that something was going to hit the fan, she was worried about the repercussions about reporting her brother . Her brother would in no way let a cop come in to his house and dictate to him what was right or wrong.

Carol had witnessed her brother's rages before, and she knew exactly what he was capable of, and knew that the police were going to have their hands full.

"Every thing okay sweetie?" Wanda asked. Carol wasn't even aware of Wanda being there, until Wanda placed her hand on her shoulder, which startled Carol out of her trance.

"Wanda ... don't sneak up on me like that, you scared me half to death!"

"I'm sorry kiddo ... you okay?"

"Yea, I'm okay." Carol replied. She didn't want to go through the whole scenario once again about her family problem, so she put on a feigned smile, and let on that everything was okay.

"Well I guess we better get back to the grindstone Carol, patients are awaiting" Wanda said, high spiritedly.

Wanda was hiding something behind her back. I have something for you sweetie.

Wanda pulled out a dozen red roses,Carol's face light right up; it was a dozen long stemmed roses, wrapped in a beautiful sheathe of heart filled crepe paper, and a huge box of chocolates.

"Are they for me?" Carol was overwhelmed.

"Well don't just stand there girl, see who they're from!"

Everyone at the nurse's station was just as anxious as Carol was to see who was the person that sent such an exuberant offering.

Carol lifted the card away from the box of chocolates and held her breath as she read it. The card read: "Beautiful flowers for a beautiful lady, from your admirer Lloyd Smith."

Carol didn't let on that she was clueless about who Lloyd Smith was. The name was totally unfamiliar to her, then she realized it, it was from a patient that came in. The one who Betty broke into their conversation that they were having, and ruined things.

Carol passed the card around to let everyone see the flattery greeting that this Lloyd Smith wrote.

Wanda and all the other staff was waiting in anticipation to find out who this Lloyd Smith was. Carol acted coy.

It was just after 1:00 a.m. when the six foot one handsome blue eyed man entered the hospital's main entrance.

Carol knew who he was at first sight, it was Lloyd Smith.

"Hello Carol," he said, softly, and in a shy manner. "I hope that you enjoyed my little token of my appreciation."

Carol was breathless and her heart was racing. Now it was hard for her to believe how she could have forgotten the name Lloyd Smith, and the face behind it, especially since he was in the back of her mind ever since the night he first came into the hospital. She thought that she would never see him again, and now, here he was standing right in front of her.

"Thank you so much Lloyd, the roses are so beautiful, and the chocolates are just wonderful."

Carol furtively lead Lloyd to one of the empty rooms for they could talk in private.

"Carol, would you care to join me for breakfast at eight and maybe we could go for a nice walk through the Lincoln County nature trails?"

Carol's heart just melted. "That would be lovely, Lloyd."

"So it's a date then, wonderful!" Lloyd looked as proud as a peacock, and his shyness quickly turned into dauntless jubilation.

"Where can I pick you up Carol?" He asked.

Carol didn't think twice, about giving Lloyd her address and phone number.

"Okay Carol, I guess I will see you at eight then."

"I'll see you then, Lloyd." Carol replied, feeling a little overcome with emotions.

Lloyd opened the door half way, then turned back toward Carol, closed the door, and said in an emotional voice, "Carol ... I have been thinking of you ever since I set eyes on you the night I came in the hospital. I hope you don't think any less of me for being so open."

Carol walked up to Lloyd and caressed the side of his face and said with glossy eyes, "No Lloyd, I think it's wonderful that you can be so open with your feelings. I have been thinking of you too, Lloyd."

"You have?"

"Yes I have." Carol said, fighting away the lump in her throat.

"Well I'll see you at eight, Carol." Lloyd said, smiling from ear to ear, so proudly, then walked out the door with a glow on his face.

Carol waited a few minutes until she knew that Lloyd was gone, then she couldn't get out of the room fast enough. She was electrified, she just had to hurry and tell someone.

Wanda was walking toward the nurses station, but Carol got there first, all ready and anxious to tell Wanda about all the details.

Carol and Lloyd were walking on the Lincoln County nature trail, holding hands and talking to each other as if they had known each other for a long time. Lloyd was like a perfect gentleman, and Carol was just loving the attention that he was giving her.

"You see that bird over there Carol? That's a morning dove. He's a symbol of peace." Lloyd cupped his hands, and placed them to his lips and made a cooing sound which raised the tentative dove's spirit, which in turn made it imitate the cooing sound that Lloyd had made.

Lloyd put his arms around Carol from her back and showed her how to make the cooing sound. Carol wasn't too interested in learning about bird calls, but she loved the feeling of Lloyd's arms around her. Something that she had yearned, for so long.

They continued their leisurely walk through the trail, talking freely and openly to each other. They felt so at ease being together.

Carol was so immersed in conversation with Lloyd that she didn't see the protruding rock ahead of her.

Carol let out a moan as she landed on the ground, twisting her ankle awkwardly. Lloyd quickly knelt down beside her and asked in a shaken voice, "Are you okay Carol?"

Carol had tears in her eyes, partly from the pain, and partly from embarrassment.

"I'm all right." She said as she sat on the ground in obvious pain.

"No, don't try and stand on it," Lloyd said, as Carol attempted to get up.

"It looks like you might have sprained or broken your ankle."

Lloyd gently lifted her up into his arms, then sat her down on a fallen tree. He removed Carol's left jogging shoe.

"Now this is a switch," Lloyd jested. "Aren't you suppose to be the nurse?"

Carol laughed, and with a red face, she said, "Well I guess the shoe is on the other foot."

"Well it doesn't seem to be broken but I'm going to carry you back to the car just in case."

"I think I can walk, it doesn't feel too bad now." Carol attempted to get up, but Lloyd gently placed his hand on her shoulder and made her stay down.

"Never you mind, love, you just stay where you are and I'm going to carry you to the car."

Lloyd lifted Carol up with such ease and they were on their way to the car, which was about a hundred feet away.

"I could get use to this real fast!" Carol said, gleefully, but thought it was witless to say. But Lloyd didn't think so at all. He smiled and said, "A fine lady like yourself deserves to be treated like a queen."

"Oh, you're so sweet." Carol said, then gave Lloyd a kiss on his cheek.

He was beginning to tire, it was a long haul carrying Carol up the flight of

stairs that led to the parking lot.

Lloyd placed Carol on the hood of the car, took out a hankie wiped the sweat off of his brow.

Lloyd opened the passenger side door and helped Carol in to the front seat.

"I better take you home for you can put some ice on that, love."

On the drive back to Carol's place, Carol and Lloyd were both very quiet. They were both in deep thought, thinking about each other.

"I had a real nice time Carol. I'm sorry that you hurt your ankle like you did."

"I had a really nice time too Lloyd. I'm sorry for being such a klutz ... I guess I have two left feet."

"There's no need to apologize love, I almost fell 'ass over teakettle' myself. And you definitely do not have two left feet."

"Tell me something Lloyd ... what the heck is 'ass over teakettle'?" Carol asked with a sheepish grin on her face.

Lloyd smiled whimsically and explained, "Ass over teakettle? Well, when I was about ten, my mom had a teakettle in her hand, ready to pour my dad a cup of tea when she slipped on the rug, her ass went flying through the air, her ass went one way, and the teakettle went another."

"Gee, I hope your mom didn't hurt herself." Carol said so seriously.

"No, only her pride, I laugh every time I think of that day.
"

Lloyd went really quiet, Carol could tell that he was in deep thought. He had a smile on his face, but a tear in his eye. Carol thought that what ever he was thinking of must be something very sad.

The impatient driver behind them sounded his horn to let Lloyd know that the light had changed to green. That was enough to snap Lloyd out of his deep thought.

"Oh… I guess I can go." Lloyd said, then sped through the intersection.

As Lloyd pulled his blue Chrysler in to Carol's drive way, they could see Sargent Johnson talking to Carol's father.

Lloyd got out of the car and walked over to Carol's side and helped Carol put her shoe back on.

Lloyd became more than a little antsy as he watched Sargent Johnson make his way toward them.

"Okay love, there you go, see if you can stand on it." Lloyd asked, anxiously.

Carol felt as if Lloyd was rushing her, but didn't think too much about it.

Carol didn't say anything to Lloyd about why the police was there, and he didn't ask, but seemed very interested.

"It feels fine Lloyd, thanks for everything." Carol gave Lloyd a quick peck on his cheek, by then, Sargent Johnson was just approaching the car. It seemed that Lloyd couldn't get in his car quick enough, and seemed as if he was trying to avoid the officer, which baffled Carol.

"I'll give you a call later on Carol."

"I would really like that, Lloyd.

Lloyd gave the officer a timorous nod, then wasted no time backing the car out of the driveway.

"Hello Sargent Johnson, how did it go with my brother?"

Carol could tell that things didn't go too well by the disheartened look on the officer's face.

"We had a rough time with your brother Miss Crawford. It took four of us to get him under control.

He's in lock-up now, but he'll be released with-in the next few hours."

Carol felt a sinking feeling in the pit of her stomach.

She knew that she stirred up a hornets nest and everyone in her family was going to suffer for it.

"I bet he feels really great about me now." Carol knew the answer to the question even before she asked.

"Miss Crawford, he's more than a little agitated and he has been warned, but I would just be a little careful for a few days until he calms down." The sympathetic cop gazed into Carol's eyes and tried to comfort her uneasiness.

"Did he threaten to do anything to me or my family, officer?"

"Well he has been warned. If you do see him anywhere near you, don't hesitate to phone us. We will arrest him again and he knows that. Just keep an eye out, that's all you can do."

"Okay, thanks officer, I really appreciate everything that you have done.

Carol's father was standing at the front door waiting for Carol to make her way up to the house.

"Everything okay pumpkin?" Jason asked, curiously.

"Yea, I'm okay dad, don't worry about me, I'm fine."

Carol's father thought that the police were talking to Carol about the black Cadillac that was following her. The last thing she wanted is to upset her father more by telling him about what his son had did.

Carol and her parents were sitting around the kitchen table contemplating about the events that took place in the last twenty four hours.

The phone rang and the three of them jumped about two inches out of their chair, but no one was in too much of a hurry to answer it. Jason stood up and took a deep breath before he answered it.

"Hello ... yes, may I ask who is calling? Okay just one minute please." Jason placed his hand over the receiver and whispered to Carol: "It's a man, he says his name is Lloyd. Do you want to talk to him?"

"It's okay dad, I'll take it." Carol couldn't get her self out of the chair fast enough once she knew it was Lloyd.

Carol talked to Lloyd for a few minutes, then went into her bedroom to talk on her bedroom phone where she could talk in private.

Jason and Jean had a look of curiosity on their faces as they silently stared at each other. They could tell that something was going on between this guy Lloyd, and Carol by the way Carol jumped up with glee when her dad told her who was on the phone.

"Yes I had a great time too Lloyd, I'm sorry that I spoiled things by tripping over my own two feet like that."

Lloyd asked Carol out for an early dinner, but Carol had to turn down his offer. She explained the situation about her brother and sister in law. Lloyd was very sympathetic.Carol thought that he was a little too interested in her families predicament by asking so many questions, but thought that he was just genuinely concerned. They both agreed to wait until everything calmed down a little before they see each other again. Lloyd let Carol know that he would be there for her if she needed him for anything at all. Carol thanked him then hung up the phone and went back into the kitchen where her mom and dad were still sitting, longing for some details about this Lloyd guy. Carol could sense this so she filled them in about Lloyd and herself.

Jean and Jason's face lit up at the thought of their daughter having a new man in her life. It had been so long since she had a date. They had always felt a little guilty, they felt that they were the reason that their daughter didn't have too much of a social life. Carol had always put her parents first before she would even think of doing anything else.

CHAPTER EIGHT

Jason just got off the phone and looked as white as a sheet.

"What's wrong dear?" Jean asked with a sense of urgency in her voice.

"It's Matthew ... he's in the hospital. They say that we should get over there right of way." Jason just stood there trembling and in a state of shock.

"I'll go wake up Carol and tell her to get dressed." Jean said with panic in her voice.

"What's wrong mom... what's going on?" Carol yelled out in a state of confusion. She vaulted out of her bed in a fury to see why her mom was in such a frenzy.

"We have to go to the hospital right away dear."

"Is it dad? Is he all right?" Carol asked in a state of exigency. They were out the door with in five minutes.

As they entered the hospital Carol went directly to the nurses station to find out where her brother was.

Doctor Burns pulled Carol to the side and explained to her what Matthew's condition was. It wasn't good.

"I'm sorry Carol, your brother has been through a rough ordeal. He has had a very bad trauma to his head and we are trying to bring the swelling down." Doctor Burns placed his band onto Carol's shoulder.

"He's comatose and on a respirator."

Carol's lips quivered and her hands were shaking.

"Is he going to be okay?"

"Carol, it doesn't look good. The next twenty-four hours will be crucial. I'm very sorry."

It made it so much harder for Carol to bear, once she found out how Matthew's neighbor had found her brother. He was found laying face down, unconscious beside his house.

Doctor Burns told Carol that he was almost beaten to death.

Carol looked into her father's eyes, he could sense that things were very serious. Jason's eyes watered up and held onto his wife, then he broke down.

As Carol and her parents entered the intensive care ward, they could see all the tubes and lines that was hooked up to Matthew. Carol had seen many patients in this condition, but no nurse or doctor could ever prepare themselves in seeing a family member in this grave condition.

"I'm here Matthew." Carol said as she took a hold of her brother's hand. There was no response, he just lay there still, with no signs of life.

Jason and Jean stood at the bottom of the bed and just stared in shock, too terrified to face the reality of what had happened to their son.

The dreadful sound of the alarm suddenly sounded from the monitors that was connected to Matthew. Doctor Burns and Betty came rushing in. Carol and her parents stood there paralyzed from shock. Betty led Carol and her parents out of the room.

With-in five minutes, Doctor Burns came out of the room with a grim look on his face.

"Hello Jason, Jean. We're doing every thing possible for Matthew. I'm very sorry."

Jason and Jean were just too shook up to say anything.

Doctor Burns led Carol to the side and told her the bad news. "Carol, it doesn't look good. I think you should prepare yourself and your family."

Carol was trying so hard not to break down. She knew that she had to be strong for her parents.

"Carol, there's a police officer here that would like to ask you a few questions."

Carol gave her parents the sorrowful details, and made arrangements for Doctor Burns to give them a sedative to help ease there anxieties. Garry was on his lunch hour, he kindly offered to take them home.

Carol walked over to the waiting officer, anxious to find out who did such a vicious thing to her brother.

"Hello officer, I am Carol Crawford, Matthew's sister. Do you know who did this to my brother?"

The stout and expressionless cop gave Carol an intimidating looking over, and had no regard for Carol's question.

"Miss Crawford, do you have any idea of who would want to harm your brother? Did he have any problems with anyone that you know of?"

"Officer, my brother had problems but he was a good man."

"Miss Crawford I asked you a question and I expect you to answer it, now did your brother have any problems with anyone, and do you have any idea who did this to him?" The irate, unsympathetic cop raised his voice.

"Well thank you for your concern, officer!" Carol snapped back.

The contemptible cop didn't even blink an eye at Carol's little eruption and her tears.

"I have a brother that's dying and you treat me like I'm the villain here. How dare you! You don't even make it as a human being, never mind a peace officer." Carol was in such a state that she poked her finger into the uncompassionate cop's chest as she berated him.

"And you can stick your questions where the sun don't shine!" Carol stormed away in tears

Let it all out, hon ... I'm so sorry." Betty held onto Carol and let all of Carol's emotions escape her heavily burdened mind.

Carol went into hysterics. All the built up anguish that she had been carrying on her shoulders for so long was now coming to the surface.

Carol was the one that had always held her emotions inside. She was now crying uncontrollably.

"It's going to be okay Carol." Betty said, compassionately.

As Betty led Carol to one of the rooms, they past the offending cop. He just looked at Carol with an expressionless look.

"You rotten bastard!" Carol yelled out.

Carol went silent when she seen her sister in law, Cathy walk by. She didn't notice Carol, which was a relief to her.

Carol's sister in-law staggered from side to side, obviously intoxicated.

She had an expression on her face as if there was nothing at all wrong.

Betty placed Carol onto a gurney. Doctor Burns administered a sedative for her. Carol would spend the night in the hospital. She was having a nervous break down.

Carol awoke at 7:00 a.m., holding her head. She felt as if she had a hangover, probably from the sedation, she thought.

She couldn't remember falling asleep in the hospital bed, but reality struck her the minute she saw the two detectives standing at the foot of the bed.

"Miss Crawford, my name is Detective Mark Jones and this is my partner Stan Barkley. I apologize for bothering you at a time like this. I understand that you and your family are going through a lot, and I'm very sorry, but we need to ask you a few questions concerning your brother's death."

If Carol wasn't laying down, she sure would have collapsed. No one had told her that her brother had died. She knew that her brother's chances of surviving was next to none, but it was a shock and so very hard to except.

"Okay gentleman, you're going to have to leave Miss Crawford alone." Betty firmly told the two detectives as she entered the room.

"It's very important that we ask Miss Crawford some questions concerning her brother's death." Detective Barkley insisted.

Betty's face turned beet red with rage. "How dare you tell her that her brother died ... she didn't even know it yet!" Betty hollered out.

The abashed detective walked past Betty to Carol's bedside.

"Miss Crawford ... I'm so sorry, I thought that you already knew. I feel so terrible about what I have done."

Carol felt sorry for the remorseful detective.

"I understand officer." Carol said in a soft pacifying voice. "I know you never meant any harm."

"Carol you're going to have to be strong. Your parents are going to need you very much now." Betty said, then gave Carol a hug. "It's going to be alright hon."

Once Carol started to settle down, the person that came to Carol's mind was Lloyd Smith.

She gave Betty Lloyd's phone number, and Betty went off to phone him."

The detectives asked Carol a few more questions, then left.

In less than an hour, Lloyd entered the room and compassionately took Carol into his arms, and comforted her. She was grateful that Lloyd showed up.

CHAPTER NINE

Reverend Kent blessed the oak coffin as it was being lowered into the grave.

It was a dismal, dreary rainy day, which was tantamount to the sorrowful discontentedness of everyone who had attended the funeral.

Carol's and Cathy's family were united together, holding on to each other, giving each other empathetic support.

Lloyd Smith held Carol in his arms trying to ease her pain. Carol's mother was in a wheel chair, sobbing in a way that Carol had never witnessed before. Jason stood over his distraught wife and silently wept.

Two police detectives sat in an unmarked car within a moral distance. They were keeping an eye out for anything or anyone suspicious. Detective Berkeley was studying everyone in attendance through his field binoculars, trying to identify everyone there and taking pictures of anyone who he couldn't identify.

The unmarked car pulled away as soon they seen that the proceedings was over.

Lloyd drove Carol and her parents home, but he didn't stay.

"Hi pumpkin." Jason said dispiritedly. His eyes teared up. He put his hand over his face to try and shield his grief from Carol.

Carol wrapped her arms around her grieving father and kissed his forehead.

"It's going to be okay dad .... " Carol said, then the room became filled with silence.

Carol could see the two detectives walking up the front steps. She greeted them before they had a chance to ring the door bell.

"Hello officers," Carol said with a quiver in her voice.

"Miss Crawford, I am Detective Mark Jones and my partner is Stan Berkeley. We would like to ask you a few more questions." Detective Jones showed so much compassion, which made Carol feel a little more at ease.

"Sure, please come in." Carol said, then led them in to the living room, where Jason was anxiously waiting to talk to them.

"Hello Mr. Crawford." Detective Jones said.

"Do you have any idea who did this to my son?"

"We don't have any suspects as yet, Mr. Crawford. Do you know of anyone that would do any harm to your son?"

"If I knew who did this to my son, I'd kill the son of a bitch myself!" Jason's fists were closed tight and his jaw clenched.

"We see in our files that your son was released from jail just four hours before his body was discovered. Could you tell us how long he was having family problems?" Detective Berkeley was trying to be as attentive as possible. He had such a soft voice for a big man.

Carol explained to the two detectives about her last encounter with her brother when she had seen the battered look of her sister in law.

Carol broke down as she tried to construe the events that took place the last time she had seen her brother alive. A sudden rush of guilt went through her weary mind. She thought to herself that this might not have happened to her brother if she would have never reported the incident to the police.

The detectives had finished their questioning, and were just walking out the door when the telephone rang. Carol walked nonchalantly to answer it. "Garry, I'm so glad you phoned. Did you hear what happened?"

Garry had just returned from a weeks vacation in the Barbados.

"Yes I did hon, I'm so sorry. How are you holding up?"

"Oh Garry, it was so horrible seeing my sister in law so battered, then finding out about my brother."

Carol could hear Garry's voice break up. He too was in tears. He had a heart of gold and really felt for Carol, and her family.

"Carol ... I'll be down as soon as I can, I love you."

"I love you too .... " Carol said then hung up the phone.

It took less than ten minutes for Garry to arrive. He wrapped his arms around Carol and held on to her. As soon as he seen Jason, he walked up to him and embraced him.

Garry bowed his head shamefully and said, "I'm sorry I missed the funeral."

"That's okay Garry, I'm sorry that you had to come back to so much bad news."

"Where's your mom, Carol? I hope she's okay." Garry asked looking very worried.

Just as he asked, Jean walked out of the bedroom. She looked extremely confused and lethargic.

It was a pure struggle for Jean to make it to the kitchen table, she tried her best to hide the fact, but it was too obvious to hide. Garry gently took a hold of her arm, and assisted her to the chair. Jean didn't even attempt to sit down. It was all that she could do was to use the chair to hold herself up. Carol could see that there was something drastically wrong with her mother.

"Are you okay mom?" Carol asked, horrified. Carol's mind raced as she waited for her mother's reply, which seemed to take an eternity for Carol.

"Mom .... ?"

"Yes! I'm okay." Jean said, in a confused state.

Garry just looked on, stunned. He too knew that there was something terribly wrong with Jean.

"Who is this nice young man?" Jean asked.

"Mom, that's Garry. you remember Garry, don't you?" Carol asked, her voice trembled with concern.

"You know who I am, don't you Mrs. Crawford?" Garry asked in a raised voice.

"I'm not deaf you know!" Jean shot back, which caught everyone off guard."

Garry? I don't think that we ever met before ... have we?" Jean asked with a puzzled look on her face.

Garry, Carol and Jason looked at each other with shock and disbelief on their faces.

Jean attempted to sit down but failed, she fell to the floor. Garry quickly came to her aid to help her up.

"Get away you fool!" Jean yelled out at Garry, with her arms whaling.

"I can get up myself. I don't need your help, now get away from me!"

Garry stepped back but was ready in case she fell again.

Jean tried to get up but failed miserably.

"Well don't everybody just stand there, help me up! Make yourself useful."

Garry and Carol helped her up off the floor, then Garry carried her to bed.

Carol picked up the phone and dialed 911 for an ambulance.

The only problem would be to convince Carol's mother to go to the hospital.

Carol walked in to the bedroom, and went on her knees. She caressed her mother's hair, and explained to her that she was going to go to the hospital.

"No, no, I don't want to go to no hospital! You're just trying to get rid of me, that's all your doing, just leave me alone, go away!" Jean yelled out, and was extremely combative.

"Mom ... no one is trying to get rid of you. We love you, and we are going to be right with you, I promise."

"It's going to be okay dear, don't you worry none." Jason said to his crying wife.

Carol could see that her father was getting very upset as well. Once again, Carol knew that she had to be strong.

The ambulance arrived and prepared Jean to go to the hospital. She put up such a struggle that it took both paramedics, as well as Garry to load her onto the stretcher.

Carol rode up front of the ambulance. Jason and Garry followed close behind in Garry's car.

Once Carol's mother was sedated, she felt more at ease and started to relax, she stopped her combativeness.

Jason just sat in the chair starring at the floor, engulfed with grief. They had never been apart in their forty-two years of marriage. Many different scenarios went through Jason's worried mind, he just could not imagine life without his best friend.

It was well after 3:00 a.m. when Wanda convinced Carol and Jason to go home. Carol wanted to stay, but she could see how exhausted her father was.. She thought it would be best to take him home, then come back later on.

Before Jason walked out of the room, he walked over to his wife's bed side, where she laid so peacefully. Jason kissed her forehead, and whispered something into his ailing wife's ear. As they walked towards the door, Jason turned and looked back at his pitiful wife. Jason felt that this might be the last time he would ever see his wife again. A tear rolled down his face as he turned and walked out the door.

The next morning, Doctor Howell had telephoned Carol. He was too vague which totally frustrated Carol that Doctor Howell wouldn't give her anymore information over the phone. He asked Carol to come to the hospital, and they would talk about her mother's condition over coffee in the hospital's cafeteria.

Carol and Dr. Howell sat in hospital's cafeteria, drinking coffee.

"So how is everyone treating you down in E.R, Carol? You should be running the place by now."

Dr. Howell had a lot of admiration for Carol. He had always felt that Carol would have made an excellent doctor.

"I love working in the E R, every shift is different, never the same repetitive stuff like you get in the other wards." Dr. Howell had always made her feel so illustrious with all his confidence and support that he gave her.

Carol glanced anxiously at her watch, then gave Dr. Howell a look of anticipation. She sat up straight, interlocked her fingers, and rested them on the table.

Every essence of her consciousness was on her dear mother.

Beads of sweat formed on her brow and she squirmed in her seat as she anticipated what Doctor Howell was about to tell her.

Dr. Howell placed his hands on to Carol's, and calmly said, "Carol, your mom is going to be fine. What I'm about to tell you, sounds a lot worse than it is."

Carol listened intensely to every word that Doctor Howell spoke.

"Carol, your mother had a stroke."

Carol gasped for air and cupped her hands over her mouth in shock.

"Oh no ... no, oh my God no!"

"Carol, calm down." Doctor Howell said, compassionately.

"We gave your mom a M.R.I. and found that she had a hemorrhagic stroke. We caught it in time. We have to give her some time to see how this is going to affect her. Right now she is stable. She is going to need special care."

"How is this going to affect her?"

"You might see a little difference in her personality, how much, we really don't know.

You will have to keep a close watch on her for awhile."

"Thank you Doctor Howell." Carol said as she stood up. Carol was in shock, and terrified.

"Are you alright, Carol?"

"Yes, I'll be okay ... I'm fine, thanks." Carol said, but Doctor Howell could see different.

"I need to see my mom. My dad is with her now. He's taking it really hard." Carol whimpered.

"Okay, Carol. I'll be up to see your mom as soon as I can. I have a patient in the ER waiting."

Carol walked in to her mother's hospital room, and was shocked to see Jean all dressed and ready to go home. She was even more astonished to see that her mother had pulled out the intravenous. There was blood on her bed, and blood was seeping through her blouse.

"Mom, you can't leave now. You have to get back into bed."

"You never mind now Carol, I'm going home and no one is going to stop me!" Jean bellowed out, throwing a merciless tantrum.

Nurse, Mary Dawson came into the room to see what all the commotion was about. She heard Jean's voice all the way at the nurses station. Jason fragrantly put his hands over his face, conscious stricken from all the ruckus his wife was making. She was thrashing her arms violently in the air. Carol and Mary had a hard time controlling her.

"Come on mom, settle down." Carol yelled out as she tried to gain control of her mother.

"What's going on in here? Why is your mother all dressed?"

"That bullshit isn't going to work with me sweet heart, now get your hands off of me and let me get the fuck out of here!"

Jason had all that he could take. He jumped out of his chair and came to the aid of his daughter.

"Now come on Jean, don't you talk that way to Carol, she's only trying to help you." Jason's spoke up to his wife, something that he seldom did, there was never a need to. Jean calmed down just long enough to let her husband's words sink in, then she bellowed out, "And you fuck off too ... if you won't take me home I'll find someone else who will. Fuck you... fuck you all!"

Jason and Carol were totally shocked at Jean's outburst, especially the vulgarity. They both took it right to heart. Tears ran down their dejected faces.

Nurse Dawson came back in with a syringe of Valium. "Okay Mrs. Crawford, this will make you feel a lot better." Mary said as she cautiously approached Jean.

"No! I don't want a needle." Jean begged. "Please let me go home ... I'm sorry."

"It's okay, sweetie." Mary compassionately said. Jean looked so sad and scared.

"It's okay, mom, I'm here." Carol said, as she stroked her petrified mother's hair.

Carol distracted her mother enough for Mary could inject the Valium into Jean's hip The Valium took affect almost immediately.

"I want to take a rest now ... just for a couple of minutes, then I want to go home." Jean said, then quickly fell off to a deep sleep, much to the relief of Carol and her dad.

CHAPTER TEN

Carol pulled up in front of the Caprice restaurant, got out of the car, and placed a quarter into the parking meter. The meter maid nodded her head at Carol and gave her a friendly smile as she walked past. Carol returned the gesture.

Carol could see Lloyd sitting at a corner table as she walked in to the dimly lit restaurant. Lloyd's face lit right up as soon as he noticed her.

Thoughts raced through Carol's mind. There was just something about Lloyd that was so magical to her about him. She adored his shyness, which helped to take the edge off of her own lack of confidence in herself.

Lloyd made her feel so at ease and she loved the way she felt when she was with him.

"Hi Lloyd," Carol said with a big eager smile.

"Hi Carol, is that a new dress?" Lloyd asked as he pulled her chair out for her.

"It sure looks nice on you ... it matches you're beautiful blue eyes."

"Why thank you, Lloyd." Carol said, her face beaming.

"That was so nice of you to say.."

"Hey, it's true, darlin', Carol, you look absolutely beautiful."
Carol blushed.

Carol looked at Lloyd in majestic wonder. She thought to herself that he had the body of a man, but the innocence of a child.

"Isn't this a wonderful table ... and so romantic?"

"Yes it is, hon."

"Well I hope so, I had to pay the guy a 'ten spot' to get this table." Lloyd's face went full flush. He was trying so hard to be gracious, and what he had said made him feel like he just stuck both feet in his mouth.

Carol could see the humiliation on his face, she spoke up and said, "Yea it ain't too shabby at all, Lloyd."

Lloyd looked up at Carol and smiled contently. Carol returned the smile. It was like a magic moment for them. Lloyd knew right then and there that he didn't need to put on any show for Carol, and that he had found himself such a special lady. Carol felt the same way as well, about him.

"What would you care to order, Carol?" Lloyd asked, still beaming. He looked at Carol as if he were starring at an Angel. In his eyes, she was.

"Everything looks so good. Why don't you order for me?"

"All right then ... let's see, okay, why don't we have the duck?" Lloyd motioned to the waiter.

"Would you like to order now?" The waiter asked.

"Yes we would. We will have the duck, with French fries and gravy."

"Sir ... you want to have french fries and gravy with your duck?" The waiter gave Lloyd a baffled look and a mocking grin.

"Would you care to see the wine list sir? We have a lovely Chateau Chablis wine from Canada, that would go superbly with your duck, french fries and gravy." The waiter was now totally belittling Lloyd. Lloyd's face went red with embarrassment.

"Yes we would like to have the Chateau Chablis, Carol shot out at the obnoxious waiter.

"Yes mam." The now flustered waiter responded, then walked away shaking his head.

Lloyd gave the waiter a 'if looks could kill' kind of glance. It was obvious that Lloyd wasn't too accustomed to dining out at such a fancy restaurant. Carol could tell that he was more than a little out of place, she thought that it was more precious than anything else. He was the one who made the reservations, and it was he who felt like a fish out of water. Carol tried to make him feel less self conscious.

"You never told me what you do for a living Lloyd.

"I work as a bartender. I know that isn't nothing to brag about, Carol, but, I'm looking for something better." Lloyd bowed his head as if he were ashamed of what he did for a living.

"Lloyd, I bet you're the best darn bartender in this country."

Lloyd was taking all this attention in. He never received so much attention from a woman or from anyone else before. He knew that Carol was not like most woman that he met, Carol was a lady.

She invited Lloyd to her place for a drink of wine.

She had a bottle of white wine that she was saving for a special occasion, and this was definitely a special occasion for her.

As they entered the front door, Jason was anxiously waiting for them.

"Hello Mr. Crawford. It's nice to see you again." Jason shook Lloyd's awaiting hand.

"Well it's really nice to see you again too Lloyd. Come on in, I will put the coffee on."

Jason brought out a tray of coffee and some cinnamon roles.

"So, how was your dinner?"

"It was wonderful, dad. Lloyd ordered duck, and it was so delicious."

"Well that is nice." Jason said, with a big grin on his face.

"I will let you two be alone. I'm off to the den, I have a new friend on my computer. She is a wonderful lady. She's from Buffalo... I wouldn't tell mom about it though, she might get the wrong impression.

Do you know anything about computers, Lloyd?"

"No, I'm afraid not, Mr. Crawford...maybe you could show me sometime."

"It would be my pleasure there, Lloyd."

I'm going to talk to Martha on my computer. She's waiting for me" Jason was overly excited. Which gave Lloyd and Carol a little giggle.

Carol took a hold of Lloyd's hand and led him in the kitchen.

"I will make us some cheese and crackers." Carol said, then gave Lloyd a bottle of white wine to open.

Lloyd stood up, he didn't say a word, he put his arms around her from behind and kissed the back of her neck. Carol's legs became weak. Carol turned around and they embraced, Lloyd's hands eased up Carol's blouse and worked his hands up to her breasts.

"Not here sweetie," she whispered. Come with me." Carol could barely breath, she was full of passion. She took Lloyd's hand and led him into her bedroom. They embraced.

Lloyd removed Carol's blouse and exposed her large aroused breasts.

They both got on to the bed.

Carol's back was arched and she was savoring the ecstasy that Lloyd was giving her. Carol grabbed hold of the sheets and tried to silence her pleasure.

"Carol, are you in there?" Jason bellowed out through the closed door.

Carol and Lloyd jumped to their feet and tried not to make such a commotion as to give away there urgency as they raced to get dressed.

"Yes dad ... I'll be right out." Carol said deceptively.

Carol opened the door and her dad was standing there peering through the half opened door in an inquisitive manner. Carol's face was two different shades of red.

Lloyd just stayed seated on the bed. Jason was well aware of what was going on, he could see that Carol's bed was in such disarray.

Even though Jason was well aware of their going-ons, he didn't make an issue of it. If it was Carol's mother, something for sure would have hit the fan.

"I'm sorry to bother you kids. Could we go see your mother?" Jason's eyes were filled with tears.

"Sure dad, we will go as soon as you're ready."

"Thank you sweetheart, I need to see her." Jason was very emotional and seemed very upset.

CHAPTER ELEVEN

Lloyd lived at the Peepers Strip Club for almost three years. It was 9 am, someone was pounding on Lloyd's door.

"Who the fuck would be knockin' at my door at this time in the fuckin' morning?" Lloyd grumbled as he made his way toward the door.

Lloyd opened it. Matt Clark stood there in his thousand dollar suit. He was the owner of Peepers Strip Club, which was just a front for him. He was a mafia boss and when he spoke everyone listened. He could put the fear of death in to anyone. He was a king pin with a large drug cartel.

Lloyd suddenly had a change of attitude when he realized who it was.

"Come on in Mr. Clark. How are you doing sir?" Lloyd put on the dog with his changed attitude.

"Cut the bullshit Smith, I have a job for you to do, and I want it done today, understand?"

"Yes sir."

Beads of sweat were rolling down Lloyd's face. He was terrified of Matt Clark.

"Okay Smith, here's what I want you to do. There is an asshole, his name is Bernardo. He owes me money big time. I want you to go and pay him a visit, and shake him up. You tell him that I want my money now. If Bernardo doesn't give you my ten grand right away, then teach him a lesson. Now don't go out there and kill the son of a bitch, just make sure that he gets the message, big time."

"Yes sir, I will make sure that it will get looked after today."

Matt took hold of Lloyd's shoulder and said: "You do things right for me Smitty and I will look after you." Matt gave Lloyd an intimidating slap on the side of his face then left after giving him the details of where to find this Bernardo guy.

Lloyd was getting in deep with Matt Clark. He owed Matt ten thousand dollars from a gambling debt. Lloyd had to do some pretty dirty blood work in order to payoff his debt off to Matt.

Lloyd was one of the lucky ones, usually when some one didn't pay a debt to Matt, they wound up crippled or dead.

Now this was one of Lloyd's jobs, to go after anyone that didn't payoff their debts.

Lloyd splashed some water in his face and got dressed and prepared to do his assignment.

Lloyd climbed into Matt's black Cadillac which he often used, and headed towards First street. A pair of black leather gloves lay beside him on the passenger's seat.

As Lloyd pulled up in front of Jim Bernardo's house. Matt always kept a snub nosed 38 in the glove department. Lloyd didn't want anything to do with it.

He put the leather gloves on to his big hands.

As Lloyd walked up the front steps he could see that there was still a morning newspaper neatly rolled up and placed in the aluminum doors handle. So it appeared to Lloyd that this Bernardo guy hadn't left the house yet this morning.

Lloyd checked to see if the door was unlocked. It was, so Lloyd prowled his way through the door and into the house. Everything was quiet except for a faint snoring noise that was coming from one of the rooms that was in Lloyd's sight.

As Lloyd made his way to Bernardo's bedroom, he could see Bernardo laying in bed and beside of him lay a blond haired woman.

Lloyd made his way towards Bernardo, taking careful steps as to not awake them.

Lloyd put a strangle hold on the unsuspecting Bernardo's throat. He awoke in total terror. Lloyd loosened up his choke hold on Bernardo just enough for he could talk. The young blond haired woman awoke in a frenzy. Trying to cover up her exposed body.

Lloyd showed no interest in the woman, he just told her to shut up and she wouldn't get hurt.

"Matt wants his ten grand, and he wants it now. So what's it going to be, you give me the money now or you are going to die a long painful death. What's it going be asshole? It's do or die."

Bernardo was now sweating profusely and was begging for his life. He was desperate and the blond that once was laying beside him was on her feet, screaming and pounding her fists on Lloyd.

This just made Lloyd more irate. He gave her a swift and hard backhand, knocking her to the floor.

"Shut the fuck up, or I'11 kill the both of you!"

The hour glassed figured woman grabbed her clothes and tried to walk out the door.

Lloyd grabbed her by the hair and tossed her back on the bed.

"Okay asshole what's it going to be?" Lloyd was losing his cool and he wanted to get things done and over with, and to get out of there.

"Please let me go." Bernardo cried out in terror. " I don't have the money I can get it tomorrow. I'11 make sure that Matt gets it."

Lloyd gave Bernardo a viscous. blow to the nose. Blood splattered on to the sheets and half way up the wall.

Bernardo's arms were now trying to shield his face.

"Tomorrow ain't good enough, Mr. Clark wants it now." Lloyd gave Bernardo another blow to his head."

"I don't have it ..... I just don't have it ... " He cried out.

"Give him the money...give him the money!" His blonde haired companion yelled out, now she was beating on Bernardo.

"And you shut the fuck up too, you stupid bitch." Lloyd yelled out, then gave her a viscous blow to the back of her head.

Lloyd lifted the defenseless Bernardo right off of the bed and slammed him against the wall..

"I have some coke in my dresser .. let me get it for you and maybe you can let me go for another day."

Lloyd was very interested in Bernardo's offer.

"Okay asshole, go get it."

Bernardo staggered towards the unpainted dresser, he opened the drawer. Lloyd noticed the devious look on his face. Lloyd rushed over towards Bernardo. Bernardo tried to fend off Lloyd as he pulled out a colt 45. Lloyd wrestled him to the ground and the gun went off shattering the ceiling light fixture and sending shards of glass across the room..

"You stupid fuck, I'll fix you, you son of a bitch!"

Now the woman was getting into the action, climbing on top of Lloyd smashing his head with her tiny fists. Lloyd had no problem knocking her off of him and on to the floor.

Lloyd had the gun in his hand now..

"Stand up mother fucker and you stay there bitch." Lloyd was jamming the barrel of the gun down Bernardo's throat. Lloyd was never in this position before and it made him feel powerful but scared.

"How would you like it if I pulled the trigger right now asshole?" Lloyd cocked the trigger and started to shake uncontrollably. Lloyd removed the gun from Bernardo's mouth and released the trigger. Then he pummeled Bernardo with massive punches and kicked him as he fell to the floor. Lloyd bent over and grabbed Bernardo by the hair and told him to pay up by tonight or he would kill him. As he stepped over Bernardo's body he peered towards the petrified woman and gave her a good stare. She sat unclothed against the bedroom wall, too terrified to move or say a word.

"And fuck you too bitch." Blood was streaming down from her nose where Lloyd had connected a hard blow.

Lloyd walked back to his car. He sat in the car, thought of what he had done, then he broke down and cried like a baby. He was never in this position before where he had to beat someone up so badly and the gun had a big part of it too.

Lloyd just sat there in a daze, reflecting at what he had just done. He wished that he had never met Matt Clark. Lloyd didn't like the way how Matt Clark changed his life. Lloyd was a peaceful man before he met him.

Lloyd reached over and opened the glove compartment and pulled out the loaded gun and held it to his temple. He cocked the revolver, then a thought came to his mind, it was about Carol. The only one that loved him. He changed his mind and placed the gun back in to the glove compartment.

Lloyd was driving down River Road, the bloodied gloves lay on the passenger seat. Lloyd had blood stains on his shirt and a couple of buttons missing from his scuffle with Bernardo. As he was turning up the volume to a Rolling Stones tune, he seen the flashers of the police cruiser in his rear view mirror. He quickly grabbed the bloodied gloves and stuffed them underneath the seat. He hated anyone who wore a badge. The impatient cop put his siren on to get Lloyd's attention and to pull over. Lloyd took his pocket knife and sliced his index finger intentionally then pulled the black Cadillac over to the side of the road.

He could see the officer exit his cruiser, and approach the Cadillac with caution.

Lloyd's mind was racing. He wasn't sure if this was just a routine traffic stop or if Bernardo had ratted him out.

Sargent Bruce Johnson gave the black Cadillac a good looking over.

"Hello officer, was I going too fast? I just have to watch that lead foot of mine." Lloyd said, obviously nervous.

"Sir can I see your drivers license and registration please?" Sargent Johnson was very stern.

"So what did I do wrong officer?"

"Sir can I have your license and registration please?" The stern cop asked the second time.

Lloyd reached for his wallet in his back pocket and Lloyd's quick maneuver was too fast for Sargent Johnson and his hand moved towards his weapon. Lloyd could sense that this was more than just a routine traffic stop. Lloyd handed the uneasy cop his driver's license, then reached over to the glove compartment for the vehicle registration. This made Sargent Johnson feel uneasy. He placed his hand on his weapon.

"There you go officer, this is my bosses car so if there is any unpaid traffic tickets it "s not my fault."

The timid cop took Lloyd's identification and went back to his cruiser.

He could see the cop talking into his microphone.

A few minutes past and another cruiser pulled up. This really made Lloyd paranoid.

"Fuck you! Fuckin' useless pigs! Why don't you go find yourselves a doughnut shop instead of getting on my fuckin' ass." Lloyd was becoming very irate.

"Fuck!" he slammed his fist on the dashboard in frustration.

Both cops walked towards the Cadillac very cautiously.

"Mr. Smith can you step out of the car for a moment please?" The officer asked with his right hand on the butt of his revolver.

"Am I under arrest or something?"

"Mr. Smith, I'm going to ask you one more time now. Would you please step outside of the car, now?" The cop was the one that was getting irate now.

"Okay okay I'll get out, but I wish you would tell me what I've done. You just can't pull me over and treat me like this, and not tell me why. I have fuckin' rights you know." Lloyd was losing his cool, he was convinced that he was going to jail. Officer Johnson pushed Lloyd against the car and told him to spread, while the other officer stayed back and observed.

Officer Johnson placed Lloyd in handcuffs and both cops lead him towards the cruiser.

They opened the rear door to the police cruiser and guided his head and then closed the door.

The two officers stood in front of the cruiser, discussing the situation.

Sargent Johnson opened the back door of the cruiser.

"Okay Mr. Smith, here's where we stand. You have a bench warrant against you in Montana, we're waiting for conformation. You failed to appear in court. Can you tell me what that was all about, Mr. Smith?"

"I don't remember nothin' about no court." Lloyd was losing his composer. He knew he was going to jail.

"Mr. Smith you're not going to help yourself very much if you don't help us get this sorted out. You know we can just bring you down to the precinct and we can let you wait it out down there." Sargent Johnson was giving Lloyd a chance to make things easier for himself.

"Okay, it was just a common assault that's all. I didn't want to go to jail for just giving some idiot a broken nose." Lloyd wasn't getting any further ahead with his attitude.

"Mr. Smith, how did you get blood all over your shirt?"

Lloyd had covered his tracks on that one when he intentionally sliced his finger with his pocket knife.

"I cut my damn finger on something in the car." Lloyd displayed his bloodied finger to the suspicious cop.

Sargent Johnson had is hand held police radio held up to his ear, then said a few words into it and replaced it back into his holster. The dispatcher gave the officers another call, which was an emergency.

"Okay Mr. Smith, Montana doesn't want you, they said that they would be happier if you stayed out of their state. Are you staying out of trouble here, Mr. Smith? Are you working?"

"I work at Peepers, I'm a bartender there." Lloyd said in such a cockily way. He knew they didn't have anything on him to arrest him.

"We are going to let you go Mr. Smith. Now you stay out of trouble. The two police officers escorted Lloyd to his car.

Lloyd put the car in drive when Sargent Bruce Johnson spoke up. "Hey wait a minute !!. " Sargent Johnson just remembered about the incident involving the Black Cadillac following Carol.

Lloyd held his breath in fear.

"What, you changed your mind now and you're going to bust me?"

The unsettled cop took his hat off and scratched the back of his neck. He gave the situation a quick thought then looked down at Lloyd. "Never mind, just get the hell out of here." Lloyd didn't need to be told twice, he was gone in a flash.

CHAPTER TWELVE

Jason was in the den, sending out e-mails to his computer friends. Carol had just awaken, and was sitting alone at the kitchen table, contemplating on how she was going to spend her day off. She knew that her dad was content in front of his computer.

Carol had Lloyd on her mind, she had such a strong desire to see him, but she knew that Cathy and her nephew David needed more of her attention right now. She hadn't visited them since her brother's death. Carol picked up the phone and dialed the number to her sister in law's house. After the sixth ring she switched the cordless phone off , then placed it back onto the table. After a moments thought, she picked the phone back' up and started to dial Lloyd's number. She had a change of heart and decided that her time should be spent with her family.

Her heart yearned so much for Lloyd. She was reminiscing about the time they spent together, ordering the French fries with the duck, and then the passionate love that they made together. She thought that Lloyd had the innocence of a child and he just needed some polishing around the edges.

Jason came into the kitchen, half crying and very upset about something.

"What's wrong dad?" Carol reached out to her distressed father. Jason could barely catch his breath and his face was contorted.

"Lucy, my computer friend and I had a disagreement. I don't want to lose her, I love her pumpkin, I really love her. I want to go see her but she lives so far away." Jason was heart broken. Carol had no idea that her dad had so much feeling towards anyone on the computer.

Carol hugged her grieving father as the tears rolled down his face.

"It's okay dad, don't you worry, everything is going to work out okay."

Carol was starting to feel the pressure, she was carrying a lot of weight on her shoulders. She was feeling very stressed and burdensome. She was reaching her limit, there was only so much pressure that she could handle before her emotions would begin to surface, but she knew that she had to be strong for her family, it was becoming so much more difficult as more and more problems kept popping up,she felt that it was her responsibility to keep every ones emotions in check.

Jason was calming down. Now it was Carol's turn, she could take any more, and the flood gates opened, her shoulders could no longer bare the weight. Carol and her dad seemed to be trying to out duel each other. The harder Carol cried her despondent father followed right along in unison. After a few minutes of venting, they both wiped their eyes, then looked at each other, then they laughed hysterically. They both didn't know what they were laughing about but it sure felt better than crying. They were both all cried out and all the pressure was gone, but for how long?

"You know what pumpkin? I'm going to get right back onto that computer and set things right with Lucy. You know what they say pumpkin, when you fall off a horse, you just climb right back on it, and that's exactly what I'm going to do." Carol smiled from her fathers adage.

"Okay dad, you get back on that horse and I think I'm going to go see if Cathy and David are home, and pay them a visit." Carol turned around, but her father was gone back to his computer.

Carol walked in to the den to tell him where she was going. "Okay dad, I hope that you don't get any saddle sores." He was so emerged in his computer that he didn't hear a word she said.

Carol pulled up into her sister in law's driveway. There was no change. The yard looked like a total scrap yard. Over turned garbage cans and an unsightly array of refuse.

Cathy's car was parked half on the driveway and half on the walkway. A big dent on the front fender made the car look twice as old as it was. Carol sauntered up to the walkway, then climbed the steps almost loosing her balance from the broken railing. She braced herself to make sure that she avoided stepping on what appeared to be was vomit. As she peered through the same old ragged curtains on the front door, she could see Cathy sitting at the kitchen table.

The scene was familiar to Carol, Cathy was sitting there, drinking a bottle of beer, with at least four empty bottles spread across the filthy table. An ashtray sat in front of her, heaping full of cigarette butts.

Carol gave two soft taps on the door, then entered, holding her breath, taking in all the putrid air a little at a time.

"What the fuck are you doing in here? Grab a beer and sit down." Cathy was more than a little intoxicated. Carol ignored Cathy's offer for a beer and just sat down. The room wreaked of cigarette smoke and the sink was overfilled with dirty dishes.

"So how is everything, Cathy?" Carol felt so uncomfortable seeing her sister in law sitting there so drunk weaving back and forth in her chair.

"Oh everything is just honky fuckin' dory sweetheart, just fuckin' honky dory. I don't want no fucking sympathy speech either. I don't need that crap. Matthew was nothing but a fuckin' bastard anyways. Do you ever think that maybe he deserved to die?" Cathy pounded her fist on the table, knocking two empty beer bottles on to the floor and she didn't even flinch at the smashing noise. There was broken shards of glass spread allover the filthy linoleum floor.

"So where is David, Cathy?"

"Now how the fuck am I suppose to know? He hasn't been home for days. He doesn't give a fuck about me, and I sure don't give a fuck about him either."

Carol knew that she wasn't going to have a civil conversation with Cathy, so she stood up and headed towards the door.

"I'm sorry I can't stay, Cathy, I just dropped by to see how you're getting along. I'11 try and stop by sometime next week and see how everything is." Carol said in a somber voice.

"Yea yea, just don't let the door hit you on your way out."

Carol walked out the door without saying anything more.

Carol sat in her car for a few minutes, trying to get her thoughts back in order. She decided to head back home to check on her dad, and take him to see her mom at the hospital.

When Carol entered the house, she was taken back with astonishment. Her mom was sitting down at the kitchen table in her pajamas and housecoat.

"Mom ... how did you get home? Did they let you out of the hospital?" Carol was in total disbelief..

"Hi sweetheart,. how are you my dear? I didn't want to stay in that place any longer, so I decided to walk home. A really nice police officer stopped and brought me home. Oh he was so handsome, you would just love him, and he is single. I wanted to give him our phone number but I just couldn't remember it. He said that he might come over to see you. He was a little confused though, he couldn't find our house."

Jean was talking in a low robotic way, which worried Carol. Her mother was never the same after she suffered the stroke.

Carol grabbed the phone on the kitchen table and was going to phone the hospital to let them know that her mom was home. Before she could dial, the phone rang, it was nurse Holiday from the Trillium ward where her mom was staying. Carol had a shaky voice and more than a little dismayed. The nurse felt at ease when Carol told her that her mom made it home safely.

The nurse told Carol that Dr. Howell wanted her mom to get back to the hospital.

Carol switched off the phone, and placed it back on the kitchen table. She didn't know how she was going to tell her parents that she had to go back to the hospital. Her dad didn't know what was going on. He was sitting there with a big grin on his face; he was happy to see his wife back home. He missed her so much.

"We have to take you back to the hospital, mom. You're not ready to come home yet."

"Your not making any sense dear. What is going on?"

"Yes, Carol...what in the Sam hell is going on?" Jason bellowed out.

" Dr. Howell wants mom to go back to the hospital."

"She is not going back to the hospital!" Jason yelled out, banging his fist on the table. Totally out of character for him.

"Yea that's right dear...what did he say?" Carol's mom didn't have a clue at what was going on.

"Okay, settle down now, and I will phone Dr. Howell."

Carol picked up the phone and brought it to the living room. She dialed the number and asked to talk to Dr. Howell. It took over ten minutes until Dr. Howell came to the phone. Carol explained to the doctor at what was going on.

With stipulations, the doctor agreed to let Carol's mom stay home.

For Carol's mom to stay home, Carol would have to take some time off of work, which it was something that would be good for her as well.

Carol's dad was ecstatic at the news..

Carol pulled up into the parking space at the hospital. Carol felt a little despondent on returning to work after having three days off. But today she felt like work would be more like a haven after looking after her mother for three days.

She entered the rear door of the hospital and headed straight for the fourth floor where her mom had stayed.

Nurse Mary Dawson was at the nurses station. Carol took a sigh of relief that there was someone that she knew.

"Hi Mary. How are you? Are you busy?"

Mary looked up and saw that it was Carol and immediately asked about her mom.

"Your mom sure made a quick disappearing act. If you would like to talk to Doctor Howell he'll be here any minute now."

"When I came home Wednesday, I was shocked to see my mother there. She was so confused. That was pretty scary. Thank God the police found her."

Mary felt a little self conscious, she was one of the nurses who was on duty when Jean had snuck her way past the nurses station.

"Your mother was really sneaky, she certainly has a lot of spunk I must say."

"Hello ladies." Forty five year old Dr. Howell came to the desk in his green surgical scrubs, wiping the sweat of his brow. He was one of the most pleasant doctors that was on the staff at the West Wood Hospital. He treated all the nurses with respect and gave them the credit that they deserved. Most doctors didn't give any credit to the nurses, they just overlooked their importance and the job that they did. AII the staff got along so well with Doctor Howell.

"Hello Dr. Howell." Nurse Mary said to Dr. Howell in a flirtatious way.

Carol my dear. How are you doing kiddo.? How is your mom doing?"

"I'm just fine, thanks Dr. Howell. My mom is holding her own, she's still pretty confused."

"To be honest with you Carol, your mom is going to be a handful to look after." Doctor Howell told things just the way the were. He was a type of doctor who wouldn't sugar coat anything.

"Just give her time, Carol. She'll come around."

"Thank you Doctor Howell." Carol said, then made her way down to the E.R.

CHAPTER THIRTEEN

Carol awoke feeling energized. She had a clear mind and it felt great to have all the weight off of her shoulders. Her family life was now tranquil. The first thing on her mind as she sprung out of her water bed was her romeo, Lloyd. She picked up her princess phone and dialed Lloyd's number.

A strange voice came through the receiver, "Hello Peepers." There was a lot of loud background noise.

Carol paused for a minute, thinking that maybe she dialed the wrong number.

"I'm sorry, I think I might have the wrong number."

"Well who the hell do you want?" The man on the other end of the line snapped back. Carol couldn't think fast enough. She didn't know if she should just hang up or not.

"I'm looking for Lloyd Smith. " Carol was feeling a bit on edge now from this guys obnoxious attitude.

"Why the fuck didn't you say that in the first place? Hold on a minute and I'll get him."

Carol could here this very rude guy holler to someone to go and get Smitty. Carol could here a crowd of people in the background cheering and whistling, really carrying on as if there was some kind of side show or some kind of party.

Carol could hear Lloyd's voice in the background as he was getting closer to the phone. Carol covered her one ear for she could here what Lloyd was saying.

"Who the fuck is bugging me know? Don't tell me it's another bitch wanting me to go and save her fuckin' ass."

Carol quickly slammed the phone down, feeling hurt and disgusted.

Carol's mood went from such a high to a rock bottom low, from what she heard Lloyd saying on the phone.

Well so much for my day, Carol thought to herself, and so much for her romeo.

Carol sat on the edge of the bed in deep thought.

She was shocked at Lloyd's crude words that she overheard. She was disgusted at him.

Carol was so livid, she vaulted from her bed and grabbed a hold of her princess phone, and pushed the redial button. She wanted to get this dilemma solved. She couldn't have this playing on her mind, she wanted to know where she stood with Lloyd. She wanted to find out if Lloyd was referring her as a bitch.

"Hello, how can I help you?" Lloyd answered in rough voice.

"Hello Lloyd."

"Yes, this is Lloyd, now what do you want?" Lloyd couldn't tell that it was Carol from all the background noise.

"Lloyd, this is Carol." Carol raised her voice.

"So how is my little angel? It's so good to hear from you Carol."

"Lloyd" Carol said in a nervous voice. "I phoned this number ten minutes ago, and this very obnoxious guy answered the phone, and when he called for you, I heard what you said. Was that directed at me?" Carol felt like she was doing more harm than good from bringing this up, but she had to confront Lloyd about his lewd outburst.

"Oh that was Jack who answered the phone before, don't worry about Jack, he didn't mean nothin', he's just having a bad day that's all."

Carol wasn't interested in the least about Jack and his bad day. She wanted Lloyd to get right to the issue of his remarks.

"Were you referring to me when you told Jack that you hope that it wasn't a bitch on the phone?"

The fifteen seconds of silence seemed like an eternity for Carol. She bit her bottom lip and waited for Lloyd's reply.

"Carol, I would never call you that, never."

Carol heard the disparity in Lloyd's voice, which made Carol feel guilty at what she was insinuating.

Lloyd was pulling the wool over her eyes and Carol was too gullible to see it.

She could hear Lloyd's faint sigh.

"I'm sorry Lloyd. I didn't mean anything by it. I just overheard someone saying ... I didn't mean to accuse you" Carol was squeezing the phone so hard that her knuckles were white. She was holding her breath in anticipation.

"Now don't you go apologizing to me sweetheart. You have nothing to apologize about, Carol. We were just goofin' off here, that's all. You should hear the kind of stuff that goes on around here, it gets pretty brutal. I'm just sorry that you had to hear it darlin'. But you must also realize, that this is a bar, and there is so much trash talk in this place. Sometimes I can barely stand it myself. If I didn't need this job, I would be out of here."

He knew that Carol was so naive, and he could manipulate her feelings so easily. It always gave him great confidence when he would wrap a woman around his little finger, and this was exactly what he was doing to Carol. Carol was too caring and too naive to see what Lloyd was doing to her. But Jack and a few of the guys that were gathered by the phone, got a kick out of listening at what Lloyd was saying, and manipulating Carol. Lloyd was coaxing them on., and they were being quite entertained about it, at Carol's expense.

Carol felt a lot more comfortable now and less hurt. It would have broken her heart if Lloyd didn't play his insincere song and dance to Carol, and pacify her insecurities.

"So how are you Lloyd?" Carol asked in such a descending way.

"Well I'm just fine sugar. How is your mom and dad doin'? Everything going okay?"

"We had a crisis with mom, but everything is getting better now.

"I'm sorry to hear that, I wish I was there for you, Carol

"Well how about if I come over there and pick you up?"

"Well ... what did you have in mind?" Carol asked in a seductive way, in which Carol was even shocked to hear it come out of her own mouth.

"How about going for another walk in the Lincoln Nature Trails?".

"Sounds great to me dear. And I promise not to be such a klutz this time, and not trip over my two left feet, like I did last time."

"Don't you worry none, I will hold you tight."

"Oh I like the sound of that."

Carol glanced in the mirror over her dresser and could see the flush on her face. She was longing for a chance to spend time with Lloyd. Just the thought of her spending time with Lloyd made her out of breath. She couldn't wait to be in Lloyd's arms once again.

"Okay hon'. How about me picking you up in about an hour?"

"Do you have to work tonight?" Lloyd was trying to talk over the noise at Peepers. All the patrons were making a big fuss over an ex Playboy centerfold, making her way on to the stage, with a cowgirl outfit on.

"Sure, an hour will be fine, and I don't have to work until Wednesday, I have two days off.

What the heck is going on there Lloyd? I can barely hear you."

"Trust me darlin', you wouldn't want to know. They are really having a party here, and things are getting pretty rowdy. I'll let you go, and I will see you in an hour, okay darlin'?" Lloyd was anxious to get off the phone, for he could take a good look at Miss Texas.

"Okay hon, I'll see you then." Carol waited for Lloyd to hang up, then she did the same.

Every one that was gathered around listening to Lloyd on the phone, gave Lloyd a high five. Lloyd ate-up all the attention that they giving him.

Carol was more than a little curious on what all the cheering and whistling was all about. She wondered what ever went on at his work, must be pretty entertaining to make all those people go so wild like that.

It was three in the afternoon. Eighty seven degrees and a very humid day. Carol and Lloyd were walking over a planked bridge. Below was a fast moving stream.

"Now you hold on real tight now sweetheart. Look over there Carol, you can see all the carp trying to swim upstream. Aren't they pretty. Look at that orange one." He was more content being away from the city. The Lincoln Nature Trails was always the place that Lloyd would come and clear his mind when everything started to get to be too much for him. A place to get away from everyone.

Carol was perplexed at the way Lloyd was so much at ease. Usually he was on the antsy side.

"So tell me Lloyd. Where did you live when you were a young boy? I bet you were a country boy."

"You're right sweetheart, I was a country boy. Back in Hillside Montana. I can remember how much fun I had living out in the country, fishing everyday. It all seems like a different world now. I'll never see those days again." Lloyd stopped talking and bowed his head, then looked up and wiped a tear from the corner of his eye.

"Yep, those were the good ole days. Just look at where I am now. No where, absolutely nowhere.

I tell ya, Carol, if I had myself some money, I would buy me a big old farm in the country. I'd have me some chickens, cows and all the land you could imagine, nothin' but wilderness sweetheart, nothin' but wilderness."

"That sounds wonderful honey When can we leave? Carol wanted to be part of this dream as well.

"You mean it sweetheart? You would come with me?" Lloyd asked enthusiastically.

"Believe me Lloyd, I wouldn't give it a second thought. I would love to live in the country. I don't know if I would make very good farmer though. Can you picture me wearing a pair of overalls, and a piece of straw in my mouth? But for you, I would trade in my nurses uniform for a pair of overalls any day." Lloyd looked at Carol in a totally different way now. He was more serious about this than Carol could ever imagine.

"You know it would only take about a hundred grand to get started. What do you think sweetheart? Do you think we really could.?" Lloyd was all ready to buy the farm and move in, but there was only one thing stopping him, and that was money

"Now you are serious about this darlin', aren't you?" Lloyd looked at Carol eagerly.

"Absolutely honey. I think this would be great for the both of us." Carol didn't give the idea a second thought, she was as anxious as Lloyd was.

"Well okay then, I guess I'm going to have to come up with some big money.

Lloyd gave Carol a hug and a kiss. I love you, I really do, so much." Lloyd took Carol into his arms. They became filled with heated passion. They were both out of breath and could no longer hold back what was inevitable.

"Come on sweetheart, there's a nice private spot over there where no one will bother us."

Lloyd lead the way to his secluded spot where they made love.

"Hey, what are you two doing over there? Can I play with you? My name is Bobby, I have a new gun. Wanna play?" Four year old Bobby Taylor asked.

"No thanks kid. Now run along ... go on. Beat it now."

"I know what you guys are doing, you know?" Bobby explained.

Little Bobby, stood there with his plastic toy gun pointed at Lloyd.

"So you think you know what were doin' here aye kid?" Lloyd was amazed with this kids intelligence.

"Yep, I do it all the time."

"You do? So tell me then. What were we doing?" Lloyd was really intrigued with this little tyke. Carol and Lloyd couldn't keep a straight face.

"Piggy back riding. That's what you were doin'. I do it all the time with my brother. Wanna meet him? I can get him for you, if you want me to. But he aint got no gun. He was bad and my daddy took it away from him." Bobby explained with such a serious expression on his face. He was such a cute and adorable little boy now standing right in front of them.

"Okay Bobby, run along now. Your parents are going to be looking for you." Carol pleaded with the little kid while she was trying to tidy her clothes back up.

"I got a daddy but my mom's not here. My daddy is over there in the bushes with his girlfriend. He told me and my brother to go fuck off for awhile. So here I am. Do you want to play or not?" Bobby sure was persistent.

"Bye Bobby, it was nice to meet you." Lloyd bellowed to the little tyke.

"Bye, nice to meet you too mister and lady." Bobby yelled out as he was going through the bushes.

"You never told me that you were so good with kids." Carol remarked to Lloyd.

"I have never been around kids before Carol. I don't know anything about kids." Lloyd said self consciously.

"You sure sounded like you did when you were talking to little Bobby. Did you see the way Bobby's eyes lit up when you talked to him? You're a natural at it. You were meant to be with kids, you would make such a good father, honey" Carol said in such a kind way to Lloyd.

"Carol, this is the first time anybody really cared for me like this. I love you. I love you so much." Lloyd didn't say a word after that. He felt love towards another person for the first time in his life. He didn't know just how to react. They both just stood there hugging each other cherishing the moment.

"I love you too Lloyd." This was a magic moment for the both of them.

CHAPTER FOURTEEN

Lloyd sat at a corner table, drinking a beer. His eyes fixed on the stripper on stage, thrashing her huge breasts over a bald headed man. The man was more embarrassed than anything else. Although Lloyd's eyes were on Tiny Tina, his mind was on Carol. He couldn't get over this feeling that she gave him. He was totally love struck. He just couldn't shake this feeling. He got a knot in the pit of his stomach, every time he thought of her.

"Something the matter there Smitty? You look like death warmed over." Roy Walters asked as he placed a shot of whiskey in front of Lloyd.

What's this for? I didn't order no fuckin' shot." Lloyd snapped at Roy.

"Well I suggest you to take the fuckin' shot, the boss sent it over for you!" Roy snapped right back at Lloyd.

Lloyd held up the shot of whiskey in the direction of Matt Clark, then nodded his head in a show of gratitude to his boss.

"What the fuck is he up to Roy? The last time he bought me a shot was when he wanted me to do some of his dirty work." Lloyd didn't want to even think of what his boss's intentions were. He knew the shot of whiskey would come at one price or another.

"I don't know what he's up to Smitty. The boss don't give anyone a free shot for nothin' you know?"

"Well thank you very much Mr. fuckin Einstein. Now get the fuck off my back and leave me alone." Lloyd was in no mood for chit-chat, and the last thing he wanted is some little runt like Roy yacking at him.

Lloyd was all smiles when he made eye contact with Matt Clark, but if his boss knew what he really thought about him, he would find his ass out in the street.

"Big man, big fuckin man. Well big man, I got my own fucking problems to deal with, never mind your own." Lloyd said under his breath. It just clicked in Lloyd's mind. Matt Clark was the big money man. Matt had the money that Lloyd needed to buy the place that he and Carol were talking about. Now Lloyd was anxious for his boss to approach him. Lloyd was ready to be confronted with what ever his boss wanted done for him. Lloyd would just about do anything to get his hands on some big money. His mind was racing as he waved off Roy's offer for a beer. Lloyd wanted a clear mind when Matt decided to come over and talk to him. He knew the time would be soon, as Matt never liked hanging around the bar. He thought he was too good for this place, even if he did own it.

"Hey Smitty."

"Now what the fuck do you want Roy?" Lloyd felt like grabbing Roy by the scruff of his neck and telling him to go away.

"Holy shit man, chill out will ya? The boss wants to see you upstairs, pronto." Roy explained.

Lloyd knew that this could be his big chance to come into some serious money.

Lloyd was Matt's only man now to do his dirty work. The last guy got his head blown away from being careless. Something Lloyd didn't plan on that happening to him.

Lloyd took the stairs two at a time, he knew Matt was just as impatient as himself.

As Lloyd opened the door, Matt was standing there waiting.

"Hello Mr. Clark. How are you doing today?" Lloyd was ready for anything that Matt had to ask of him.

"Never mind the formalities Smitty. I got a big job for you to do. Do you think you can handle it.?"

"Yes sir, Mr. Clark. I can handle anything." Lloyd hated to play the part of a yes man.

"Okay Smitty, I'm going to give you a chance to earn some big money. How well do you know Cedar Rapids?"

"Very good, Mr. Clark. I know it like the back of my hand."

"Okay Lloyd. Now I'm not talking about roughing someone up here. I want this son of a bitch dead. Can you handle it?" Matt came right to the point. Matt gave Lloyd a photograph of twenty nine year old Frankie Ramsey.

"This is the son of a bitch that I want you to take out. He's a sneaky prick, so you will have to watch your ass.

"What did he do Mr. Smith?" Lloyd nervously asked.

"Never mind what he did. You don't need to know. You just do this job for me and don't worry about anything else. He is expected to be in Cedar Rapids some time within the next two weeks. He hangs around a bar called Cedar's Pub. You go up to Cedar Rapids in the next couple of days and rent a cottage. Spend as long as you need to up there and enjoy yourself. But don't come back here until you finish the job." Matt handed Lloyd five thousand dollars, with a promise to double it when Lloyd finished the job.

"Okay Mr. Clark, consider it done." Lloyd spoke with a crackle in his voice.

"Don't start getting too cocky about this now Smitty. If you fuck this up, I'll send someone after your ass." For a small man, he had no problems of getting his point across.

"Yes sir Mr. Clark. I'll make sure things get looked after."

Carol and Lloyd were sitting in the doughnut shop having a coffee and discussing the trip to Cedar Rapids.

"I don't know if I can get the time off, honey. It sounds so wonderful but I have to give at least a weeks notice before I can take a vacation."

"I know sweetie, I'm sorry for giving you such short notice, but my boss just decided to give me a couple of weeks off. I would of asked you earlier but I didn't know myself. I just thought that you would love the idea of spending some time with me that's all." Lloyd was trying to play on Carols heart strings.

"Okay Lloyd, I'll ask my supervisor and see if she will give me a break. I just can't drop everything and take off."

"I'm sorry Carol, I didn't mean for you to get all upset about this. How about it if I go to Cedar Rapids and get everything all ready, and when the time is right for you I'll come and pick you up?"

"Okay honey, that sounds a lot better. I sure could use a week off. I just love it in Cedar Rapids." Carol was thrilled at the thought of spending at least a week with Lloyd.

"Okay then, it's all settled. I '11 drive you home and I'll head out to Cedar Rapids and get everything organized. I'll give you a call tomorrow morning."

Lloyd was all smiles now. He was thrilled at the thought of having his new found love with him for a week and this way it gave him time to scout the area for Frankie Ramsey, the thought of taking someone's life terrified him. He knew that he didn't have it in him but he needed the money.

Lloyd sat in his Blue Chrysler for a moment to gather his thoughts. His mind was racing. Every thing was going so fast for him. He had second thoughts now about bringing Carol along with him. He wanted her there with him, but he didn't want her to get in his way, or get mixed up in anything.

He was nervous as it was. Carol might just be a big distraction for him. Beating the hell out of some one was one thing but Lloyd was having his doubts about being able to kill someone. Especially when he didn't know the reason behind it.

Lloyd pulled into the parking lot of Cedar's Pub, eyeing all the cars in the parking lot. He sat in the car for thirty minutes before he got up the nerve to go in the bar.

As he entered, he could see two men in the middle of a fist fight. The bartender standing over them with a baseball bat in his hands, threatening to use it.

This was a great way for Lloyd to enter the bar because all the attention was on the two combatants.

Lloyd went unnoticed entering the bar. He took a seat in a dark isolated part of the room. The jukebox was thunderously playing.

"What will it be partner?" The skinny long haired waiter asked.

"Just give me a couple shots of Jack Daniels." Lloyd asked without making any eye contact with the scruffy waiter. He took out the small photo of Frankie Ramsey. Studied it, then took a quick survey of the place. The bar was nearly empty now. No one there even remotely resembled Frankie Ramsey.

Lloyd knew that this wasn't going to be that easy.

"There you go partner." The waiter placed Lloyd's two shots down in front of him. Lloyd didn't say a word to the waiter. He didn't like the sound of this skinny punk calling him partner.

A tall Deputy Sheriff entered the bar to make sure everything was calmed down. The fight had already been over and the combatants were long gone.

Lloyd didn't know how to play his cards. He didn't know if he should play Dick Tracy and start flashing the photo around the bar and ask questions, or just sit back and see if this Frankie Ramsey was going to show. He decided on the latter, he didn't want to start stirring things up and one of Ramses' buddies warn him that there was someone looking for him.

As Lloyd made his way to the exit, a very attractive young red haired woman approached him.

"Hi handsome. You look like you're lost....I can show you around town if you like. Martha Gilmore was soliciting her services. She was well known as the towns working girl. She was a very bright and good looking woman, but the drugs had gotten the best of her, and she turned to prostitution to feed her heroin addiction. Martha Gilmore definitely got Lloyd's attention.

"Whatever you're selling sweetheart, I'm buying." Lloyd replied while flashing a wad of money.

"Well then let's go sweetheart." Lloyd spoke up as he held the door open for his new found companion.

As they made their way towards the exit, a loud outburst from the bartender could be heard throughout the bar.

"John, the towns drunk slapped his knee in laughter. He himself had been with Martha on several occasions.

Who was that guy anyway Bud? He looked a little familiar." John asked as if he had seen Lloyd before.

"Don't you know who that guy was, Bud? That was Muhammad fuckin' Ali." They all broke out in laughter once again.

Lloyd made his first big mistake by drawing attention to himself.

"So where to toots?". He asked his new companion.

"Well where are you staying handsome? Martha asked Lloyd in her best flirtatious way.

"I'm from out of town sweetheart. I don't have a place to stay as of yet. Now where can I get a nice cottage that's close to a lake and not too far away from Cedars Pub?"

"Oh you're looking for a cottage? What are you, a fisherman?"

"No sweetheart. I just got some business to look after that's all."

"What kind of business, handsome? The scantly dressed prostitute asked very interested.

"Well lets just say that I'm here to look after someone that's all."

"Oh ... are you a hit man or something?" Martha asked, acting coy. She was good at getting information out of anyone.

Her tricks usually opened up to her. They felt that she was only a two bit hooker and that there would be no harm in opening up and telling her anything that they would not dare to tell anyone else.

"Are you some kind of reporter or something?" Lloyd asked facetiously.

"Oh calm down tiger. You're going to be a live one, aren't ya?" Martha was intrigued by his loftiness and she wanted to find out more what Lloyd was up to.

Martha moved closer to Lloyd and started to fondle him, but Lloyd wasn't looking for anything like that so he pushed her back to her side of the car.

"Okay sweetheart, we got a lot of time to play around, but let's find us that cottage now."

"Let's get us a bottle of whiskey before we find us a cottage." Martha was talking as if she was going to spend the two weeks with Lloyd. Just as long as Lloyd had that big wad of money, she would stick right with him.

He was willing to keep her around at least until Carol was ready to come join him.

Lloyd stopped off at the liquor store and purchased a forty ouncer of five star whiskey. He climbed in the drivers seat, and his new companion grabbed it away from him.

"Man, a five start forty ouncer of whiskey. She was quick to open it up and started drinking it.

"Hey bitch! Put that bottle under the seat, do you want us to get busted?"

Lloyd could see that she was upset.

"You okay, sugar?"

'No I'm not. You didn't have to call me bitch...I'm not a bitch!"

"No, you're not a bitch. I'm sorry for calling you that. Lloyd reached over and stroked her long silky hair.

The cottage was old and run down, but it was situated in front of the lake which made it look a lot nicer than it really was. It was about two miles away from Cedars Pub.

Right off the bat Martha sprawled on the bed with the whiskey bottle,

"Well come on handsome, don't be shy." The dauntless prostitute taunted Lloyd into joining her. Martha lay on the bed, her legs spread just enough to give Lloyd a tease. Lloyd seemed to be uninterested by her antics. Lloyd looked through the tattered screen door and stared at the lake.

"Hey handsome. I need a fix before we do anything." Martha was in need of a shot of heroin. She was starting to come down from her last high.

"What kind of shit do you got yourself on?"

"Fuck man, this stuff isn't shit. This is what keeps me goin'." Martha moved over to the side of the bed to retrieve her purse where she kept her drug paraphernalia. Lloyd was fascinated watching Martha giving herself the injection. Martha fell back on the bed, the needle was still intact in her arm. Her body began to spasm. Her eyes rolled up into her head.

Lloyd panicked. "What the fuck is going on?"

He pulled the needle out of her arm, then slapped her to try and bring her around.

"Fuck ... don't you die on me bitch." Lloyd did not have any idea of what to do. It took all his strength to hold her spasmodic body down. He thought that she would be dead any minute. He seen junkies when they had an overdosed and died with the needle still stuck in their arm.

After a few minutes, Martha's body became as limp as a rag doll. Lloyd checked for a pulse. She was still alive, but barely.

It was six o'clock in the morning, Lloyd had stayed up all night watching over Martha. She lay still as a corpse.

He was satisfied that she would survive now that she had made it through the night.

Lloyd climbed onto the bed next to the debilitated Martha. He rapped his arm around her and fell fast asleep.

Lloyd was startled awake, when he felt Martha climb out of the bed. He made it look like he was still asleep. He wanted to see what she was up to. She was walking around in her panties. Staggering from the effects of the heroin overdose, she walked around in a big daze.

"You got to get of off that fuckin' stuff. You could have died last night."

"I had a pimp that got me hooked on that stuff. He use to beat the hell out of me." It was the only thing that stopped her pain, mentally and physically. As a prostitute, she was beaten up several times.

"If I gave you a thousand dollars, would you go to detox and get off of that crap?"

"You would really do that for me?"

"Yes I would. I seen too many people die from that stuff, and you are a beautiful woman, and you are still young.

Martha started to cry. Lloyd was quick to hold her. After a few minutes Martha stopped crying. She looked up at Lloyd, and said, "You really care, don't you?"

"Yes I do...I really do. Now how about me taking us out for breakfast. I am starving."

Martha was now smiling. Lloyd was really good for her.

Martha walked up to Lloyd and hugged him. They looked into each others eyes, then they kissed. They ended up on the bed. They didn't have sex; they made love.

CHAPTER FIFTEEN

Carol was laying down, trying to get to sleep, but was unable to, her mind was on Lloyd. Carol was anxious for him to call. She had good news to tell him, her vacation started in two days. Wanda knew that Carol went through a rough couple of months, with the death of her brother, and her mother having a stroke, so she figured that bending the rules was justified, and she let Carol have her vacation without the proper notice.

Carol lay in bed, thinking how wonderful it has been with Lloyd in her life. And the couple times that they went to the nature trails, it was so romantic. Carol laughed out loud, she was thinking about Bobby, the little boy that caught them in the act. He was so cute, so adorable.

Carol nodded off with a content smile on her face.

Two and a half hours later Carol awoke. She looked at the digital alarm clock and seen that it was three thirty.

She sprung out of bed, put her house coat on and headed for the kitchen.

"Hi dad, did Lloyd phone?" Carol startled her father, he nearly jumped out of his chair.

"Oh pumpkin, you scared the heck out of me."

"I'm sorry dad., did Lloyd phone?" Jason sat there with a clueless expression on his face.

Carol was becoming impatient with her father.

"Lloyd ..? Oh Lloyd, I'm sorry pumpkin, my mind was wandering.

"No, I don't think Lloyd phoned, let me go ask your mom." Jason got up and walked to the bedroom where Jean was. Carol was getting more than a little anxious.

"I'm sorry pumpkin, your mother says that he didn't phone."

Carol was disappointed. She walked back to her bedroom now feeling depressed.

Lloyd and Martha lay cuddled in bed, sharing a joint, it was like they didn't have a care in the world.

"So are you going to tell me what you're doing in Cedar Rapids handsome?" Martha was determined to find out what Lloyd was up to. She had suspicions that Lloyd was up to no good.

"Now aren't you a nosy little thing? Grab my shirt over there darlin." She leaned over the side of the bed and picked Lloyd's shirt off the floor. Lloyd reached into his pocket and pulled out the picture of Frankie Ramsey and showed it to Martha.

Martha could not believe her eyes. "Frankie, that's Frankie." Lloyd felt a sinking feeling deep in his stomach.

"You know this guy?" Lloyd asked in a shock.

"Yes that's Frankie Ramsey. We used to live together. Frankie and I are very close. You're after him, aren't you?" Martha was full of fear.. This put her in a vulnerable position. She felt scared not knowing what Lloyd would do to her.

Lloyd sat up on the bed. He put his hands over his face and thought for a minute. He gave Martha an evil stare.

"My boss sent me down here to get him. Frankie fucked up, and my boss wants him dead. I have to do all his fuckin' dirty work." Lloyd smashed his fist on the night table, breaking the corner off of it and knocked over the lamp.

Martha sat there holding the sheet over her, using them like a child would use them as a security blanket.

"How many men have you killed Lloyd?"

"I never killed anyone in my life, and I don't know if I'm going to start now." Lloyd had doubts all along about killing Frankie Ramsey. The only one he wanted to kill now was Matt Clark. He was the one who got him in this mess in the first place.

"I know Frankie has a lot of money. Maybe you could work something out with him."

"If I don't kill him, my fuckin ass is history. Shit!" Lloyd was working himself up into a frenzy. Martha was starting to shake now, and Lloyd could see it. He put his arms around her, she was trembling. Lloyd tried to calm her down.

"Don't worry darlin', you're safe with me, I could never hurt you." Lloyd was really in a jam. He couldn't let Martha go, knowing what she knew.

"Did you say that this Frankie guy has a lot of money?"

"Yea, he does. He ripped somebody off of about twenty grand. Some guy wanted to buy a shit load of coke. The guy gave him the twenty grand and Frankie gave him a shit load of flour."

"Holy fuck, I can see why they want him dead. This Frankie guy must have some really big balls. Do you know where he is now?" Lloyd was hoping that Martha would open up and tell him everything she knew.

"I sure do. He vanished one night, completely disappeared. About a week after he disappeared he phoned me. He wanted me to take a bus to Virginia and meet him there. He's staying at his brothers place up there in a small town called ... Mount Hope. Martha was eager to help Lloyd and Frankie. She would rather help Lloyd work something out with Frankie.

"Well darlin', it looks like we're going to Mount Hope."

Lloyd was appeased, he knew exactly what had to be done now. He was truly grateful to Martha, she helped Lloyd immensely.

"You're not going up there to kill him are you?" Martha feared that she told Lloyd too much. But she knew that there was no way that Lloyd would do her any harm.

"No darlin', I'm not a killer. Here's what we'll do. We'll take a ride to Mount Hope and pay Frankie a visit.

I'm sure that we can make a deal. Frankie will be glad to see you too." Lloyd was trying to make everything sound like it was going to be easy, he knew himself that it was going to be a very tense situation.

Lloyd had to watch out that Martha didn't warn him that they were coming. Lloyd wanted to take him buy surprise, catch him off guard.

"Okay darlin', let's get dressed and get on the road."

Martha was thrilled at the thought of going to Mount Hope. She missed Frankie so much. She and Frankie lived together for a year, she left him when he started beating her. She blamed herself for all his aggression. It was her that was so heavy into the drugs, and running around on him. Martha never wanted to be tied down with just one man. Now she regretted not going to Mount Hope when she had the chance. She was able to earn just enough money from prostituting to buy her heroin. It was the heroin that she was living day to day for. She had no love in her life since Frankie had gone, even that wasn't true love, it was just another means of survival. It was a lot better living with Frankie and being beaten every other night than selling her body to all the low lifes in Cedar Rapids. She had been beaten more than a few times by her tricks, and the ones that usually beat her, with out giving her a dime. She felt more love in this one day with Lloyd than she ever did.. The first thing that she needed to do was to kick her heroin addiction. But in her mind she knew how hard that was going to be.

They were driving down highway 58, traffic was light. The blue Chrysler cruised along at about seventy five, the rear end shimmied and the springs were bad, it made an uncomfortable ride. The car always got Lloyd to where he was going.

"Well darlin', we should be there in four, maybe five hours. What do ya say if I put some tunes on."

Lloyd reached over and turned on the radio to an oldies station. Trying to liven things up a bit.

Do Wah Diddy Diddy by Manfred Mann was playing, Lloyd cranked the volume up, their once placid mood quickly changed to a rhapsody of impetuous singing.

They both were singing at the top of their lungs, emptying their minds of all their dilemmas.

The song ended and it was followed by the news. Lloyd turned the volume back down and once again there was silence. Martha unbuckled her seat belt then moved over to Lloyd's side. She rested her head on his bulky shoulder. Lloyd put his arm around her.

Things were different, he knew that all Martha had on her mind was Frankie.

Different scenarios played through Lloyd's mind at what he was going to do to Frankie.

"Are you going back with Frankie?" Lloyd asked harshly, taking his arm off of Martha, and pushing her back to her own side of the seat.

"Yes, I'm going back with Frankie." Martha snapped back at Lloyd,

"Well than fuck you too."

"I'm sorry Lloyd, I'm still in love with him. I didn't mean to hurt you."

"Hurt me? I don't give a shit if you go back with him. What would I want from a whore like you!."

In reality, Lloyd felt rejected, he never took rejection very well.

Lloyd hurt Martha's feelings, she was upset.

"Well fuck you too. Don't you think that I have feelings for you too?"

Lloyd's eyes teared up. "I'm sorry hon, I didn't mean it. You know how much pressure I'm under."

Martha just turned away from Lloyd and starred out the window.

An eighteen wheeler cut right in front of him. He slammed his foot on the brake, the car fishtailed into the oncoming traffic narrowly missing a guy on a Harley.

"I'm sorry darlin, I didn't mean it."

"Fuck you, you son of a bitch." Martha yelled out.

For the next hour there was nothing but silence. No music, no talking.

Lloyd could no longer suppress his thoughts. "I'm sorry damn it! I just have so much on my mind that's all. There is no excuse for me to jump on you like I did."

Martha didn't say a word, she just kept starring out the window.

They were a little more than half way, Lloyd figured if he could speed it up a little more than they would be there in less than two hours.

"You okay darlin'?" Lloyd asked, after hearing Martha mumble something.

"Look, you're a young woman with your whole life ahead of you, get off the fuckin' drugs and quit peddling your ass and make something out of yourself."

Lloyd could see the emotion in Martha's eyes. She was about to break down. He held his arm out to comfort her.

"Come over here darlin'. You just need some good loven' that's all." Martha accepted Lloyd's offer and slid over to his side and laid her head on Lloyd's shoulder.

A guy driving an eighteen wheeler stretched his neck to get a good view of what was going on in the front seat between Lloyd and Martha, Lloyd looked up to the zealous driver."What the fuck are you looking at? Martha sat up and lifted her top, exposing her breasts to much of the delight to the red face trucker.

Lloyd was so shocked that he almost lost control of the car. "Holy shit,that was good darlin'. Did you see the look in that guys face. Lloyd had to wipe the tears from his eyes from laughing so hard.

"Well what do ya say if we go grab a coffee and pick us up a map and see where this Mount Hope place is?"

"I know where it is, you don't need a map."

Lloyd gave Martha a surprised look. "You know where it is'?"

"Yea, I know where it is, my uncle use to live there.

Mount Hope was a small town with a total population of twenty two thousand. Not a very good place to hide out, it had all the traits as any other small town, every one knew every one, and anyone that was new drew all the towns attention.

Driving down Main street at a snails pace, there wasn't much going on. Lloyd and Martha stuck out like a sore thumb. Every time the blue Chrysler drove past someone on the street, they gave them a distrustful stare.

"Well darlin',I wouldn't want to rob a bank in this town. Look at all the nosy hicks starring at us.

Martha went quiet, all Martha could think of was seeing Frankie.

Lloyd pulled over and parked in front of a barber shop. All the patrons turned their heads as if the blue Chrysler was a stretch limo or something.

"I bet you if I asked these hicks if they know where Frankie lives they would tell me in a second. I grew up in a small town like this, and believe me, they know everybody and their brother. Well let's go in and ask.

Okay, we'll both go in, and you just play along with what I say. Don't start no long winded conversation with them. We just want to go in there and find out where Frankie lives and get the fuck out."

Lloyd and Martha entered the barber shop, all the chattering came to a sudden halt. Lloyd felt like he was the grim reaper walking into a funeral home, no one would acknowledge that he and Martha was standing there.

Two old men sat studying their next move in a checker game.

"Good afternoon gentleman ... "

"Good day." The barber said in a low and cautious voice. Everyone else just sat quiet, sneaking a glance at the two strangers.

Martha had to hold back her laughter. This got Lloyd going as well. They had no other choice but to leave the melancholy place, they just couldn't hold back their hilarity.

As they made their way out side they unleashed their hilarity and roared with laughter.

"Are you sure that this isn't Mayberry? That barber had to be Floyd ... " Lloyd was having a real belly laugh.

"What the hell were they so scared of? If you would have said boo, those guys would have shit their pants and headed for the hills."

Tears were running down their faces, she could barely catch her breath.

Now the both of them cracked up laughing even more. Everyone in the barber shop was now standing at the front window with their mouths wide open, vying for position to gawk at them.

They both got back in the car and waved goodbye to Floyd and his gang. The thing that really got to Lloyd and Martha was that they waved right back with huge smiles on their faces.

Lloyd drove down the block until he seen a phone booth. He pulled over and told Martha to see if Frankie's address would be in the phone book.

Martha got out of the car and went in to the phone booth. The phone book had Frankie's phone number and address in it. She ripped the page out and brought it back to the car,

"It says F. Ramsey 555-6436, he lives at 6982 Bellevue Street."

Bingo, let's ask someone were Bellevue Street is." Lloyd said, feeling pretty antsy, sweat was running down his face. He didn't know what was going to happen.

Lloyd pulled the car in front of a bus bench where an old man was sitting.

"Sir, could you tell me where Bellevue Street is?"

The man told Lloyd that Bellevue Street was just six blocks over, less than five minutes away.

Although he really didn't know how it's going to be between him and Frankie. He might not have a choice. It all came down to Frankie, at what he was going to do.

I don't want you to say anything to Frankie, let me do the talking. If we fuck this up, it could cost Frankie his life.

Martha was horror-struck, she didn't want anything to happen to Frankie or Lloyd.

They turned left onto Bellevue Street. Lloyd parked the car directly across the street from Frankie's house.

There was a black late model Oldsmobile parked in the driveway. They presumed that it was Frankie's.

After a few minuets they walked across the street and climbed up the four stairs to the front door.

Lloyd gave the door a hard knock. Frankie opened the door and Lloyd grabbed Frankie by the scruff of the neck, practically lifting the 6'1" unsuspecting Frankie up off his feet. He gave Frankie a viscous blow to the nose, blood gushed out of Frankie's nose.

"Well Frankie, you fucked up really bad. Your buddy Matt Clark is missing twenty grand, someone ripped him off. I suppose you don't know anything about that. He sent me here to kill your ugly fuckin' ass. Okay pal,we can do this the easy way,or we can do the hard way. What's it going to be?" Lloyd had him pinned up against the wall,.

"Fuck, man, you broke my fuckin' nose."

"Please don't kill me please don't kill me ... I'll make it worth your while if you let me go." Frankie was terrified.

"Okay, I'm listening asshole. What's it going to be?"

"I'll give you two grand and five kilos of weed, that's twelve thousand dollars.

Martha came rushing to Frankie's aid. "Leave him alone" Martha screamed out. Then she started beating on Lloyd.

"Get your fuckin' hands off of me, bitch" Lloyd pushed her out of the way, she fell to the floor.

Lloyd waited until Frankie regained his composer, he gave him a hankie for his nose and helped him get up from the floor.

"Okay, here is what you're going to do, Frankie. I don't want your weed. I am going to leave, and I'm taking Martha with me, and I will be back in two hours. I want you to sell the weed. You give me the money, plus your two grand, and I will see if Matt will except it. And if you don't have it by the time I get back, I will kill the both of you..

"My partner will kill me. The weed is half his!"

"What will it be,Frankie?"

"Do it Frankie...do it." Martha screamed out, in hysterics.

"Okay okay, I'll do it." Frankie yelled out. "But I'm dead either way."

"That's your problem buddy, not mine."

"I'll tell you one thing Frankie, you must have more guts than brains to rip Matt off like you did."

Lloyd took Martha aggressively by the arm and led her to the car. Martha yelled out: "I love you Frankie" Frankie didn't say a word, he just gave her an evil look.

Lloyd forced Martha into the passenger seat, he was worried that she would try to run back to Frankie.

"Fuck you." Martha yelled out at Lloyd. "You didn't have to hurt him like you did."

"You should be grateful that I didn't kill him."

"Fuck you!" She shot back. Lloyd slapped her across the face, knocking her against the car door.

"Don't you disrespect me, bitch!"

Driving down Drummond Road, Lloyd was looking for a place to eat. He spotted Joe's Diner. He pulled into the parking lot and parked in front.

"Now don't you think of doing anything stupid now."

Martha didn't say a word.

They both ordered a hamburg and fries with a chocolate milk shake.

Once they were finished eating, Lloyd drove back to Frankie's place. He parked across the street, keeping a close eye on the house. Frankie's car was gone. Lloyd knew he wouldn't try to flee, not when Lloyd had Martha. Frankie still had feelings for her.

Fifteen minutes had past, when Frankie pulled into the driveway. Lloyd waited for him to enter the house.

Lloyd opened the door without knocking. Frankie was standing in the hallway.

"Okay Frankie, where's my money?"

Frankie handed Lloyd a small duffel bag. Lloyd opened it, it was full of money.

"Use your head next time, don't fuck around with Matt. And if I ever hear that you are abusing Martha in any way, I will come back and I will kill you.

Lloyd walked towards the door and never looked back..

Lloyd was heading back to Cedar Rapids, not even realizing that Carol was now on vacation and was sitting dishearteningly at home, still waiting for his call.

CHAPTER SIXTEEN

Carol sat at the kitchen table, gazing out the window in deep thought. She sat there for hours on end racking her brain, trying to figure out what might of happened to Lloyd. Could he have been in an accident? Should she phone the Cedar Springs Sheriffs office? Or should she take a drive and see if she could find him?

"Pumpkin, are you going to sit there all day like that?" Carol didn't hear him, her mind was so busy playing out all the scenarios.

Her dad didn't realize what his daughter was going through until he saw the tears roll down her face.

"Are you okay pumpkin?"

"Oh dad,why doesn't he phone? Where in heck could he be?" Carol was worried sick.

"Don't you worry he'll phone. He must of had some kind of car trouble, maybe a flat tire or fan belt." Jason's assumptions didn't help Carol any, she was grateful for her dad's concern but he didn't help her worrying any.

Jason could no longer take seeing his daughter suffer like this and not do anything about it.

"Where did you say he was going pumpkin?" Jason reached for the phone book.

"Cedar Rapids. Who you going to call, dad?"

"I'll give the sheriffs office up there a call and see if they know anything."

As soon as Jason found the number, the phone rang. Carol jumped to her feet, hoping that this was the call that she was so desperately waiting for.

"Hello ... "

"Hello darlin', I missed you so much, are you coming up to Cedar Rapids?"

"Yes, I'm coming, but what happened to the phone call you were suppose to give me. I've been sitting here for two days waiting for you to phone, I didn't know what to think." Carol's two days of built up tension was starting to surface, and Lloyd could sense that in her tone.

"Sorry about that sugar, I just made it to Cedar Rapids and my damn engine blew in the car.

"I'm sorry for being so inconsiderate, it's just that I was so worried about you." Once again the blame switched to Carol.

"That's all right hon, I'm just happy that I have someone that cares about me. I'll come and pick you up as soon as I can, and we'll go out for a nice dinner. I'll get a move on, I'll see you in a little while. I love you."

"I love you too Lloyd ... bye."

Carol held the phone to her heart, entranced by Lloyd's three words 'I love you', she thought the day would never come when a man would say that to her. She placed the cordless phone back on the table. She looked up and there sat her father, making it look like he was reading a Time Life magazine, Carol knew all his interest was on her conversation with Lloyd.

"Every thing okay pumpkin?" Jason asked, not even raising his head.

"Yea just great dad, Lloyd's picking me up pretty soon." Carol was grinning from ear to ear.

"That's nice pumpkin, have a good time." Jason replied with a big smirk on his face.

Carol placed her suitcases at the door. She was ready to go.

Carol's mother was sitting in the living room with one eye on the T.V. and the other on Carol.

"Carol will you sit down, you are going to wear the carpet out pacing back and forth like that. How do you expect me to watch my Oprah with you distracting me for fuck sake."

Jean's profanity was a red flag for Carol. This was a sign that her mother hadn't taken her medication.

"Mom, have you been taking your medicine like you're suppose to?"

"Hey, you just worry about your fuckin' trip with lover boy, and you can take the damn pills with you too. I don't need no pills"

This just made things more burdensome for Carol, and added to her stress level. She went to the refrigerator where her mother's medication was kept. She took the pills from the top of the fridge and gave them to her dad.

"Dad, you're going to have to make sure mom takes these pills every day, and if she doesn't she's going to end up back in the hospital." She was very stern with her father, totally out of the ordinary for Carol.

"Okay, I'll make sure she gets them every day when you're..." Jason was only half finished talking when Carol made a mad dash to the front door, hollering out that she thought that Lloyd had arrived. Her mother was yelling one thing at her, the T.V. was turned up to a deafening level, and now her dad was right behind her explaining to her about the medication all over again.

Carol just felt like screaming, she could take no more of this circus like atmosphere, her head was spinning from all the confusion. She stood there gazing out the window, squinting her sorrow pervaded eyes from the blinding afternoon sun. She felt so disappointed that the car door that she heard shut was not Lloyd, it was some one visiting next door closing their car door.

She sat down on the front stairs, taking in all the wonderful silence and trying to clear her heavily troubled mind.

"Come on Lloyd, hurry up and get here, will ya?"

Lloyd climbed up the stairs to the cottage, his size ten boots almost going right through the rotted and bug infested steps. He entered the front door and could see the unsightly mess that he and his harlot had left. There were bath towels, dirty clothes, discarded fast food wrappers just thrown heedlessly onto the hardwood floor.

Lloyd didn't know where to start, he didn't want to bring Carol there and have her think that he was some kind of slob. His room at Peepers was always immaculate.

After about an hour of tidying up, Lloyd was ready to go and get Carol. He gave the place one last good looking over to make sure he didn't miss anything, then he left feeling so proud of himself, as if he had done something so special.

Jason never seen his daughter move so fast as she did when Lloyd pulled into the drive way. As Lloyd climbed out of the car, Carol was standing there anxiously awaiting for Lloyd's affections. She didn't say a word, she wrapped her arms around him and held him tight, savoring the moment,

"Oh I missed you so." She said.

"Hey, how are you Lloyd?" Jason asked as he walked up towards the two love birds.

"Well I'm just fine Mr. Crawford. And how's yourself?"

"Really good there Lloyd. So you're going up to Cedar Rapids for the week. I hear their catching some good size pickerel up there. Are you planning to do any fishing?"

"Oh I think we should be able to get out in the lake a couple of times anyway. I rented a nice cottage up there, it's right on the lake. Well, why don't you come up and see us on Sunday, and bring Mrs. Crawford. Maybe you and I can go out on the lake and catch us some of those pickerels, and the ladies can go shopping or whatever they'd like to do."

Jason's face lit right up at the idea. Carol knew how good this would be for her dad.

Jason looked at his daughter for reassurance, she gave him an assuring nod and a warm hearted smile, and that was enough to persuade her dad to accept Lloyd's offer.

"Well, that sounds just great Lloyd, I'll be there." Jason shook Lloyd's hand then walked back to the house wearing a huge radiant smile.

"That was so nice of you to invite my parents over like that, look at my dads smile, I never seen him smile like that for a long time." Carol gave Lloyd a hug and a kiss for his thoughtfulness.

"Well darlin',are you all ready?" Lloyd asked, feeling on top of the world.

Lloyd snickered to himself over Carol's overabundance of baggage, it looked like she was going to stay for a couple months..

"Are you sure you didn't forget anything?" Lloyd asked, mockingly.

"Yes I think I got everything, thank you very much .Mr. smarty pants.." Carol snickered.

"We're not even there yet and you're pickin' on me already, well I'll just have to teach you a lesson or two as soon as we get there ... think you can handle it?" Carol seductively shot back at Lloyd, her eye brows rapidly moving up and down, flirtatiously.

"Oh I don't know if I can handle it, but I sure am willing to give it a try."

They got in the car and they made their way to Cedar Rapids.

"You're going to love the cottage I got for us darlin'. it's right on the lake, and there's a nice forest for we can take a walk through."

"Oh that sounds so wonderful, it's going to be so great to get away from every thing. I just can't believe that I'm going to be free for over a week." Carol was beaming and she could feel all the tension releasing from her heavy shoulders. She did feel a little guilty leaving her parents to tend for themselves, they depended on her so much, but they had to know that there would come a time when she would leave home, and Carol knew that the time was near.

Lloyd pulled off the highway to the Shell service station, the oil warning light was on for the last two miles.

The service attendant was sitting inside the kiosk reading a magazine, not even acknowledging that he had a customer.

Lloyd beeped the horn a couple of times, then the lackadaisical attendant looked up and slowly made his way to the car.

"Yea, what will it be?"

"How you doing there speedy? Fill it up and give me a quart of oil will ya?"

"These old junkers can really suck up the oil. I must have put three quarts in it this month alone."

"I thought you just had a new engine put in yesterday?" Carol asked, curiously, with a dumbfounded look on her face

The color drained from Lloyd's face. His mind was racing and he began to sweat.

"Awe ... did I say it was a new engine? I meant that it was a used one. That damn guy told me that, it wouldn't burn oil, but I'm not going to worry about it sweetheart, I got the engine for next to nothin' anyway." Lloyd was lying through his teeth, and hoped that Carol would buy his fabrication.

"That will be twenty dollars."The yawning attendant uttered in a low voice.

"Okay there lightning, take it easy. Lloyd's sarcasms just went over the young attendants head, but Carol got quite a kick out of it.

"You're just a big bully,that's what you are. Picking on the poor young kid like that." Carol said facetiously, grinning from ear to ear.

"Awe that guy and I are buddies.

"Well here we are darlin', Cedar Rapids,population 24,875."

They pulled off the main road onto the dirt road that led to the cottage.

"Well there's the lake darlin'. Doesn't it seem like another world here? Everything is so peaceful here, just you, me and nature darlin'. What else could anyone ask for?" The country boy was coming out in Lloyd once again, he seemed like a total different person.

"Every thing is so beautiful here, look at all the leafs changing color and look over there, it's a raccoon with all her little ones. Oh Lloyd, I'm never going back. Carol was in a state of awe.

When they pulled up in front of the cottage, Carol got out of the car and was taken back by the setting.

The sunset tinted the sky a brilliant pink that beamed down onto the trees. It was a photographers fantasy. To Carol it was heavenly paradise. Lloyd took Carol's hand into his and led her to the lake. It was so romantic for the both of them. Not a word was spoken, they just stood there taking in the majestic view.

"What do you think darlin'?" Lloyd asked in such a mellow voice as he wrapped his arms around her.

"Oh Lloyd, I think it is so wonderful, heaven couldn't be any better than this. I love you so much."

"I love you too Carol."

"There's no one out here but us, darlin',we got the whole lake to ourselves.

Lloyd picked up Carol and was going to carry her into the cottage.

"Oh how romantic hon." Carol was loving every moment of it.

As soon as Lloyd's foot stepped onto the third step it gave way, he went crashing through it. Trying to regain his balance and making sure he didn't drop Carol, he couldn't do anything.

"Son of a bitch, I'm stuck!" Lloyd's shouted out, making Carol burst out in laughter.

"Okay honey, let me down, and I'll help you out." Carol said, doing her best not to laugh. She could see Lloyd was getting more than a little aggravated, which made Carol more than a little nervous.

"I'm sorry for laughing, hon."

"Well, it wasn't funny at all." He snapped back at Carol.

She went really quiet. He hurt her feelings.

"Hello. Are you guys alright?" Jim Parker the owner of the cottage was making his way towards them.

"Oh for damn sakes, this is just what we need." Lloyd gave one more attempt to try and free himself and he did.

"Good evening, I was out for a walk and I heard you guys out hear and I thought you might have had some trouble or something. Well I must say it's a beautiful night for a walk.

Usually I bring the dog with me, but not tonight. Yep, left him at home, he's getting a little old. It's his eyes, poor thing is going blind."

"Is this guy going to come up for air and shut up?" Lloyd whispered to Carol, not really caring if Jim heard him or not.

"Oh dear that's too bad, you know, I've been meaning to put a new set of stairs there. Yep, those stairs are made of pine, I should-of used cedar. But then .... "

"Holy shit gramps, do you suppose you could shut up tor one minute!" Lloyd could take no more of this guys rambling on. Carol didn't like the way Lloyd was talking to the owner..

"Lloyd, that wasn't very nice. Carol spoke up.

Lloyd didn't say a word to Carol, but he gave her an evil look.

"Okay there, let me take a closer look !.. Yep, you broke through alright."

"Well we already know that for fuck sakes. Lloyd shot back.

"I'll leave you alone folks. Have a good night." Jim said, then walked through the woods, still carrying on, mumbling away.

Lloyd sat on the bed, while Carol tended to his swollen ankle.

Carol went really quiet. First Lloyd didn't call her for a couple of days, which made her a nervous wreck, and now seeing a different side of Lloyd when he snapped at her, and being very mean to the owner of the cottage.

Carol also didn't like Lloyd's vulgarity,

She just didn't know what to make of it. In the back of her mind, she wished that she never came.

"Did you here that old fart rambling on the way he did, he went on and on, for fuck sake, I didn't think he would ever shut up. What the hell was he saying anyway, something about his dog going blind?"

"Who cares about his fucking dog."

Lloyd stood up, his ankle was still only half wrapped, but he had the desire for something a little more amorous. Lloyd ran his hand down Carol's thigh, He gently caressed his hands across her breasts.

This was the last thing Carol wanted to do. She spoke up and told Lloyd that she had a headache, then walked in to the bathroom. She sat on the toilet seat and thought real hard at what she could tell Lloyd that she wanted to go home.

Lloyd apologized to her about his rampage. He gave Carol a hug and whispered I'm sorry in her ear.

"I need to lay down, hon. It's been a long day for me."

"Me too, I will join you, I'm exhausted."

They were just falling asleep when they heard a hammering noise that was coming from outside the door. Then they could hear the sound of someone singing 'Onward Christian Soldiers' so way off tune. This was too much of a distraction for Lloyd, he rolled over in frustration. Carol went back to the bathroom and turned the tap on full for Lloyd would not hear her outburst of laughter. It took her a good ten minutes to get it out of her system.

It wasn't really laughter, Carol was in hysterics.

"Are you all right in there Carol?" Lloyd asked as he gave a gentle tap at the bathroom door.

"Yea, I'm all right... I'11 be out in a minute."

Carol came out of the bathroom, more composed than what she was when she went in. Her eyes were completely red and puffy,

"Carol, did I do something wrong, were you crying?" Lloyd had a genuine look of concern on his face.

"No, I'm just really tired."

"Do you know who was making all that racket out there? It was that damn old fool that owns this place.

He wanted to start fixing the broken stair now. Son of a bitch, I shooed him away.

"I hope that you weren't too mean with the poor guy, he means well.

Lloyd didn't say a word.

CHAPTER SEVENTEEN

Lloyd and Carol slept in until 10:45, the only sounds that could be heard was from the tranquilizing serenades from the morning doves, and the faint sound of a motor boat far off in the distance on Lake Gaston. Carol lay snuggled up beside Lloyd.

Lloyd got out of bed and walked in to the bathroom to have a shave and a shower.

Carol was laying in bed, thinking about the night before. She was thinking that she was too hard on Lloyd, and today she was going to make it up to him.

Carol could hear the shower running. She jumped out of bed and joined Lloyd, much to his delight.

After a thirty minute shower, they went back to bed and made love.

After making love, Lloyd fell asleep. Carol laid there thinking, she was thinking of what a future she and Lloyd would have, how nice it would be to have a house in the country, just like the one they were in now. Maybe a couple of kids, a few animals. She laughed to herself, thinking about what they had discussed about a farm, it now seemed so far fetched and definitely not in her interest. She hoped Lloyd shared the same sentiments now as well as she did. Then she thought about a wedding, would it be a big wedding... no she thought, maybe they could elope.

She just couldn't believe at how much she loved Lloyd. She had waited a long time for a man to come in to her life. In her mind she thought that she found the best.

Lloyd had been awake for a couple of minutes. He lay there watching Carol in her trance,wondering what she was so mesmerized about.

"What are you thinking about, sweetie?" Lloyd asked.

"About us." Carol softly said .Do you think we'll be together in the next fifty years?"

"Fifty years?" Lloyd looked into Carol's eyes and took hold of her hand. "Yes darlin', I would love to spend the next fifty years with you."

"Oh Lloyd,I love you so much." Carol wrapped her arms around him, put her head on his shoulder and savored the moment. She longed for this moment, and this made her morning fantasy come a little closer to reality.

"So what did you want to do today sweetie, anything special?"

"Yea, your parents are coming over tomorrow, so I'd like to go into town and pick up some fishing supplies. Maybe while I'm doing that you could pick us up some groceries. Maybe get a couple of nice big steaks. Your mom and dad like steak, don't they?"

"Sure, hon, steaks would be great." Carol said in a low tone.

She was a little hurt that Lloyd didn't want to do everything together.

"You okay, sweetie?"

"Yes, I'm fine. I'm a little tired, that's all."

It would be a good thing for you and dad to go out fishing by yourselves. It would give you guys a chance to really get to know each other." Carol didn't want to let on that she was terrified of going out in a boat. She had two cousins that drowned when their boat capsized, and she never really got over it.

"Okay darlin', I'll take you out in the lake Monday, how does that sound?" Lloyd sounded too eager for her to say no, so she agreed, even though she hated the thought of it.

"Well, what do you say about us hitting the road now? Maybe we'll stop off somewhere and get us a nice lunch first."

"Okay hon, that's sounds good, I'm starving."

Before they went anywhere, Carol insisted on making the bed and washing the coffee cups out. It was important to her to show Lloyd that she was a good house keeper.

As Lloyd and Carol came out of Katie's Kitchen restaurant, Lloyd bumped into Bud Simpson, the bartender at Cedars Pub. Lloyd knew exactly who he was, Bud Simpson just stood there giving Lloyd a good looking over, he knew Lloyd's face, but he just couldn't figure out where he had seen him before. Lloyd acted as cool as a cucumber, he didn't say a word and just kept walking.

When they got into the car, Lloyd turned around to see if the bewildered Bud Simpson was still standing there. He was starring right back at Lloyd, now with a mean evil look in his eyes. Lloyd realized that Bud had remembered where he had seen him now, and this probably would mean trouble for Lloyd once word got around that he was still in town,

Lloyd pulled the car into the parking lot of Super Save Supermarket.

"Are you going to be all right shopping by your self darlin'?" Lloyd asked with a little hint of guilt in his voice.

"Yes, no problem hon, Carol said. "I'll be okay, don't worry about me none. You go do what you have to do, and I'll be here when you're done." It was obvious that Carol was a little upset from Lloyd leaving her on her own like this. Lloyd could see this, but he just let things slide, he handed her a couple of hundred dollar bills, and gave her a kiss on the side of the cheek. Carol opened the car door, turned towards Lloyd with such a sad look on her face, it almost made Lloyd change his mind about leaving her on her own.

She shut the car door rather hard, then headed for the Freshmart Supermarket, not even turning around to see Lloyd drive off. Lloyd pulled out of the parking lot and headed for the bait and tackle shop that he had seen just a couple of stores past Katie's Kitchen.

He made a u-turn and pulled into the parking lot . He felt an arm grab his shoulder, he quickly turned around in a defensive way, it was Bud Simpson. He stood about 6'1", 220 pounds, and very muscular, some one that Lloyd would not like to tangle with.

"Hey, what the fuck are you doing in this town anyways?" Bud asked, poking his finger into Lloyd's shoulder, trying to intimate him. Normally Lloyd wouldn't take such abuse from any one, no matter how big the guy was.

"Hey, your the bartender at Cedars Pub aren't you?"

"Yes I am, and I asked you a fuckin' question, asshole. What the fuck are you doing in this town?" Bud Simpson was pushing his luck, if he only knew what Lloyd was capable of, then he wouldn't have been so bold.

"Me and a few of my buddies came up here to do some partying and some fishing, I was just heading over to the fishing shop to pick up some supplies. Say do you know what the pickerel are biting on?"

"Fishing aye? Well I seen you leave the bar with Martha, and we never seen her since. Now what the fuck did you do to her, a lot a guys are wondering pal?" The over confident Bud still poking his fingers into Lloyd's shoulder. Lloyd just about loosing his cool.

"I'll tell ya pal, you keep poking me with that finger, and you're going to lose it. I took Martha out for a nice dinner, then we rented a motel, then she asked me to drive her to the bus station, she said she wanted to go to Kentucky to get back with her old boyfriend. So what's the big fuckin' deal about that?"

Lloyd's sudden change of temperament caught Bud off guard, he didn't feel so tough any more.

"Okay pal, no problem,we're all worried about Martha that's all, she was the best lay in this town, every one in this town is going to miss her, that's for damn sure. Okay pal ... Oh yea,use a worm harness, that's what their biting on now. Good fishin' pal, come over to the bar and I'll buy you a couple of beers."

"Yea, I might do that, thanks for the tip."

Bud turned around and went his way, and Lloyd made his way to the fishing shop.

He walked in to the bait shop, went right up to the rack that held all the fishing rods, he wasn't too choosy, he grabbed the first two rods that he seen. He picked out an Old Pal tackle box, picked out some tackle, including a worm harness and a Mepps Spinner. He brought them to the counter where seventy two year old fishing shop owner Sam Cook sat at the counter, reading a Field And Stream magazine.

"Hello there young feller, looks like you're going to do some fishin'. The pickerel are biting pretty good, you should do pretty good with this worm harness, my boys went out last night and brought back their limit."

"That's great, I hope I'll have the same luck." Lloyd eagerly said.

"Hey, do ya wanna see some pictures of some of the fish that I caught through the years?"

"I'm sorry pops, maybe next time, the wife is in the car waiting for me. You know how woman are, you're gone for five minutes and they say you're gone an hour."

"Okay I'll ring it up for you."

Lloyd could see the big look of disappointment on the old guys face. Lloyd was conscience-stricken.

"No wait a minute there pops, I'd love to see those pictures." Lloyd knew that Carol would be incensed from all the time he had been taking.

By the time Lloyd and the old timer looked through all of pictures it was well after two o'clock.

"Well those are great pictures pops, but I really have to get going now."

"Oh, I'm sorry for keeping you here so long, son, you tell the misses that it was my fault."

"Hey, you don't need to apologize pops, I loved seeing those pictures." Lloyd treated Sam with kindness.

Lloyd paid Sam $125.00 for the fishing gear, shook his hand, then went out the door and walked briskly down the street to his car. He tossed the fishing gear into the back seat and headed out to pick up Carol.

He pulled into the supermarket parking lot, Carol was standing out side in the hot sun with a fully loaded grocery cart. He could see the languid look on her face.

Carol smiled when she seen Lloyd, her smile made Lloyd realize what a real gem she was. He was expecting that she would be in an agitated state for being made to wait so long.

Lloyd opened the door before the car even stopped, he walked up to Carol, and gave her a kiss, then apologized to her for being so long.

He explained to Carol about the old guy wanting him to look at some pictures.

"That was so sweet of you to stay with him like that, you have such a big heart, you know that?"

Lloyd just smiled at Carol, and continued to load the car with the groceries.

Lloyd didn't know how to respond to Carol's praises. No one had ever gave him praise and reassurance, like the way Carol did.

They finished loading the car up, then Lloyd returned the grocery cart back to the store, something that the average person would never think of doing. He sauntered his way back to the car, whistling so contently.

"Well darlin', I have to make one more quick stop. Don't worry, it shouldn't take me as long as before. I'm going to drop you off at Katie's Kitchen so you can have a coffee, and I'll join you in a few minutes. Is that okay darlin'?"

Carol sat at a window seat, for she could keep an eye out for Lloyd. She had an odd feeling that Lloyd was up to something. Leaving her on her own to do the shopping was one thing, but leaving her alone again for the second time really irked her.

After forty long minutes, two Cokes and half her French fries, she was startled to see Lloyd staring at her from out side, pressing his face to the window, making funny faces at her. She wasn't amused in the least.

Lloyd walked towards Carol with a happy-go-lucky grin on his face, this didn't bode too well with Carol. She was a little incensed at the thought that she sat there for almost an hour, depressed and on her own for the second time, and he comes in so chipper.

Lloyd could see that Carol was a little upset, so he toned down his high spirits, and sat down across from her.

"What's wrong darling?" Lloyd asked sympathetically.

"Nothing, I'm fine." She sarcastically said.

"Lloyd, can we just. get out of here?"

"Sure, let's go." Lloyd tossed a five dollar bill on the table, more than enough to cover Carol's coffee.

Once they were in the car, Lloyd asked Carol what was wrong again. She just stared out the window, not saying a word.

The silence seemed like an eternity, it seemed as if it didn't bother Lloyd in the least.. Nothing was said between them until Carol spoke up. "Lloyd,I just don't like to be dropped off like that. If there is something to be done, don't you think that it would be nicer if we could do it together?"

Lloyd thought to himself for a couple of minutes before replying.

"I'm sorry darlin', I just didn't think that you would be interested in coming with me to pick up fishing supplies and stuff like that. I should have been more considerate. Do you forgive me?"

The look on Lloyd's face was expressionless.

"I'm sorry for being such a bitch sweetie. I just love you so much and I was only thinking about my self. I should realize that you need some time to your self too." Carol felt ashamed at herself from her little tirade.

"You just never mind darlin', don't you be so hard on yourself. You had a right to be upset. We should have did every thing together today. I'm going to make everything up to you tonight. Now come over here and give me a kiss."

Carol slid over to Lloyd's side, gave him a sensuous kiss.

Carol was in better spirits now.

They pulled up in front of the cottage, they could see that the eccentric owner Jim Parker had replaced the broken stairs. They unloaded the car together, Lloyd had his arms full of groceries, and Carol in her gaiety playful mood was chasing after Lloyd as he struggled with the groceries, laughing and jeering her on. He couldn't move fast enough to make it into the cottage before she could catch him. She caught up to him and playfully tried to kick him in the butt, she missed and she fell flat on her backside, Lloyd laughed so hard he dropped half his groceries and fell to his knees roaring with hilarity.

Once inside, and settled down, and the groceries were put away, Carol went to have a shower, while Lloyd went out to the car to get all the fishing equipment. He wanted to make sure every thing was ready for when he and Jason went out on the lake in the morning. Once he had the rods and tackle set up, he went for a walk in the woods to gather up some fire wood. He enjoyed sitting in front of a campfire, and it would be so romantic for the both of them, gazing at the stars in the cool night air. Lloyd even picked up a bottle of wine while Carol had been waiting in the restaurant. He had the evening all planned out, if things were going to turn out the way he had planned, then it would be a wonderful night, and one that they would both remember for a long time. As Lloyd opened the door to the cottage, Carol was just getting out of the shower, drying herself off, giving Lloyd a desire that he had to suppress, he wanted to wait for when the moment was right

"Did you get everything ready for tomorrow sweetie?"

"Yea, everything is all set to go. I just have to go see Jim to see if I can use a boat. I got everything ready outside for a nice campfire. So you better put something warm on, cause even with a fire, it still gets cold out there."

"A campfire? Oh that's a wonderful idea. Okay I'll get dressed and I'll be ready by the time you get back."

Lloyd walked out the door, and Carol pranced around with glee, she thought that it would be so romantic, sitting around a camp fire, all snuggled up close to the man she loved so very much,

Carol was dressed and anxiously awaiting sitting out on the front steps gazing at the breathtaking sunset, which tinted the sky a brilliant pink. She could hear Lloyd in the distance, whistling away in merriment.

They were sitting in front of a roaring fire, hypnotized by the flames, and by the love that they felt for each other. To them, heaven couldn't be any better.

"Look at that sky darlin', isn't it beautiful? You know what they say about a pink sky?

Pink sky at night, sailors delight. Pink sky at morning, sailors warning."

"So that means that it's going to be a nice day tomorrow."
"Yea, that's exactly what it means darlin', and it also means that it should be good fishin' tomorrow too."

Lloyd opened up a whole new world for her.

"This is so wonderful out here honey. Wouldn't it be so nice to be able to get out of the city and settle down in a place like this?"

"It would be wonderful darlin', just wonderful.

Well darlin', I have to go in for a minute, I 'll be right back, don't you go anywhere now." Lloyd gave Carol a gentle kiss on her lips, then sprinted his way to the cottage.

Carol tossed another log onto the fire, listening to the popping sounds of the wood burning and watching the sparks disappear into the darkness of the night. She was startled by something that brushed her leg. To her own surprise she was more curious than frightened. She casually leaned forward to see what it was. It was a skunk. She watched in fascination as the intrepid skunk made it's way closer to the fire. To her, it posed no threat, she felt the urge to reach down and pet it as if it were a cat, but she knew better. The putrid stench changed her notion very fast.

Didn't you see the skunk, it was right in front of me?" Carol excitedly asked.

"Skunk! Where's the skunk? Lloyd acted like it had been a bear or some ferocious creature. From the way Lloyd reacted, Carol thought that he was going to jump right into her arms. Carol had to laugh at Lloyd's reaction, she thought that Lloyd would be the last person to be so frightened of such a small helpless animal. Outside of the foul stench, she thought that there was nothing to fear, it seemed so harmless.

"Don't worry sweetie, it's gone now."

Carol grinned as she thought to herself. Who was more scared, the skunk or Lloyd.

"Do you know what a skunk can do to you Carol? If you get sprayed by one, you'll be scrubbing the stink off of you for a week.

"Carol, I love you so much, and I want to spend the rest of my life with you; will you marry me"?

Carol sat on her chair trembling, her lips quivering and the tears started to fall.

"Yes...yes I will."

Lloyd went down on one knee, his hands shaking, he opened the blue velvet ring box, looked deeply into Carol's eyes and placed the ring on her finger.

"Carol, I love you so much, and I know that we haven't known each other for a very long, but just in the short time that we have been together, it has been the best part of my life.

You to know, I'll treat you just like a queen, and I promise to never let you down, I'll always be there for you." Lloyd was tearing up.

He placed the ring on her finger.

"Ya-hooo." Lloyd lifted Carol off her chair and swung her around ecstatically.

"Oh Lloyd, you have made me so happy, we're going to have a wonderful life together. I just can't believe it, I feel like this is all a dream.

"Oh Lloyd, it's so beautiful, look at it, just look at it, I'll never take it off as long as I live. Oh sweetie, I love you. It's so wonderful!" Carol was overwhelmed. She thought the day would never come.

"Here you go sweetheart, let's have a drink." Lloyd popped open the bottle of Champagne, the cork went flying through the air at such a high velocity, and it hit Carol right in the forehead, knocking her off her chair. She lay there stunned for a few seconds, then got up realizing what had happened, this brought on the hilarity, she laughed so hard that she wet herself. This only made her laugh even harder now. She turned towards Lloyd, and he was bent over laughing just as hard.

Carol held out her glass, trying to regain her composure.

"To the most wonderful lady in the world. I love you darlin'."

"I love you too, sweetheart. " They made their toast to each other, and then drank their Champagne.

Lloyd gracefully lifted Carol off of her feet and, carried her back to the cottage. He gently laid her onto the bed. Other than asking Carol to marry him, this is what Lloyd had been yearning for, to make love to the most wonderful lady in the world.

The alarm went of at 6:30 am, two hours after Lloyd and Carol fell asleep. Lloyd sat up on the edge of the bed, rubbing his tired eyes. He staggered his way to the bathroom, his eyes still half closed.

It was lightning and thundering and pouring rain, so much for the red sky theory he thought to himself.

Figuring that his soon to be future mother and father in law would know enough not to come and expect to go fishing in this weather. He crawled back into bed, and was sound asleep as soon his head hit the pillow.

They were awaken by someone pounding on the door, Lloyd looked at the clock, it was noon, Lloyd quickly got dressed and headed for the front door. He knew it had to be Jason. He opened the door, and sure enough it was Jason.

"Come on in Mr. Crawford."

"Hello there Lloyd, I was wondering if you guys were even home, I was just about ready to leave when you opened the door.

"I'm sorry,we had a late night last night, I was up earlier and I seen that it was raining so I went back to bed."

" Yes, I figured that fishing would be out of the question,so I thought I'd come up anyway to pay you guys a visit."

"Well that's great, I'm glad you did, Mr. Crawford."

"Lloyd,you're part of our family now, you can stop with the mister, call me Jason."

"Okay mist ... Jason."

"Hi dad, come sit down and I'll make us a coffee.

"How do you like steak, Jason?" Carol picked up some real nice thick sirloins?"

"Oh I love steak Lloyd, and I like-em nice and rare."

"Hopefully the rain will stop for I can barbecue them.

Lloyd was feeling a little on edge, thinking about how Jason was going to react to his proposal to his daughter.

"Dad, we have a surprise for you." Carol said, putting her left arm behind her back.

Dad....Lloyd proposed to me last night."

Before Carol could show her dad the ring, her dad yelled out. "Well I hope that you said yes."

"Yes I did, dad."

Carol showed her father the ring.

"Look at the size of that rock. Congratulations to the both of you."

Jason was smiling from ear to ear.

After playing bridge for an hour and a half, the rain stopped and the sun came out.

Lloyd went outside to get ready for the barbecue. Lloyd picked up the picnic table with ease and carried it over towards the barbecue pit. Every thing looked presentable, so Lloyd cleaned out the barbecue pit, found some good kindling and lit the fire.

"You sure have a nice set up here, Lloyd, lots of privacy, and right by the lake too. Lloyd's future father inlaw said.

"Okay, you two stay here and have a nice chat while I clean everything up. I 'll bring out a pot of coffee." Carol gave Lloyd a wink as she walked by him.

"You're a bartender aren't you Lloyd?"

"Yes I am, but I'm looking for a better job, there's just not too much out there right now that pays anymore than what I'm getting now."

"Do you own a house, there Lloyd?'

"No, Jason, not yet, but I'm looking for one."

"Lloyd felt like he was in the hot seat with all the questions that his soon to be father in law was asking.

Carol came with the pot of coffee and a tray of cookies.

"So how are you boys getting along?" Carol could see that Lloyd was very uncomfortable, so she walked over to him and gave him a peck on the cheek.

"Let's see that ring again pumpkin. Sweet Jesus, Lloyd that must have set you back a few dollars. Look at the size of that diamond."

Jason was giving Lloyd's confidence a big boost, it made all the difference in the world to him, to have so much of Jason's support. He felt like a million dollars now.

Carol and Lloyd were sitting on the picnic table, discussing their wedding plans and their future. They both had decided that it would best for the both of them to elope, since Lloyd had no family to think of.

Carol was admiring her engagement ring, turning her hand in all directions to see the brilliant sparkle.

"The ring is so beautiful sweetheart, you must have paid a fortune for it. Did you buy this ring yesterday when you dropped me off at the super market?"

"I was going to buy it after I came out of the bait shop, but that nice old guy kept me there for so long that I couldn't, cause I knew that you were waiting for so long. So that's why I dropped you off at the restaurant, for I could go over to the jewelers and pick it out."

"Oh Lloyd, I'm so sorry for getting so upset at you yesterday, here I was feeling sorry for myself, from being dropped off like that, and all along you were out looking for a ring for me. You're the greatest guy in the world honey, and I love you so much. We are going to have a wonderful life together."

CHAPTER EIGHTEEN

A frantic mother came rushing through the emergency doors, carrying her lifeless child in her arms.

"My baby my baby, some one help me!" She screamed out in panic.

Carol was the first one to come to the aid of the hysteric mother. She grabbed the limp child from the mother, and rushed him into resuscitation.

"Okay what happened to your son?"

"I don't know ...we were just driving to my mothers house and he was fine, by the time we got there, I went to take him out of his car seat and he was all blue and ... oh my God, is he dead? Oh my poor baby ... " Linda Speck was becoming more hysterical by the minute.

"Okay Linda calm down now... is he allergic to anything?"

"No, I don't think so."

"What's his name?"

"Bobby, his name his Bobby!"

"Carol, Doctor Burns will be in as soon as he can, he's with a V.S.A. (vital signs absent) patient." There was only one doctor on the floor, he was tending to a motorcycle accident victim, and the other doctor was in surgery, helping out with an emergency appendectomy.

"Call for a code blue Carol. Linda, I'm sorry, but you'll have to go wait in the waiting room."

"Come on Bobby, come on sweetie." Carol knew that the boy was about to go into cardiac arrest, from what the heart monitor was showing.

"Okay, get me a suction tube, I can see something lodged in his throat, and it's blocking his airway." Carol carefully inserted the suction tube down into boys throat, she could hear the suction tube had a hold of something, she eased the tube back out, and at the end of it was a button, about the size of a dime, enough to totally block a small child's airway. Wanda placed an oxygen mask onto the still lifeless child. There was still no change on his condition, he was still critical.

Two nurses entered the room with a crash cart, ready for the worst.

"Come on Bobby, wake up sweetie, come on Bobby you can do it." Carol and Wanda were doing everything they could to bring the boy back to life. When Carol gave his chubby thigh a pinch, to her delight, Bobby started to cry, it was the most wonderful sound for everyone in the room. Everyone cheered, they were so happy for little Bobby, and so proud of Carol for doing what she did.

Doctor Burns entered the room, he could hear the loud crying from little Bobby, he looked up and seen all the beaming faces, all except for Carol's, she was out of the room, telling Bobby's mother the good news. Carol came back in with Bobby's mother. Carol handed the child to her.

Everyone was so impressed at the way Carol took charge and saved the life of the child that was knocking on deaths door. The offending button turned out to be off of Bobby's jacket.

It was a typical Friday night at the Westwood Hospital, everything happened all at once, the rooms were filled with patients suffering from anything from the most serious cases to the pathetically minor health problems.. This was the most frustrating thing for all the staff, half of the rooms were filled with such insignificant cases, they robbed the bed space for the much more serious cases.

A hour had past since the arrival of little Bobby, and all the rooms were finally empty. This gave Carol a chance to take her long awaited break.

As she entered the cafeteria she could see Mary Dawson, the nurse who helped take care of Carol's mom when she was in the hospital. Their friendship stayed in the confines of the hospital.

Carol picked out an egg salad sandwich and a coffee. She seen Nurse Mary Dawson siting three tables down.

She just waved at her and smiled. Carol wanted to sit by herself. She liked Mary, but she did nothing but gossip, and Carol was not in the mood hear any gossip.

When Mary was finished her lunch, she walked over to Carol. "How is your mom doing, Carol?"

"Oh, she's coming around pretty well."

"Oh my gosh Carol. what a beautiful ring. Did you get engaged?"

"Yes I did."

Who's the lucky guy?"

Carol perked right up.

"His name is Lloyd Smith. We met here at the hospital,when he came in with a broken hand. A couple of days later, he sent me a dozen long stemmed roses and a huge box of candy. It was almost love at first sight for me. He's so sweet and I just love him to death."

"Have you set a date yet?"

"No we haven't yet."

Mary looked at her watch, then said "Oh I have to get back on my floor, I'm late for a procedure.

Take care Carol, and don't forget to invite me to your wedding."

Now every one will know about our engagement, Carol thought to herself.

Carol was just about finished her lunch, when she heard: code blue, E.R .code blue, E.R. Carol quickly got out of her chair and raced to the E.R.

Lloyd was tending the bar. It was getting close to closing time at Peepers. Lloyd generally never drank while he was tending the bar, but tonight was an exception. He was more than a little drunk, and feeling very low. He was still in the same rut that he was in the last two and a half years. Still working in a place that feigned the urges of drunken lonely men, who would come in just to look at the beautiful naked woman dancing on the stage, thinking that this would fill the void in their lives, but instead going home drunk and twice as lonely and depressed as when they first came in.

Lloyd felt like he was a pathetic failure all his life, and he was only going to drag Carol down in the end. He knew that Carol deserved better, and he wasn't worthy to have her.

But no matter how bad things looked now to Lloyd, there was nothing that couldn't change his mind about marrying Carol.

CHAPTER NINETEEN

Jason had his kiss the cook apron on, flipping burgers and really enjoying himself. It was more like a small friendly gathering than a party.

Carol's eyes lit up when she seen Garry making his way toward the backyard.

He walked up to Carol and gave her a big hug.

"Hi, you must be the lucky man, I'm Garry Simpson." Garry held out his hand, Lloyd obliged and shook his hand.

"Yea, I'm the lucky guy, good to finally meet you Garry, Carol told me so much about you."

"Well it's good to meet you too Lloyd. She's a great lady Lloyd, you're a very lucky man.

He didn't like Garry hugging Carol. He thought it was very bold of him to hug her in front of him.. It made Lloyd's insides filled with rage. He hastily grabbed Carol's arm, and led her away from Garry towards the side of the house. Garry just stood there with a stunned look on his face, he didn't know how to react, his natural instincts told him to go after him, and straighten this guys act out.

"Lloyd! What the hell do you think you're doing? Get your hands off of me!. What's wrong with you?"

"Carol, you had your hands all over Garry, what the hell did you think I was going to do? He's lucky that I didn't drop him right then and there."

"Lloyd you made an ass out of yourself. Let me tell you, big shot, Garry and I have known each other for years, we're best friends damn it,and I love him very much. He's my best friend, so you better get use to it."

"Carol, I don't give a damn if he's you're friends or not. You just keep your hands off of him, and if I see him flirting with you one more time, so help me God, I'll drop him."

"Come on now Lloyd, don't be such an idiot. Didn't you see his earring in his right ear, which means he's gay?"

"Carol, any man that wears an earring must be a fagot."

"Don't you ever call him that, he's gay, so does that make him any less of a person? Garry is a wonderful human being, and if you think he is any less of a person just because he's gay, then I guess you're not the same person that I thought you were." Carol was in tears, Lloyd went to hug Carol, but she just turned away and headed for the house.

Lloyd felt like some one had just put a knife through his heart, he thought that everything was over between he and Carol.

"Hey there Lloyd, how you doing son?"

"Just fine, Jason, just fine." He lied.

"Well you don't sound fine to me, is there anything wrong, you guys aren't getting cold feet are you?"

"No nothing like that,we just had a little disagreement that's all,Carol's in the house."

Jason could see the look of despair on Lloyd's face.

"Don't you worry none there Lloyd, every couple goes through this just before their wedding, it's only natural to have cold feet, you'll see son, everything will turn out okay."

"Thanks Jason, I'll go in and see Carol and get things straightened out."

Lloyd walked into the house, he could see Carol sitting on the sofa crying. He sat along beside her and put his arms around her.

"I'm sorry darlin', I acted like a fool, I'm just so much in love with you.I'm going to freshen up, and then I'm going right out and apologize to Garry. Please forgive me sweetheart, It will never happen again. I know Garry's a great guy, if you want we'll invite him to our wedding."

"I'd like that."

Lloyd came out of the bathroom, Carol was still sitting on the sofa.

"You go back outside hon, and I'll see you in a couple of minutes. I'm going to go freshen up." Carol's eyes were all red and puffy, it looked obvious that she'd been crying. Lloyd gave Carol a long compassionate hug, they looked into each others eyes, they were too choked up to say anything to each other, so Lloyd gave her a gentle kiss on her forehead, then he walked out the door,feeling remorseful, and very depressed.

Once he composed himself, he made his way toward the barbecue where Garry was talking to Jason. Lloyd felt belittled about apologizing to Garry, but he knew it had to be done, he still felt that his tirade was justified.

"Hey Lloyd, you better get over here and get yourself a burger before they run out. Jason could see that Lloyd was feeling down.

"No thanks, Jason, maybe a little bit later. "

"Hey Garry, could I talk with you a minute?"

"Sure Lloyd."

"Garry, I just want to apologize for acting like such an idiot, I know it's no excuse but Carol means the world to me, and I guess that I just lost it."

"You don't have to apologize to me Lloyd, if I was in your shoes, I think that I would have socked me one, I'm the one that should apologize." Lloyd made a motion to shake Garry's hand, but instead of Garry accepting his hand, he through

Lloyd a curve and gave him a hug. Even though this was out of Lloyd's character, he welcomed Garry's show of affection, and even embellished it.

Carol was standing back, peering at the two of them, it meant so much to her, seeing the two of them back on good terms, and she was astounded at the sight of them hugging, if she hadn't seen them with her own eyes, she would have never believed it.

"Well come over here Carol, there's lots to go around." Garry refrained from giving Carol too much attention, he didn't want to rock the boat any more than he had already done. Carol also made sure that Lloyd was the first one that she went to.

"Okay ladies and gentleman, can I have your attention please?

At this time I would like everyone to join me and raise their glass to congratulate Lloyd and Carol's engagement."

" Everyone raised their glass and gave a gracious toast to the two lovebirds. After the toast, they all cheered, then gathered around Lloyd and Carol, congratulating them with all their hugs and kisses and support.

Get over here and give mom a big kiss on the lips you handsome devil you." It was obvious that Jean was into the champagne, she staggered into Lloyd's arms, her kiss didn't exactly come in contact with Lloyd's lips, from the way that she was weaving, it was more like a face wash for Lloyd. He ended up with bright red lipstick just under his eye, his nose, and cheek, but nowhere near his anticipating lips.

"Welcome to the family Floyd." Jean slurred.

"Thank you. Mrs. Crawford" Lloyd said, feeling a little embarrassed.

"Mother, his name is Lloyd, not Floyd." Carol blurted out, trying to keep a straight face.

"Well what the hell do you think I called him? You got to get those ears of yours checked out Carol. Isn't that right there Floyd?" Jean was the entertainment of the day, everyone was getting quite a kick out of her escapade.

"You're exactly right Mrs. Crawford, I'll make sure she gets those ears of hers checked out as soon as we can."

"And cut the bullshit out too Floyd, you call me mother now, no more of this Mrs. Crawford crap."

"Okay,I promise mom." Lloyd thought Jean was so adorable, she knew that they were going to get along very well together.

The guests gave their final best wishes to Lloyd and Carol, and thanked Jason and Jean for the lovely time that they had. They made their way to their cars, all with smiles and a content look on their faces.

When all of the guests had left and every thing was cleaned up, Carol, Lloyd and Jason sat out on the front porch, relaxing over a cup of coffee and a piece of cake.

"Well Lloyd, it looks like you're going to be living with us for awhile."

"Yes sir,I know it's a lot to ask, and I'm really grateful to you and Mrs. Crawford, but I'm going to see if I can get a better paying job and see if Carol and I can get a nice place in the country."

"Don't you worry none there Lloyd, you two can stay here as long as you like, it will be a pleasure having you around.

I'm going to see if your mother is feeling up to coming out and sit with us for a while."

While Jason went in to the house, it gave Carol a chance to give to give Lloyd a hug and a kiss.

"I love you so much darlin', and I promise you that I'll be the best husband, and treat you like a queen every day of our lives."

"I love you too, Lloyd, and don't you worry, we're going to get that house out in the country."

They both knew that their dream house was just exactly that, a dream.. It would take at least a good year to earn enough money just for a down payment, but they knew that they had a whole lifetime together, and that was the most important thing.

Jason and Jean came through the door, Jason was carrying a good size nicely gift wrapped package with a wonderful little plastic bride and groom placed on the top of it.

"Your mother and I got you something that we thought that you guys could use. It's not very much, I just wish we could have gotten you guys something better." Jason handed them the heavy box.

"Oh dad, I'm sure that it's going to be lovely, don't be so hard on yourself."

"Well come on you two, open it up." Jason was more exited than anyone.

"Oh dad it's so heavy, what is it?" Carol was anxious.

Carol removed the plastic bride and groom and placed it gently on the table. She laid the box on the porch, and her and Lloyd got right down on their knees to open it up. Lloyd pulled his pocket knife out, and ever so gently cut the box up the middle. They anxiously opened up the flaps of the box, and seen that it was filled with small popcorn like packing.

"Come on you two, reach in there, don't worry it won't break." Jean was getting more excited now.

Lloyd finally put his hand fully into the box, he felt around until he grabbed onto something.

"I got something here Carol." Lloyd uttered, sounding so excited.

Lloyd finally pulled out what his hand had grasped on to. It was a brick, Lloyd didn't know what to say or how to react, so he just held out the brick and smiled. He was dumbfounded.

"Now how in the heck did that get in there?" Jason asked with a big smirk on his face.

Lloyd and Carol couldn't stand the suspense any longer, they just tipped the box over and emptied everything out in a fury. On top of the pile of all the packing was a large manila envelope.

"Hey, you finally found it. Go ahead open it up." Jason was just as eager.

Carol handed the envelope to Lloyd to open. He cut the envelope open with his pocket knife, then paused a moment, took a deep breath, then pulled out the content.

Lloyd and Carol studied the document, their bodies went limp, and they broke down, they held each other in their arms, crying like a baby.

What was in the envelope, was the deed for the cottage that they stayed in, in Cedar Rapids, stamped; paid in full.

"Oh thank you guys so much, you made us the happiest couple in the whole world, oh if you only knew how much this means to us, I love you both so much." Carol and Lloyd walked up to Jason and Jean and gave them a big hug.

Lloyd was so overcome with emotion, that he couldn't even talk.

CHAPTER TWENTY

The Limousine pulled up into the Holy Trinity Church parking lot. The chauffeur exited the lustrous black limo, and opened the rear passenger door. Lloyd stepped out, dressed in a black tuxedo, with a red carnation pinned to his lapel, looking and feeling like a million dollars, and as proud as can be. He held out his hand to Carol as she stepped out of the limo with a bouquet of white baby-breath . She was wearing a beautiful white wedding dress, with a string of pearls. They entered the church and was greeted by Reverend Dale Steen.

He led them to the church's front door. The silence was eerie, Carol could hear her own heartbeat, and every breath she took.

Lloyd tightened his grip on Carol's hand, trying to ease his shaking, and to give solace to his apprehensive feelings.

Jason, Jean and Garry were in a state of awe as Lloyd and Carol entered the chapel.

It was time for the ceremony to begin, Carol and Lloyd stood in front of the Reverend, anxiously awaiting for him to proceed.

"Dearly Beloved, we are assembled here in the presence of God, to join this man and this woman in holy marriage. Those who enter into this relation to cherish a mutual esteem and love, to bear with each others infirmities and weaknesses, to comfort each other in sickness, trouble, and sorrow. Love can be one of the highest experiences that comes to humankind. At its best it reduces our selfishness, deepens our personalities, and makes life far more meaningful. Its very nature is to want to give to one another, and to feel joy, and live in harmony. Such love can call forth the best qualities in each of you.

Lloyd Robert Smith, do you take Carol Lynne Crawford, whom you hold by the hand to be your lawfully wedded wife, and do you covenant to be true to her, to love, cherish, and protect her, in sickness and in health, in poverty or in wealth, until death do you part?"

"I do. Lloyd placed the ring onto Carol's finger.

"Carol Lynne Crawford, do you take Lloyd Robert Smith, whom you hold by the hand to be your lawfully wedded husband, covenanting to be true to him, to love, cherish, and honor him, in sickness and in health, in poverty or in wealth, until death do you part?

"I do." Carol placed the ring onto Lloyd's finger.

"As a minister of the gospel, and by the authority invested in me by the state of North Carolina, I pronounce you to be to each other, husband and wife. Whom therefore God hath joined together, let no man put asunder. You may kiss the bride."

Lloyd gently took Carol into his arms, they kissed, to them, this moment was heaven sent. Lloyd could taste the salt from the tear that rolled down Carol's face. He so delicately caressed her tender cheek.

"I love you Carol."

"I love you too sweetheart."

"Congratulations ... you two ... we're so happy for you. "Jason was so overcome with emotion that he could barely get the words out. Garry gave Carol a hug, and a kiss on her cheek.

"Well there Floyd, now you went out and got hitched on me aye? Get over here and give mama a kiss damn it." Jean said, slurring her words,

Jean could lighten up any moment, she was a real gem and a true treasure to Lloyd.

He obliged and gave his mother in law a big hug and a kiss right on the lips. Jean's face lit up like a Christmas tree, she loved the extra attention that Lloyd gave to her.

They made their way out of the church to the awaiting limousine, Lloyd and Carol gave everyone a farewell hug before climbing into the limo to head out to the airport to catch their plane to Canada. Just before the limo pulled away, Carol opened the window, yelled out and tossed her bouquet . She made sure that she tossed it towards Garry, much to his delight, he caught it.

"You're next Garry." Carol yelled out.

They stood and watched as the limo drove away, Carol was waving gloriously, until they were no more in sight.

CHAPTER TWENTY ONE

Carol and Lloyd arrived at the Pearson International Airport in Toronto Canada. It was a frigid ten degrees, the wind made it feel more like ten below.

Lloyd walked up to an awaiting taxi and asked the cabby if he would take them to Niagara Falls. The cheerful cabby concurred and stepped out of his cab and loaded their luggage into the trunk.

"So where are you two from?" The smiling cabby asked.

"We're from Cedar Rapids, North Carolina." Carol grinned at Lloyd when he said Cedar Rapids. They hadn't even moved in there yet and Lloyd was already saying that they were from there.

"Oh that's a nice place . I bet you don't get any weather like this down there."

"No sir, we rarely get any snow, and it never gets this cold." Lloyd and Carol were both still shaking from the cold. The cab driver noticed and kindly turned the heat up.

As the cab turned on to the Queen Elizabeth Highway, Lloyd pointed out to Carol the sign that said Niagara Falls 100 kilometers.

"My name is Tyrone, welcome to Canada. We should be in Niagara Falls in about a hour more or less. I bet you guys are here for your honeymoon?"

"Yes we are,we just got married this morning." Lloyd said so proudly.

"Good for you, I hope you have a wonderful life together.

You're going to love Niagara Falls. You know it's the honeymoon capital of the world. I take my wife and kids up there at least once a year. The falls is one thing that you never get tired of seeing."

It was starting to snow heavily, and the closer they got to Niagara Falls, the snow seemed to be coming down faster. The wind started to pick up and the cab slowed down to a snails pace. They could barely see ten feet ahead of them, it was like someone was holding a white sheet in front of the car.

Carol and Lloyd were very nervous at the weather. North Carolina had tornadoes but nothing like this. They could feel the car fishtailing. Lloyd felt like his heart was in his stomach, Carol just sat there nervously staring out the window. The cabby was really concentrating on his driving, so much that his nose was almost touching the windshield, probably the only way that he could see where he was going. They both dared not say a word to him, in fright that they might distract him enough to cause an accident.

The snow started to taper off a little as soon as they made it over the Burlington Sky Way Bridge

The cabby turned his head and looked back at the anxious Lloyd and Carol, and smiled.

"Oh don't worry too much about the weather, this is always a bad spot in the winter. We get it a lot worse than that, in 1977 we had such a blizzard that they had to close the highways right down. People were left stranded in their cars, a lot of the cars were completely buried in snow. Some of the snow drifts were as high as the telephone poles. There weren't many casualties thank God."

The cabby's little story wasn't too much of a comfort for Carol and Lloyd, but the wind had died down by now and the snow that was now falling was more hypnotic, and less intimidating.

"Well we're just coming into St. Catherines, once we get over this sky way, we will be pretty close to Niagara Falls. Is there a special motel that you want to go to?"

"Yea, we have reservations for the Micheal's Inn."

"Oh your going to like it there, that's really close to the falls. You'll be able to hear the roar of the falls right from your hotel room."

They were finally in Niagara Falls, they could see the Skylon Tower in the distance, all lit up with Christmas lights. The next sign that they seen was the one that they were waiting for, it said: Niagara Falls population, 79,000. They were ecstatic that they were finally there.

The cab drove down Clifton Hill,where all the museums were. Lloyd rolled his window down, they could hear the thunderous roar of the mighty falls.

Their room was on the tenth floor, there was a beautiful heart shaped water bed, and a heart shaped jacuzzi to match.

They were astonished when they looked out the window and seen the spectacular view of the falls.

They stood at the window taking in the breathtaking view for a few minutes then Lloyd took Carol by the hand and led her to the awaiting bed. They didn't make love, they were just content on holding on to each other and sharing the moment.

"I love you so much."

"I love you too, sweetie."

Did you ever make love on a water bed before darlin'?"

"No, I never did. How about you?"

"No, I never did either."

"Then what are we waiting for?"

They started to make passionate love. The water bed moved along with every movement that they made. Carol was in a state of ecstasy, when Lloyd suddenly pulled away. He sat at the edge of the bed, soaked with sweat and as white as a sheet.

"Lloyd what's wrong?" Carol asked with a sound of fright in her voice. She thought that he might be having a heart attack from the way he looked.

"Do you want me to call 911?"

"No darlin',this happened to me before, I should have told you. Damn it!" Lloyd was really in a bad state. He looked like death warmed over.

"Tell me what's wrong. What happened to you before? Tell me!" Carol had the sound of panic in her voice.

"Carol ... It's the water bed. I'm fucking sea sick. I just can't stand all those waves ...

"Lloyd made a mad dash to the bathroom, Carol could hear him being sick, her panic turned into sheer laughter. She pushed her head into the pillow for Lloyd would not hear her laughter. She felt so sorry for Lloyd that such a thing would happen to him on their wedding night, but the hilarity took over the sympathy. Tears rolled down her face from laughing so hard. She tried to regain control of her hilarity but with no avail, she just couldn't stop laughing, the thought of Lloyd getting seasick on a water bed and on the first night of his honeymoon was something that one would see in the movies, not in real life, but it did happen and she was part of the cause.

Lloyd made his way out of the bathroom, Carol bit her bottom lip and took one look at him and realized how sick he really was, this made her feel guilty. Lloyd had a wet towel draped over his head and he didn't say a word, he just grabbed a pillow, tossed it on the floor and went right to sleep.

Lloyd slept the rest of the night on the rock hard floor with the cold towel on his head. Carol emphatically slept uncomfortably next to him the whole night.

They awoke at dawn, both of them suffering from a sore back.

"How do you feel now honey?" Carol asked, sympathetically.

"I'm okay darlin', I feel so bad that I spoiled our wedding night."

"Oh sweetie, don't be so hard on yourself, you didn't spoil anything. I'll tell you what stud muffin, we'll make up for it tonight, how does that sound?"

"Sounds great darlin', I just hope that I don't get seasick from looking at the falls and be useless again tonight." Lloyd said with such a serious look on his face, but actually, he was being facetious.

"Well if looking at the falls is going to make you sea sick again sweetie, then we won't even go near it. There's a lot of other sights that we can see besides the falls."

Lloyd couldn't keep a straight face any longer, he bursted out into laughter. Carol just stood there looking so bewildered.

"I was only pulling your leg darlin', the falls isn't going to make me seasick, just keep me the hell away from that damn water bed that's all."

"Oh you joker you, I'll fix yea you son-of-a-gun, I'll teach you not to fool with me ..." Carol playfully wrestled Lloyd onto the bed. Carol was on top of him playfully badgering and slapping him around, not even realizing what she was doing to his poor stomach. Lloyd could feel every little wave from the water bed, he turned to two different shades of green. Carol finally noticed and stopped, Lloyd raced to the bathroom, where once again he was sick.

This' time, Carol didn't think that it was so funny, she felt so guilty from her thoughtless actions. She nervously waited for Lloyd to come out of the bathroom, and when he did, he looked up at her, and to her surprise, he was the one who bursted out in laughter, much to her relief, she half heartily laughed along with him.

"Well darlin', are you going to buy me some breakfast or what? I got nothin' left in my stomach."

"Yea, I'll buy you breakfast sweetie, but maybe we should go and see the falls first. I wouldn't want you to waste a perfectly good breakfast." Carol said with a huge mocking grin on her face.

"You just never mind there smart ass. I'll just get me some Gravol for my stomach, then we'll see who gets sea sick tonight."

"Oh hon, that sounds like fun, but I think we should get you some breakfast first, you're going to need a lot of nourishment for tonight, lover boy."

After a hearty breakfast they were on their way to see the falls. The sun was out and the sky was clear, and even though the temperature was frigid, it felt so good for them to get out into the fresh air. The snow made a crunching sound as they walked, they could see their breath as they spoke to each other. All winter the Niagara Parks Commission put on a wonderful festival of lights. Everywhere they looked they could see a dazzling display of Christmas lights. All the trees were lit and covered with snow, there was a sleigh and rein dears, snowmen and so many other different designs all lit up. They walked to the railings and looked down at the swift current of the Niagara River, the view was spectacular, the ice jams were breaking apart and being swept away by the aggressive river. There was a steady stream of avid tourists, some gazing over the railing at the Niagara River and the rest were in a hurried pace to see the mighty falls. The air was filled with a cold blustery mist that was coming from the falls, and the thunderous roar gave them the sense of the real power that the falls had. They could see the American Falls and they were no farther than a hundred feet away from the Canadian Horseshoe Falls.

"Can you imagine going over the falls in a barrel, darlin'?

"It makes me nervous just to stand this close."

Lloyd was so intimidated by the falls that he held on to the railings with both hands.

"Did anyone ever live from going over the falls in a barrel sweetie?"

"Oh yea, a few did, but a lot more died. There was a little kid that went over the falls and he is still living to tell about it. Some kind of boating accident."

Carol was pleasantly surprised at how much knowledge Lloyd had about the falls.

They went up the Skylon Tower which they could see a perfect view of the whole city and right across to the American side.

The rest of the day they spent their time going to all the museums on Clifton Hill. They went to the worlds famous Ripley's Believe It Or Not, and the Tussuad's museum, where Lloyd had his picture taken with a life like wax figure of Michel Jackson.

Carol was absolutely terrified going through all the different horror chambers of the museums, this was Lloyd's favorite part, so she didn't put up too much of a fuss.

After they had visited all of the museums, they finished the day by going out to dinner at the China Dragon restaurant. They ordered enough Chinese food to feed five people. When they finished their dinner they ordered a coffee and talked all about the comical things that had happened to them together.

They both got into a laughing gag when Carol brought up about the night at the cottage when Lloyd was so scared of the skunk, and Carol ended up wetting herself. In the short time that they knew each other, they had so many comical stories that had happened to them.

The waiter gave Lloyd a friendly smile when they made eye contact. He came to the table and placed the bill in the middle of the table, along with a couple of fortune cookies.

Carol opened up hers first and read it to herself before she read it to Lloyd.

"Oh how true this is sweetie. Listen to this: "you will have a long life that is filled with love, wealth and happiness.""

Lloyd leaned over the table and gave Carol a tender kiss.

"Darlin', I promise you that our life will be filled with love and happiness"

"Well what about the wealth? The fortune cookie said love, wealth, and happiness."

"Well two out of three aint bad."

"Come on sweetie, read yours."

Lloyd ever so gently opened the cookie up and read his fortune to himself. He just shook his head and laughed at what it had said.

"If you think that yours is true, then listen to this one: "one who makes waves, will suffer the consequences.""

Carol almost fell off of her chair from laughing so hard. "Oh ... Lloyd .... " Carol just couldn't get the words out from her hilarity.

Once Lloyd regained his composer he got up and paid the bill, while Carol walked out the door still in glee. The young waiter must have surely thought that they had been drinking from the way that they were carrying on.

"You two, very funny, very funny." The young Chinese waiter remarked to Lloyd, with such a strange look on his face.

"Thanks pal, have a nice night." Lloyd handed him a generous ten dollar tip, then walked out the door.

"Lloyd, we have to go back to the hotel now, I did it again."

"What did you do again?"

"Lloyd I'm soaked." Carol said, still laughing away.

Lloyd looked at Carol in a puzzled way, until he realized what she meant by the way she was walking.

"Oh Carol, don't tell me you did it again. What is it with you, can't you hold your water?"

"I can't help it, you had me laughing so hard in there. You and your darn fortune cookie."

"Oh come on pissy pants. We're going to have to get you some diapers, you know that?"

Carol and Lloyd lay cuddled on the water bed, they just finished making love on the hard rock floor.

"Lloyd do you think that it's always going to be like this for us?"

"Sure darlin', why wouldn't it be?"

"I don't know sweetie, everything is going so wonderful, it just feels like a dream to me that's all."

"Yea, I know what you mean darlin', it does feel like it is something from out of a dream, but why couldn't it be like this all the time? I wouldn't want any thing to change, I love everything about you, everything that you are and everything that you do and say"

"When 1 was a kid, I know that my dad loved me very much, but that was all, we didn't do anything together, we never had any fun together and I missed that so much. He was the same way with my mother. Love isn't enough. They say that love is good for the soul, but so is laughter. So I don't want anything to change darlin'."

"Oh sweetie who could ever ask for a better husband than you? I love you so much sweetheart."

"1 love you too darlin'." They held each other in their arms, feeling so grateful to have someone to love, someone so special.

"Well darlin' I'm going to shut the light off, I'm absolutely bushed, we did a lot of walking today."

"Okay sweetie, I'm really tired too."

Lloyd reached over and shut the lamp off, gave Carol a kiss, and said he loved her, then rolled over.

Carol cuddled up close to him.

Carol had a hard time getting to sleep from the roar of the falls. She was thinking about what it's going to be like when they go home to their new cottage. She wondered how her parents were doing, and was pretty worried about them. First thing in the morning she was going to call them.

"Goodnight pissy pants." Lloyd jested.

"Pissy pants? Who you calling pissy pants?" Carol took her pillow and gave Lloyd a good whack, they were laughing away. Lloyd countered with a couple of whacks with his pillow in return.

They tired out pretty fast, and with in minutes, they settled down and went to sleep.

CHAPTER TWENTY TWO

"Welcome back you two, how was Niagara Falls?" Jason asked as soon as Carol and Lloyd walked into the house.

"Oh dad it was absolutely wonderful, we loved it so much that we want to go back there in the summer. The falls was so incredible, there's so much water falling and it's so fast and powerful, you would never believe how loud the roar is. We could hear it in our motel room even with the windows closed. You and mom would just love it." Carol was filled with enthusiasm, while Lloyd just sat there quietly, he was thoroughly exhausted.

"Well how did you like it there Lloyd?"

"Niagara Falls is a great city, Jason, there's so much to see and do there. If Carol and I ever go back there this summer, maybe you and mom would like to come with us. You guys would love it, there's so many great museums and so much more to see than just the falls, but the falls is the best thing to see, a person could just stand there for hours looking at the falls."

Lloyd felt a lot more energetic now, recounting their trip.

" How is mom doing dad?" Carol nervously asked.

"Carol, your mother is fine, in fact I think she is feeling a little too fine. She has so much piss and vinegar lately, I don't know where the sam hell she's getting all the energy from.

You know she's acting like a damn teenager. She should be back any time now, she's at the hairdressers, she knows that you guys were coming back today, so she wanted to get her hair done.

Jean walked in the doorway with such a fury, she took one look at Lloyd and went right to him with open arms.

"Hi there handsome, give mama some sugar will ya?" She rushed to Lloyd and gave him long kiss on the lips, Lloyd's face was as red as a beet and he was grinning from ear to ear.

"How are you doing there sexy? We sure missed you, you know that? Did you miss me Floyd, cause I sure missed you?"

"We sure we missed you, just ask Carol how many times we mentioned your name, in fact you are all that was on my mind the whole week." Jean was taking this all in, she flourished from all of Lloyd's kind attention that he was giving her.

"Lloyd's right mom, we did miss you and dad so much."

"Your dad and I missed you too. Didn't we dear?" Jason agreed.

Carol could really see a big change in her mother, and it made her feel so good to hear her mother call her sweetie, their closeness seemed to fade away just after she suffered the stroke, and she missed all of her mother's affectionate and kind words.

"Now you didn't get all snazzied up for me did you?" Lloyd asked. If I had a camera I'd take a picture of you right now. Your hair looks so nice, and look at those fingernails, they look so pretty, what color is that? It matches your dress perfectly?" The more Lloyd said, the more excited Jean got.

"Awe Floyd, I bet you say that to all the woman."

"No mom, just you ... and your lovely daughter here."

"Well honey, why don't you give mom and dad the things that we brought back for them." Carol asked Lloyd.

"We brought you guys some snow back from Canada." Lloyd handed Jason a Pepsi bottle half full of water.

"Is this what Canadian snow looks like, sure looks like water to me?" Jason said jokingly to Lloyd.

"Well I can't figure that one out Jason, it sure didn't look like that when we put it in there." Lloyd went right along with Jason. Jean just sat there bewildered.

Lloyd pulled out a beautiful wall plate with a picture of Niagara Falls on it. He proudly handed it to Jean, her face lit right up. She jumped to her feet and asked Lloyd to hang it on the wall right away.

"Come on mom, you show me where you want me to hang it and I'll hang it up for you." Jean eagerly led Lloyd into the kitchen.

"Well your mother has sure taken a liken to Lloyd, that's one thing for sure pumpkin." Jason said with his head down low.

"You got that right dad, Lloyd just loves mom .... Oh he loves you too dad. He told me that he feels that you're the father that he never had." Carol needed to say something like this to her father, they were giving Jean all the attention.

"You really mean that pumpkin, he really said that?" Jason perked up.

"Why sure he did dad, Lloyd really has a lot of respect for you, he really looks up to you."

"Well he's a real fine son in law pumpkin!, a real fine son in law." Jason had watery eyes, he took it to heart. Carol got up and gave her father a nice hug and a kiss on his cheek.

"Carol will you get in here and find the hammer and a nail for us, now?" Lloyd impudently hollered out harshly from the kitchen.

"Carol, what the hell are you doing? I want the hammer and nail now!" Lloyd yelled at Carol.

Lloyd's mood changed like day and night.

Carol rolled her eyes and walked towards the kitchen.

She grabbed the hammer and a nail from the drawer and angrily tossed them onto the kitchen table, she gave Lloyd an if looks could kill kind of stare, then walked out of the room.

He didn't like the thought of Carol doing what she did and embarrassing him.

He hung up the plate on the wall, then marched into the living room and bluntly told Carol to get ready that they were going home.

"Lloyd, we don't even have any furniture moved into our place yet." Carol replied.

"Pumpkin, go in your bedroom and see what's in there will ya?" Jason said.

"Okay dad." Jason followed her right into the bedroom. She was shocked to see that the room was totally empty. Every piece of her furniture was gone.

"What happened to all my things dad?"

"Well pumpkin, while you and Lloyd were on your honeymoon, Garry and I moved all your things into your new place."

Carol was too overwhelmed to say anything. She just stood there with her mouth opened, then wrapped her arms around her father, and held on so tightl1y.

"What's goin' on in here?" Lloyd asked, crudely.

"Garry and I moved all of Carol's things into your new place."

Carol refused to even look at Lloyd.

"Thanks dad, you're the best ... what would we ever do with out you?" She gave her gratified father another kiss on his cheek.

"Well what do you say if we all take a drive to Cedar Rapids and see your new place?"

"That sounds wonderful to me, dad." Carol in no way wanted to be alone with Lloyd after his tirades.

"That was so thoughtful of you guys to go to all that trouble for us, thanks a lot, we really appreciate everything that you and mom have done for us." Lloyd went quiet, Carol could still sense the anger in him. She knew that this was going to spoil everything that her father and Garry had done for them.

They all were headed for Cedar Rapids. Carol gave Lloyd the cold shoulder all the way up to the cottage.

By the time they entered the town of Cedar Rapids, Carol had calmed down some, and gave Lloyd a smile. He didn't return the gesture, he gave her such an evil stare that she almost broke down.

They all stepped out of the car, Carol was the first one to the door, but Lloyd was the one that had the keys. He just brushed past her and unlocked the door. They all stepped inside, Carol and Lloyd just stood there in awe, there were new curtains on every window, a new kitchen table, and the walls had been wallpapered and painted.

"Oh dad, what did you and Garry do, it looks absolutely wonderful?" She rushed into the bedroom and seen that everything looked like it was placed with a woman's touch.

"Well what do you think Lloyd?" Jason asked, it was obvious that he was a little nervous with Lloyd now, from his antics.

"Well Jason, I think you guys did a wonderful job, thanks so much." Lloyd answered, without any sincerity in his voice. Carol felt so embarrassed, not only for herself but for her mom and dad too. Jason sympathetically caressed her back to try to console her.

"Hey what's that I hear coming from the back yard?"

"I don't hear anything dad."

"Well I do, let's go out there and see what the heck it is." Everyone went along with Jason, even though they didn't hear anything what so ever.

Carol almost fainted when she seen what was in the back yard .

Lloyd didn't appear too happy about it.

Carol was on her hands and knees with her arm around one of the most beautiful animals that she had ever seen. It was a full size Saint Bernard, and as gentle as a lamb.

"Oh you guys are going to get along just fine, look at how much she loves you Carol." The loving dog was giving her a good face wash. It made Jason feel so much better seeing his daughter happy and laughing again.

"What's her name dad?"

"Sasha, her name is Sasha dear. Jason was getting a big kick out of seeing his daughter and the dog showing so much affection to each other. Carol was still on her hands and knees, and Sasha was higher then she was.

"That looks like a fuckin' horse to me." Jean shouted out. Everyone just roared with laughter, even Lloyd. Jean just laughed along with everyone else, even though she didn't know what every one was laughing about.

"Go ahead Lloyd, go give her a pat, she won't bite, she wouldn't hurt a fly."

Lloyd got with in two feet of Sasha and she growled and lunged at him, Lloyd jumped back in fear.

"Well I'm staying the hell away from that dog, that's for damn sure." Lloyd walked disgustingly back into the house. Carol couldn't hold back her smile from what Sasha had done, she now felt a little more at ease knowing that Sasha was so protective of her already.

Jason and Jean didn't feel comfortable at all from what they could see what was going on between their daughter and Lloyd. Jason walked to Carol, he knelt down and petted Sasha, and tentatively explained to Carol that he and Jean had to go home because they were expecting Cliff and his wife over for dinner. Carol knew that this was far from the truth but she knew how uncomfortable her dad was feeling, so she didn't make a big issue out of it.

"Are you going to be all right pumpkin?" Her dad asked, feeling worried about his daughter.

"Yes, I'm fine dad, don't worry about me, Lloyd's just warn out that's all, we've done so much in this past week. I can't blame him for being a little cranky. You guys go home and have a wonderful night, besides, I got ole Sasha here, she's on my side." Carol said jokingly, but inside she really felt grateful that she did have Sasha, at the way Lloyd acted put a good scare into her, and she was more than a little nervous about not knowing what was going to happen when she walked into the house alone.

Jason quietly opened the door to the cottage, the bedroom door was closed, so he figured that Lloyd went in to lay down. He felt relieved that he didn't have to face Lloyd to say goodbye. He walked down the steps where Jean and Carol were standing talking to each other.

"Thanks for everything that you have done for us. Lloyd and I really appreciate it. Everything looks so wonderful. We're going to have you over for dinner one of these days as soon as we get settled in."

"Okay pumpkin, you call us if you need anything."

Jason gave his daughter a stern look.

"I'll give you a call as soon as we get the phone put in, hopefully we can get it put in soon."

"I can't go until I go tell Floyd goodbye."

Jean was half way up the stairs before Jason could get her and tell her that Lloyd had gone to sleep. She was determined to go anyways but Jason coaxed her not to go in and bother him.

They gave their daughter one last hug before they got into the car, then they pulled out of the driveway and was out of sight within a minute. Instead of going straight inside, Carol went to the back yard to see her new friend Sasha.

She knelt down and gave Sasha a hug and broke down and cried. She tried her best to control her emotions, but the tears just wouldn't stop. Sasha whimpered along with her, it was just as if she could feel her pain.

"Oh Sasha, you're a bigger suck than I am." Sasha licked the tears from Carol's face.

Carol gained control of herself and gave Sasha one last hug and walked to the front of the cottage. She was still too nervous to go in, she sat on the stairs, thinking what the rest of the night was going to be like.

"What the fuck are you doing sitting there. Get your fuckin' ass off the stairs and get in here!"

Carol froze in terror.

"I'll be in a couple of minutes sweetie, I just got a little head ache that's all."

Carol was hoping that her sweet talk would settle him down, and he'd leave her be.

"Listen, I just about had enough of your bullshit, now get your fuckin' ass in here or I'll drag you in!"

Carol was terrified, she wanted to get up and run but she felt too numb to move. She knew that Lloyd was upset with her, but nothing like this. She shook like a leaf, her mind racing. She managed to stand up. She turned to face him and she could see the fire in his eyes.

"Lloyd, I'm not coming in the house until you settle down. What's wrong with you, I never seen you like this before?"

"Carol, I'm not going to ask you again, now get the fuck in this fucking house now!"

"I'll come in the house when you settle down .... " Carol answered in a low tone, her lips quivering.

"Then fuck you then!" Lloyd slammed the door shut, much to the relief of Carol.

Carol walked to the back of the house, one place that she new that she'd be safe, Lloyd wouldn't come near her just as long she was with Sasha. Sasha was whining, she could sense the fear and the distress that Carol was feeling.

Lloyd had scared her so much that she wet herself once again, but this time it was out of fear instead from laughter. Sasha began to bark. Carol turned around, Lloyd was standing behind her. She let out a loud scream, Lloyd grabbed a hold of her arm before she could even attempt to run.

"Oh Lloyd, don't hurt me, please don't hurt me." Carol did everything she possibly could to try and break free from his tight hold but to no avail, he was just too strong for her.

She quickly ran out of strength and had nothing left in her to resist him. She was crying hysterically. Lloyd let go of her and she fell to her knees. She looked up at Lloyd, giving him a look that was begging for mercy.

They could see the pain in each others eyes. It was as if they were looking into each others souls.

"I'm sorry baby, I'm so sorry. I just don't know what the heck came over me."

He offered his hand to Carol to help her get up, she was still too terrified to accept his offering. He bent down and gently helped her up. They embraced in a profound emotional state. They both wept in each others arms and slowly made their way back into the house.

As they walked past the two cars, Carol could see that her front tire was completely flat. It was obvious that someone had slashed it with a knife, and she knew it had to be Lloyd. As they walked into the house, Carol kept her distance from him, she sat down on the couch, after seeing the flat tire she felt just as fearful as she did before, she knew if she wanted to escape that she would have to go by foot. Lloyd was pacing back and forth, no longer crying, he had a fierce look of anger on his face once again.

"Carol, why did you embarrass me like that in front of your parents? You made me feel like a asshole."

Carol was too scared to answer, this only made Lloyd more enraged. He picked up a lamp from an end table, and viciously threw it against the wall, shattering it into pieces. He walked towards Carol in such a rage, that Carol rolled up into a ball, crying at the top of her lungs, flailing her arms erratically in defense.

Lloyd lifted his hand to strike her, then pulled his hand back.

"Fuck this bullshit, I'm going out and you better be here when I come back!" He slammed the door so hard that the glass on the door shattered. Carol could hear the car speed away.

She opened the door, and stepped over the shards of glass.

She had thoughts of leaving and go to look for a phone, but she was just too scared, just in case Lloyd changed his mind and was on his way back. She thought if he caught her trying to leave then he would be so irate that he'd probably beat her. She decided to stay. She had to keep busy to keep her anguished mind occupied, she cleaned up all the glass from the shattered window, and lamp. She was in such a state that she didn't even realize that she had a deep gash on her hand from were the glass had sliced into her. She went into hysterics once again when she seen all the blood that was pouring out of her wound. The blood was all over her and onto the floor.

She rushed into the bathroom leaving a trail of blood behind her. She ran cold water onto the cut, she was going to need stitches. She rapped a towel around the wound, then proceeded to finish cleaning up, which now included wiping up all the blood.

Carol had everything cleaned up and put in a green plastic trash bag. She opened the door to put the bag outside in the trash can, she got half way down the stairs when she saw the outline of someone standing at the bottom of the stairs, she let out a loud scream dropped the garbage bag and ran back up the stairs and into the house.

"Hey what the darn hell is going on in there, are you alright?"

Carol recognized the voice right away, it was Jim Parker, the man that use to own the cottage.

He walked up the stairs, took one look at the window, then took a good look at her.

"Hello Jim, I'm alright, just like me, clumsy as an ox, I put my hand right through the window."

"I'll say ya did .... ah looks like you went and hurt yourself, you better let me take a good look at that."

"No! ... It's okay Jim, it's only a small cut, besides I'm a nurse, but thanks anyway." Carol didn't feel too comfortable being around Jim Parker, especially being alone with him, but he could be her savior if he could change her tire.

"Jim, could you change my tire on my car?"

"No, I don't do that...I don't know how." Jim said, deflating all hope from Carol.

"Well I was sure surprised when your father offered to buy this place, yep ... he paid some good money for it too."

"Yes Jim, we just love this house ... I don't mean to be rude or anything Jim, but I have some things to do before my husband comes home." Carol asked him assertively, this was the only way to get rid of him, he would be there for hours if she didn't speak up.

"So you love this house, aye? Well my dear, it's not really a house, it's a cottage, but I guess you could call it a house if you wanted to."

"Well thanks for dropping by Jim, we'll see you again." She pretty well had to push him out the door, he was still talking when he reached the bottom of the stairs.

Lloyd had been gone for over an hour now, Carol was anxious to take a shower and get into bed before he did come home. She didn't know what frame of mind he would be in when he did come home. She quickly got undressed, took a fast shower and was in bed with all the lights off. She lay in bed, thinking of the days events. She tried her best to keep her emotions in check, but it was just too much for her to bear. She just couldn't believe how fast things changed with Lloyd.. She played things over and over in her mind. She felt that it was her that brought everything on by the way that she acted at her parents house, but there was no way that Lloyd could justify his actions.

She suddenly heard a big crashing noise, then sudden silence. She didn't know what to do, she just held on to the blankets and lay there in fright. Then she could hear Lloyd, cursing away, using every profanity there was to be said.

She rolled over, and tried to lay as still as she could, but with the way she was shaking it would be obvious to Lloyd that she wasn't really sleeping.

Lloyd barged into the bedroom and turned on the light, Carol didn't even move a muscle, she was so terrified.

She lay there with her eyes closed so tightly, she could actually feel the breath from Lloyd, she knew that he had to be leaning right over her, she could smell the putrid odor of alcohol on his breath, it was so bad that she almost gagged.

"Yea, sleep you bitch, you don't love me now and you probably never did, so fuck you, fuck you and your whole damn family too."

Carol was getting to the point were she just about had all that she could take of Lloyd's abuse. He switched the light off, then mumbled something as he left the room.

Carol waited for a few minutes until she knew for sure that he was out of the room.

She could here him walking around in the kitchen. She quietly crept out of bed to see if she could see what he was up to, and to see what kind of shape he was really in. Her heart was racing, and she couldn't catch her breath. She could see the back of him in the kitchen, she was sure that there was no way that he could see her from the darkness of the room and from the bright light of the kitchen. When he turned around, the sight of him made her skin crawl, his face looked like it was beaten to a pulp, it didn't even look like Lloyd. His eye was completely swollen shut, and his top lip was split open and was swollen to twice the size. He was staggering so much that he had to lean against the wall to hold himself up. Carol froze when he peered into the bedroom, it looked as if he was staring her right at her. He started to stagger his way towards the bedroom. Carol made sure that the bedroom door was slightly open, for she could see him coming.

She made a beeline back into bed.

She watched him struggle his way towards the bedroom, he was about four feet away from the door when he just dropped to the floor, to her surprise he got right back up and continued his way towards the bedroom..

"Sweetheart ... are you awake? I'm sorry for hollering at you like that, come on darlin', get up and give me a hug, I said I'm sorry." He was standing right over her, weaving back and forth. He fell right on top of her, Carol jumped out of bed and went for the door, Lloyd tackled her to the floor.

Lloyd was holding her down. He tried to kiss her, but she was thrashing around too much.

Lloyd fell over, and Carol got up.

"Okay honey, you get into bed and go to sleep, we'll talk about this in the morning" Lloyd said, then he got into bed.

He was out like a light as soon as his head hit the pillow. She removed his shoes and covered him up the best that she could, then took herself a pillow and a blanket and went into the living room and laid down on the couch, making sure that she kept the hall light on just in case he decided to try and get up again.

Carol was up at the crack of dawn. She was unable to sleep the whole night, she was just too scared that he might have gotten up through the night. She tried her best to prepare herself for when he did wake up.

Carol made herself a coffee and went outside to sit on the stairs. The morning sun made it feel warmer than it actually was, there was still a heavy frost on the two cars. Her encumbered mind contemplated what she was going to say to Lloyd when he awoke, and what he was going to say to her.

Her now swollen hand, looked a lot worse than it did the night before, she needed to get it properly cleansed and stitched, and by the way Lloyd looked he was going to need some medical attention as well.

She put her empty cup down then walked to the back to see Sasha. Sasha was more than a little excited to see Carol, she rolled over on her back and sneezed about five times.

Carol unhooked Sasha's chain and they went for a walk through the woods..

"Come on Sasha, let's go for a run ... come on Sasha, never mind the chipmunk let's go."

Carol ran off ahead of Sasha and hid behind a tree. She sniffed her way right to Carol.

Sasha was so excited she sneezed another five times and she shook flinging horrid slobber all over Carol, "Yuck, Sasha, I didn't need a shower."

They lay cuddled on the ground for awhile then started to head back to the house. Carol felt so much better from having her mind off her troubles, even if it was only temporally. As they came up to the house, Carol could see no movement from the inside, she was sure that Lloyd would still be sleeping. She tied Sasha back up, and slowly made her way back to the front of the house.

She walked up the first three steps, seen that her coffee cup that she had laid down was gone, she knew now that Lloyd was up. She hesitated for a moment then walked up the rest of the stairs and into the house.

Lloyd was sitting at the kitchen table with his head down.

"Good morning Lloyd," she nervously said.

Lloyd didn't say a word, he looked into Carol's eyes then hung his head back down with a look of shame.

Carol walked over to him and placed her hand on his shoulder, he placed his hand on top of hers.

"Carol what did I do? I'm so sorry, you must hate me for what I did."

"I don't hate you Lloyd, but what got into you last night, that's what I want to know? I know I acted like a child at my mom and dad's place, but nothing to get you that upset."

"Everything is just happening way too fast for me. I just lost it I guess, I just couldn't stand all the pressure any longer, and you embarrassed me in front of your parents like that, and when we came home and I seen all the things that your dad and Garry did to the house ... damn it Carol, I got pride you know, that was my job, I was suppose to do all that work, not somebody else, this is our house.

I know that your parents bought this place for us, but, I want to be the man of the house here, and if there is anything that needs fixing, then damn it, I want to do it. I don't want anyone else doing things around here that suits their taste, this is our place, and I have dreams of what I want this place to look like."

"I know how you feel sweetie, but you have to realize that they meant well, they would never do anything to hurt you or me, besides, you can do what ever you want to this place, if you don't like what they have done, then change it the way that you like it, that's all.

No one is going to come in here and take over, hon. This is our place, and from now on, if there is anything that has to be done, you will be the one that does it, and no one else, I promise." Carol sympathized with Lloyd, it was obvious that her dad and Garry had shattered his plans and pride.

"Carol, I have to know one thing, did I hit you last night? I'd never forgive myself if I did."

"No Lloyd, you didn't hit me, but you had me scared to death. When you came into the bedroom last night I really thought that you were going to kill me, you were in a rage and I never want to feel that way again."

Lloyd was barely able to get up off of his chair, he was in so much pain from the beating he took the night before.

They had a nap and woke up together an hour later. Lloyd moaned in pain with every move that he made.

"Oh you look terrible honey, I think we should get you to the hospital."

"No I'll be all right,' don't worry about me."

"Who did this to you?"

"Shit, I thought you did this to me." Lloyd groaned with pain from laughing. Carol even laughed at what he said.

"Sweetie, if I hit you, you would look a lot worse than that, now are you going to tell me what happened to you when you left here last night, or do I have to get rough with you?" Carol spiritedly put her dukes up and taunted Lloyd.

"Darlin', I remember having a few beers, and after that, all I can remember is waking up in bed this morning. And that scared the hell out of me, a lot more than when I looked in the mirror this morning. I didn't know where you were, and what I might have done to you, that scared me the most." Lloyd was trembling.

"It's okay sweetheart, it's all done and forgotten about now.

CHAPTER TWENTY THREE

Carol pulled in to the empty parking space. She took a quick look in the rear view mirror to see if she looked as rough as she felt. She felt totally worn out, physically as well as mentally. She dreaded the thought of her first day back to work, knowing that everyone would be asking her about her wedding and the honeymoon.

She stayed in the car, waiting until she settled down, but she only felt worse from her morbid thinking.

Wanda was just pulling out of the parking lot, when she noticed Carol. She turned her car around, and pulled into the parking space beside Carol.

She gave Carol a big excited grin. Her elation turned to cheerlessness, she could see that Carol was very upset about something.

Carol got out of her car, and greeted Wanda.

She gave Carol a heartfelt hug and a kiss on her cheek.

"You okay, hon?"

Carol wanted every thing to sound so good, but she choked up and just about burst into tears.

"Want to talk about it sweetie?"

"Yes, I do Wanda, I have to talk to some one about it. I don't think that I'm going to be able to face everyone with all their questions, Wanda, I just can't do it." Carol was deeply depressed. Wanda could see that she was in no frame of mind to work.

"It's okay sweetie, don't you worry none, you go sit in your car and I'll be back in a minute." Wanda gave Carol a hug. Carol got back into her car.

Carol really felt like this was one of her lowest times that she had ever felt. She was suppose to have bragging rights on her first day back to work, but instead she was conscience-stricken, she was questioning herself if she made a mistake of marrying Lloyd too fast.

"Okay hon, everything is looked after, you don't have to worry about work until you get everything sorted out, okay?"

"Oh I hope that you didn't say anything about me being upset, Wanda".

"No Carol I didn't, but I did tell them that you were sicker than a dog and that I had to fight with you to change your mind about wanting to work today."

"Thanks Wanda, what would I ever do with out you?"

"Don't you worry about it sweetie, do you want to follow me, and we'll go to the coffee shop and we'll have a chat?"

"Okay, thanks Wanda."

Carol cried all the way to the coffee shop, by the time they found a parking spot, she had regained her composer and was trying to wipe the tears out of her red and puffy eyes.

They walked into the coffee shop, Wanda asked the waitress for two coffees as they walked by her. They sat at a booth in a darkened corner were they would have the most privacy.

"So tell me sweetie, why are you so upset?" Wanda said, very sternly.

"Wanda, every thing went so wonderful in Niagara Falls, Lloyd and I had such a great time, it was so romantic, we had a hotel so close to the falls and everything. But as soon as we got home, all hell broke loose. My mom and dad bought us a cottage, and my dad and Garry moved all our furniture into our new place, and they painted and wallpapered it. Every thing looked so good, they did a really nice job, but Lloyd was really upset about what they did, and boy did he get mad. He smashed a lamp against the wall then stormed out of the house and shattered the front door window. That's how I cut my hand." She showed Wanda her cut which was starting to fester.

"Carol that looks pretty bad, you're going to need that looked after before it gets any worse. Tell me Carol, did he hit you at all?" Wanda asked harshly. which didn't make Carol feel any better.

"No Wanda he didn't! I don't know why I'm making such a big fuss over it when it was mostly my fault to begin with. I embarrassed him at my parents house, and he just took it to heart that's all. I guess that I'm feeling a little sorry for myself. He said he was sorry, and I know that he feels really bad about what happened."

"So you're saying that you are to blame, and it's not that assholes fault. That's a load of crap!"

Wanda was making Carol feel worse than she already did, and was holding back the tears once again.

"Carol, I want you to promise me that you'll get that hand looked after."

"Yes, I'll go see my doctor tomorrow.

"Take a couple of more days off, and get your emotions under control. You know you can't be coming into work with your mind on something else. You need to get things straightened out. Wanda said, brazenly. Carol just felt like walking out on her.

It seemed that Wanda was lecturing her instead of helping her. But Carol thought that it was just herself interpreting things that way.

So if you're all right, I'll go to work and do your shift. You know we all can't just take time off when we feel like it?" Wanda shot back.

Wanda's sudden change of disposition gave Carol's emotions a jolt. She couldn't figure out how Wanda was so compassionate one minute, then being so mean and sarcastic the next. She just sat there feeling totally numb for a few minutes, then walked to the window to make sure that Wanda had left. Carol paid the bill, then walked out the door and to her car.

She sat in her car for a few minutes feeling more angry than hurt, towards Wanda.

Carol decided to go Garry's, to thank him for all he had done for her and Lloyd, and to have a good heart to heart with him,

Carol parked her car in the underground parking lot, she entered the lobby and pressed 1501 on the intercom.

"Hello .... "

"Hi sweetie, it's me, Carol."

"Carol? Wonderful! Come on up sugar."

As soon as the buzzer sounded, she opened the door and stepped into the waiting elevator where a middle aged man stood smoking a cigar. The putrid smell turned Carol's stomach. He gave Carol a friendly nod and she returned the gesture. She was relieved when he got off on the fourth floor, a big cloud of smoke followed him as he exited. The elevator went right to the fifteenth floor without stopping. As soon as the elevator door opened she was startled to see Garry standing there waiting for her.

"Hi sweetheart, it seems as if I haven't seen you in a decade, I missed you."

"I know sweetie, I really missed you too."

Gary could tell that Carol had been crying, but he didn't say anything. He knew that if she had a problem, she would open up to him.

They went into Garry's apartment, Carol told him all about their time in Niagara Falls, and what had happened the night when they came home. Garry wasn't the kind to over react, he really listened to what Carol had to say, and wasn't judgmental in the least. Carol could see the hurt look in his eyes when she told him about Lloyd getting upset from what he and her dad had done to the cottage, but even though he took it to heart, he understood why Lloyd had taken it so hard. He put Lloyd's feelings ahead of his own.

"So you think that everything is okay between you and Lloyd now, hon?"

"Yea, I don't think that we're going to have any more problems, it was just a little too much for him to go through with the wedding and all. You know, Garry, he really had a hard life, I don't really think that he ever had any love at all in his life."

"That's a real shame honey, he is such a great guy too. Well don't you worry none my dear, he's going to have all the love he can handle now, you know I really like Lloyd, he's a wonderful guy. Did you see him give me a big hug at the party?"

"Yes I seen it sweetie, that meant so much to me, more than you'll ever know."

"I know, Carol, it really meant a lot to me too. Okay, now let's get you to the hospital now and get that hand looked after."

"Oh Garry I don't want to go to Westwood, I'm suppose to be working tonight, they think I'm sick."

"Oh playing hooky are we ... labor faker haw? Well I guess your secret is safe with me sugar. We'll just take a drive over to Saint Joseph's Hospital, it will be nice to go for a long drive. Oh what about Lloyd, I don't want him to get upset with me again, is he working?"

"Yes, he's working until midnight."

By the time Carol and Garry got out of Saint Joseph Hospital it was after ten o'clock, it took five stitches to close Carol's wound, her hand was all wrapped up.

On the way back to Garry's place, he had mentioned to Carol, that he would like to come over in the morning and have a cup of coffee with Carol and Lloyd.

Carol dreaded the thought, she was totally baffled, she couldn't figure out why he would want to go and see Lloyd so soon, just after explaining to him about everything that had happened between them and that he was so beaten up. Carol's mind was racing

Garry was a very smart man, from what Carol had told him about Lloyd, he knew what was really going on with Lloyd and Carol, and it wasn't good. He was terrified that Lloyd was going to hurt her physically. He already hurt her emotionally. The only thing Garry could do is to agree with Carol, and not to tell her what he really thought about Lloyd. At some point he was going to have to do some intervention. Right now, what he needed to do was to get Carol settled down, and hopefully Carol could really see that she was in danger.

Even though Carol didn't believe in cell phones, Garry gave her his phone until they got their phone put in.

It was just after noon, when Garry pulled up in front of Lloyd's and Carol's cottage. He knocked lightly on the screen door, he could see Lloyd and Carol sitting at the kitchen table.

"Oh look hon, it's Garry." Carol said. She could see the anger on Lloyd's face, and she could tell by the look on Garry's face that he wasn't there for just a friendly visit.

"I'm sorry for just popping in on you like this."

"Nonsense Garry, I'm glad you came. Come on in, the coffee is on."

Lloyd put on a good act, which was obvious to Garry and Carol.

"Hi, Garry." Lloyd said, with a devious smile.

"Good to see ya again pal, thanks a lot for what you and Jason did to the place, you sure did a great job, the place sure looks great."

"Lloyd, what happened to you?" Garry sounded concerned, but he wasn't.

"Oh, I got a little drunk at the bar, and someone took advantage and beat me up pretty bad."

"That's just terrible, Lloyd." Garry said, sounding like he really cared.

"I just popped in to tell you about my brother in-law. He's in the intensive care."

"That's terrible, Garry. What happened?" Carol asked.

"Well, he beat up my sister Karen pretty bad, and you know we have good connections with a motorcycle gang. They took care of things. No one likes a wife beater."

Lloyd squirmed in his chair. Carol knew better, she knew that Garry didn't have a sister.

Lloyd just sat there in silence.

"I hope that your sister is going to be alright."

"She's going to be okay, physically anyway. I'm off to see her now."

Garry and Carol looked at each other. When Lloyd wasn't looking, Garry gave Carol a wink.

Garry got up and walked to the door.

Lloyd's face was full of sweat, and he went very quiet.

"Thanks for coming over. All the best to your sister. And if your brother in-law gets better, I hope he gets his act straightened up.

Garry got into his car and said "You asshole."

It was in the middle of the night when Carol woke up with an eerie feeling that someone was standing over her. She wanted to scream but she just couldn't get it out from such fear. She could see the outline of someone. She frantically reached over to wake up Lloyd, he wasn't there.

"What the fuck are you going to do now bitch? You went and got me all pissed off again tonight didn't you? You and that asshole friend of yours. You know, he's got a big mouth, and you're the one that's going to suffer for it. I'm going to teach you the meaning of respect. Now get the fuck over here."

"Lloyd what's wrong with you? Please don't hurt me."

She darted to the open bedroom door to try and escape, but Lloyd grabbed her and viciously flung her onto the bed. He grabbed her by the hair, then struck her with a closed fist, he held his fist up ready to wield another blow, but instead he just picked her up like a rag doll and tossed her across the room. She lay on the floor stunned, and terrified.

"What the fuck you looking at, you want some more, I'll give you some more?" Lloyd's rage was escalating, Carol knew she had to get out of the house, he was so out of control that he was liable to kill her. She scrambled to her feet and bolted towards the front door, she tripped over the scatter rug and went crashing down hitting her forehead on the table on the way down. She lay on the floor dazed and confused, not even aware of her surroundings. Blood was gushing from her forehead.

"Where are you bitch? Come on, I'm not finished with you yet!"

Carol's mind was in chaos.

The sound of Lloyd coming at her made her come to her senses, she was just barely able to get up off the floor and ran out the front door and made her escape. Once she made it down the stairs, she just kept running. She ran for her life not realizing how far she had ran. She ran in wind driven pouring rain and the streaks of lightning and the loud crackles of the thunder. Some how she ended up in the middle of the road, the screeching brakes and the blinding light of the cars high beams made her freeze on the spot. She fell to the ground, she lay in the middle of the highway only scantly dressed in her night gown. Forty eight year old Mike Hicks, rushed out of his car, terrified thinking that he might have struck her with his car. He bent down to see what kind of shape she was in. At first there was no response from her, then all of a sudden she became combative swinging her arms erratically and screaming incoherently. All Mike Hicks could do is hold her down so she wouldn't hurt herself any more than what she already was, he put pressure on Carol's bleeding head with his hankie. He couldn't stop the bleeding.

With in minutes more cars had stopped to give aid, and an ambulance and the sheriffs office had been called.

Deputy Brian Kemp pulled up to the scene along with an ambulance. They quickly placed Carol onto the stretcher and into the ambulance, then headed for the Westwood General Hospital.

By the time they arrived at the hospital, Carol was coherent, and talking to the paramedics.

They wheeled her into the emergency ward, Wanda was the first one to see her. As soon as their eyes met, Carol broke down, she held her shaking hand out for Wanda.

"It's okay sweetie, I'm here, we're going to take good care of you." Wanda held onto her hand as they wheeled her into room four. Deputy Brian Kemp followed them, anxious to find out what had happened to her. Everyone who worked in the E.R. was very upset that Carol was the one who was brought in. Doctor Howell was paged immediately.

She was given an injection of Demerol, right away, she was barely able to explain at what had happened to her, to Deputy Kemp. He wrote down all the particulars, then headed out to make an arrest. Spousal abuse in the state of North Carolina was taken very seriously.

Carol had calmed down considerably, once the Demerol got into her system. She was whimpering. She had a deep gash on the back of her head and to her forehead, her left eye was black and blue and was completely swollen shut.

"I'm so sorry for being so ruthless with you at the coffee shop, if I would've been more sensitive then maybe this wouldn't have happened." Wanda felt more than a little guilty, from just walking out on Carol like she did at the coffee shop.

"Oh Wanda ... there's nothing that you could have done to prevent what happened to me tonight. You should of seen him Wanda ... he was like an animal. Everything was going good, we went to bed, and we were both in a good mood. Then in the middle of the night he was just standing over me ... and ... oh Wanda, he hit me! I thought he was going to kill me. I can't go..." Carol was so distraught that Wanda had Doctor Howell paged, to see if she could get Carol something more, to calm her down.

When Wanda came back into the room, Carol was really worked up and trembling.

"Wanda ... please don't leave me alone again, I don't want to be alone, please don't leave me."

It was just before dawn when Deputy Kemp, along with three other deputies pulled up in front of the cottage. They walked up the stairs to the front door. Deputy Kemp peered through the front window to see if he could see any sign that Lloyd was there. After seeing no signs, the six foot four, two hundred pound deputy took out his baton and gave the door three heavy intimidating knocks. They could see Lloyd slowly making his way to the door, in a daze from being woken up. Lloyd was totally surprised to see that it was the Sheriffs department. "Hello officers, is there something wrong?" Lloyd said with such a baffled look on his face.

"Are you Lloyd Smith, husband of Carol Smith, sir?"

"Yes I am, Carol's my wife, do you want me to get her for you. What's going on?"

The deputies were just as baffled as Lloyd was, from the way he appeared so clueless to what they were there for.

"Okay Mr. Smith, we would appreciate it if you would get Mrs. Smith for us."

"Sure, no problem, but I sure as hell would like to know what's going on." Lloyd walked to the bedroom, the deputies followed right behind him, with their hands close to their side arms. When Lloyd discovered that Carol was not in bed, he turned as white as a sheet, from fearing the unknown.

"I was sure that she was laying right beside me when you guys woke me up. Now are you going to tell me what the hell happened to my wife or not?"

"Mr. Smith, will you place your hands behind your back for us please?"

"Sure, but tell me what happened to my wife for fuck sake."

"Mr. Smith, your wife is in the Westwood Hospital. Do you remember what happened last night?"

Lloyd tried his best to remember, but all he could remember is going to bed with Carol.

"No sir. All I can remember is my wife and I went to bed around midnight, and that's all."

"We'll, right now, you are under arrest for aggravated assault and spousal abuse."

"What the hell are you talking about spousal abuse? I didn't do nothing to my wife damn it, I love her, I'd never do anything to hurt her." Lloyd yelled out in anger.

Two of the deputies took a hold of Lloyd's arms, and placed Lloyd in handcuffs then lead him to the patrol car, and placed him in the back seat.

They converged in front of the patrol car to discuss the situation. They didn't believe Lloyd was as innocent as he was letting on. They could see right through Lloyd's act from the moment he came out of the bedroom, by his eyes, and by his tone that he was lying through his teeth.

"Well boys, what do you think about this guys story?"

"A guy just doesn't beat the hell out of his wife like that, and then just forget all about it."

"Yea, you got that right Jack."

That sucker is going down I'll tell yea that. He's just lucky that we didn't give him the same treatment as he gave his wife."

"I tell yea, if that ass hole gave us a hard time, I would have kicked his ass, and good."

Lloyd was getting totally agitated, and his temper was beginning to show from watching the deputies looking back at him.

"Fuck you too assholes, I'll fucking drop you like a hot fuckin' potato, then we'll see who's fucking who."

Lloyd really started to lose it now, he just couldn't take the ridiculing any longer. He started thrashing around, and kicked out the door window.

"Come on assholes, you think it's a joke, come on I'll kick all you're fuckin' asses right now." Lloyd had his legs out the smashed window, trying his best to try and get out of the patrol car. The four Deputies were on him right away. They grabbed his legs that were hanging out, and viciously pulled him out of the patrol car through the smashed window. It took a lot of force to get his large frame through the small opening. Lloyd put up a good struggle, especially with his hands cuffed behind him. They threw him to the ground, but Lloyd still wasn't through, he got back up and charged after the deputies, knocking Deputy Howard to the ground. The other three Deputies grabbed Lloyd and tried their best to tackle him to the ground, but Lloyd wasn't so easy to put down, he gave Deputy Jim Rice a head butt, rendering him helpless. Deputy Kemp and Deputy Crisp took over and had Lloyd pinned against the patrol car. Lloyd still refused to give up, and was still so filled with rage. Deputy Rice came at Lloyd with his billy club, giving him a viscous jab to his ribs, then struck a swift blow to his knee. Lloyd just dropped to the ground, moaning in pain. The battle was over, they put Lloyd back into the patrol car.

Deputies Rice and Howard, got into one patrol car, and Kemp, and Crisp got into the other one with Lloyd in the back seat.

"Okay Mr. Smith, we're going to take you to the Westwood Police Detachment, where you will be formally charged."

Lloyd just sat quietly on the back seat. Lloyd's feet were now shackled.

"Tell me Mr. Smith, what the heck happened to your face, you're not going to tell me that your wife did that to you, are you?" Deputy Crisp heckled Lloyd. Lloyd still stayed quiet.

"She was in pretty rough shape when we first found her, physically she'll be fine, but a woman never gets over the trauma of being beaten. This is going to stay with her for a long time. How long have you two been married Mr. Smith?"

"It hasn't even been a month yet."

It took twenty five stitches to close Carol's wounds, and she suffered a concussion.

But what concerned Dr. Howell and the nursing staff, was her emotional well being. They had seen many woman come in from being victims of domestic violence, and end up coming back to the hospital, do to their emotional state from the trauma that they endured. It wasn't always the physical violence that brought these woman, children, and even men in to Westwood General, a lot of times it was mental abuse that was bestowed onto them. Carol would be scared for life emotionally.

Carol instructed Wanda not to contact her parents about what had happened to her. She felt totally ashamed of herself for letting this happen.

Garry had been in to see her, he took it very hard seeing his best friend in such a state. She accepted Garry's offer for her to go home with him.

Deputy Brian Kemp came in to see Carol. He asked her what had happened, Carol explained how Lloyd has been very aggressive lately.

Carol broke down, she knew her marriage was over, but she still loved Lloyd with all her heart. She just couldn't accept what had happen.

CHAPTER TWENTY FOUR

Lloyd was held in custody for twenty four hours. His boss Matt Clark came within an hour to bail him out.

"So what in the hell did you get yourself into Lloyd, and who did that to your face?"

"You'd never believe it if I told you Mr. Clark. I really got my self in a real mess."

"Look, I have no time for your bullshit, now tell me why you were in jail." Matt had no patience with Lloyd.

Lloyd explained to him about being beat up in Cedar Rapids, and that he allegedly beat Carol up, and he had no recollection of the incidents.

"Who in the hell is Carol?"

"Carol is my wife."

"Why in the hell would you get married.?" Matt despised woman.

Now Lloyd was getting frustrated with Matt. He wished that he would have never called Matt to bail him out, but he was the only one that he could call.

Matt lectured Lloyd all the way to Peepers Bar, where he dropped Lloyd off. The last thing he wanted to tell Matt about them buying the cottage. He took a taxi to the cottage.

The taxi pulled up in front of the cottage, where Deputy Crisp was waiting for Lloyd.

"Hello asshole, what are you doing out here, looking for little old ladies to beat up? Get your fuckin' hands on the hood, and spread-em." Deputy Crisp slammed Lloyd on the hood of the patrol car, Lloyd moaned in pain.

"I asked you a question asshole, what the fuck are you doing back here?" He viciously slammed Lloyd's head down onto the hood again.

"I live here, asshole!" Lloyd spoke up. He wasn't in the least scared of the roughhoused deputy.

"Shut the fuck up asshole. You thought you were going to get away with beating up a defenseless woman, didn't you?"

"No sir"

"No sir, is that all you can say for yourself is no sir? Well, I don't think you're as tough as you think you are. " The deputy speared his billy club into Lloyd's ribs, Lloyd groaned in pain, he was at the deputies mercy, there was nothing he could do to defend himself or escape, the deputy had him pinned to the hood of the patrol car, pushing down the back of his neck with his forearm.

Lloyd could have fought back, but he knew that he would end up back in jail.

The deputy took a quick look around, then gave him another crack with his billy club. Lloyd's body went totally limp. He was in sever pain.

"See asshole you're not so tough. Come on, get up and show me what you're made of, come on candy ass." The deputy egged him on.

The deputy tried to stand Lloyd back up, but Lloyd was unable to, he just fell limp to the ground.

"If I ever hear of you laying your hands on a woman again, I'll hunt you down and I'll kill you, do you hear me asshole?"

He leaned over and grabbed Lloyd by the hair, stretching Lloyd's neck back, "I'll be watching you asshole."

The deputy gave Lloyd a swift kick in the ribs, then he got into his patrol car and sped away.

Lloyd laid there as still as dead until he found the strength to get up and get himself into the cottage.

Garry stayed up all night with Carol, She had not spoken a word since she was released from the hospital. Garry felt that the hospital should have kept her in longer, she was still in a state of shock.

Garry felt that he was the one who was responsible for what had happened, since he was the one that got Lloyd so riled up when he dropped in the cottage and more or less threatened him.

Carol had fallen asleep by the time Garry had to leave for work, so he let her sleep, and left her a note on the bedroom door.

Carol slept past noon, feeling a little better, but still very depressed, and in a lot of pain. She couldn't help but snicker as she read what Garry had wrote on his note. "Oh Garry, you're such a nut .... "

After a soothing shower and a cup of coffee, she decided to give her dad a call, and let him know what was going on, just in case Lloyd decided to drop by.

"Hi dad."

"Hi pumpkin, how is every thing? I was thinking about coming down to see you guys this afternoon."

"Oh that's not a good idea, dad. Lloyd and I had a little disagreement and I'm staying at Garry's for a couple of days. But don't worry dad, it's nothing to worry about."

"Come on now Carol, there's got to be more to it than that, you wouldn't be staying at Garry's if it were just a little disagreement now tell me what's really going on. Did he hit you Carol?"

Carol couldn't hold back the tears. "Yes ... he hit me dad, but it was my fault, I'm the one who got him all riled up, it's not his fault. I don't want you to think any less of Lloyd, you know that he's a good man dad."

"You listen to me Carol and you listen good, it doesn't matter what you did, no man has the right to lay a hand on a woman. Are you okay, did you call the police?" Her dad was irate.

"I'm okay dad, I don't want you to get all worked up over what happened. He didn't hit me that hard dad, and he really didn't mean to. Things have been going a little rough for Lloyd lately, and he's going through a lot of stress, he needs a lot of support dad, I love him so much."

"Yea I know you do pumpkin. So how long are you going to be staying at Garry's?"

"Not too long dad, I'm going to give Lloyd a call as soon as I find out if he's still in ... I mean if he's working today." Carol didn't want to tell her dad that Lloyd was arrested.

"Well you be careful now pumpkin, don't get him all riled up, and if he starts getting abusive, then you phone the police right away."

"I will dad, I promise. How's mom?"

"Oh the teeny bopper is fine, you know I wish she'd act her age. You know I just can't keep up with her, she's gone and joined an aerobics class, can you believe that, at her age?"

"An aerobics class ... are you kidding me? Oh dad ... an aerobics class ... oh I got to go dad....Carol was laughing so hard, the only thing was that she couldn't stop. She went in hysterics.

"I have to go dad." She hung up the phone while her dad was still talking.

Tears were just running down her face," Aerobic class .... oh mother."

It took Carol about an hour to settle down.

Carol sat on the couch contemplating what she was going to say to Lloyd if he did happen to be at home all ready.

She picked up the phone, but couldn't remember the number. The phone was just installed a couple of days ago. She had wrote the number down and she found it in her purse.

"Hello."

"Lloyd, is that you?" His voice sounded so rough, it didn't even sound like him.

"Yea it's me Carol. Are you okay?" He sounded so sad.

"Yea, I'm okay. How are you doing hon?"

"Carol, I'm so sorry for what I did. I wouldn't blame you if you never came back, but I want you to know that I love you so much, and you mean every thing to me, and I just couldn't go on with out you." Lloyd was trying his best not to cry, but it was obvious to Carol that he was.

"But Carol, please believe me, I honestly don't remember doing the things to you that they say I did." Lloyd pleaded.

Carol wanted to believe him, but she just couldn't.

"I know you love me and I love you too, so much, and I couldn't go on with out you either. I'm sorry that Garry and I got you all upset like that. We had no right to do that to you."

"Oh darlin', it's not your fault or Garry's. Do you really mean it, do you still love me?"

"Yes Lloyd, I love you, but I'm scared ... I'm so scared, I just don't know what to do.

"Listen darlin', please don't be scared, I love you so much and I promise you, that I'm going to take one of those anger management classes that they have. The sheriffs department gave me their number, and I called them, and some one is going to call me back to tell me where I have to go for it."

"Really Lloyd, you really phoned them?" Carol was very impressed.

"Yes I did darlin', and I'm really serious about this. I promise you, if you come back, every thing will be wonderful, you don't have to worry."

"Okay hon, as soon as Garry comes home from work, I'll ask him if he'll bring me home. Okay?"

"Why don't you just let me come and pick you up now instead of waiting? I miss you so much darlin'."

"No honey, I think that it would be best to wait until Garry comes home."

"Okay darlin', what ever you think what's best. I just can't wait to see you that's all."

"Okay honey, I love you, and I'll see you later."

"All right darlin', I love you too."

Carol hung the phone up, and scurried in her purse to get her pain medication. It was way to early to take her medication, but she took two any ways.

She cleaned all the apartment up, then anxiously waited for Garry to come home.

It was getting close to eight o'clock, Carol was pacing the floor waiting for Garry.

She came out the bathroom, Garry was in the living room waiting for her.

"Hi hon, how was work?" Carol asked, with a slur from the medication.

"It was work, that's for sure. How are you feeling?"

"I'm feeling a lot better now thanks."

"That's great hon, you look a lot better. I hope you're hungry, I picked us up a bucket of chicken."

"Yes, I'm starving."

"I talked to Lloyd on the phone this afternoon, we talked things over, and I decided that I'm going to go back home tonight."

"Are you sure you want to do this Carol?" Garry was beside himself, and furious at Carol for just thinking about doing so. Carol didn't realize how Garry felt.

Gary had seen this before; it is called battered wife syndrome, a psychological symptom that battered woman believe that everything was their fault. Spouses who have this, needs counseling , in which most spouses refuse to believe in.

"Yes I am sure... I love him Garry."

"I know you love him Carol. You know that I would never interfere with you and Lloyd, but are you sure that you're ready to go back? I just don't want you getting hurt again that's all."

"I'm ready to go home Garry, Lloyd's going to go to one of those anger management classes, he phoned the guy this morning. You know Garry, Lloyd's really hurting, he really feels bad from what happened."

"Sure, I don't doubt that he's hurting, Carol, but what about you, look at yourself, you know he could have easily killed you, you know that." Garry was trying to be as rational as he could, but he was sure that she was making a huge mistake in planning to go back to Lloyd so fast.

"I'm scared, but I just have to go back, I need him as much as he needs me. I think he learned his lesson this time. If anything happens, I'll phone the police."

"Okay Carol, I know it's hard for you, I just don't want anything to happen to you, don't forget I love you too."

"Oh Garry ... I love you too, please don't think any less of me because I'm going back so soon, I'll be all right."

"No, I don't think any less of you, hon, I understand how you feel.

Garry knew that Carol wasn't in the right state of mind but he couldn't do anything about it. He felt helpless.

"Well I guess you're pretty anxious to go home."

"Yes I am, hon."

"Well then we better get you home then, are you ready?"

"Oh Garry, you're the greatest. Thanks for being so understanding."

Carol was very quiet and more than a little nervous, on the way home.

"Garry, do you think I'm doing the right thing in going back so soon?" She asked, breaking the silence.

"Well sugar, I can't answer that for you. You're the only one who really knows the answer. I would say follow your heart, but my dear, your heart has no common sense does it?"

"What do you mean, my heart doesn't have any common sense?" Carol snapped back.

"I don't mean it that way sugar, I mean all your heart can do is feel, right? Your heart can't judge, it can't distinguish between what's wrong or right, your heart can only feel, and I can imagine how it's feeling now ... pretty rough isn't it?" Garry asked sympathetically.

"Yea, pretty rough all right, it's really hurting, hon"

"Well what's your mind saying?"

"That's another story, my minds going a hundred miles an hour, first I think that I must be out of my mind for going back, then on the other hand, I'm thinking that I should go back. My heart feels like it's broken Garry."

"I know it hurts sugar, I just wish there was something that I could do for you to take the hurt away. You mentioned that Lloyd is going to take an anger management class, well that really shows that he wants to change."

"That's true, and he does say that it's all his fault, even though it's not."

"I know, hon, I feel really bad for being so cocky with him that night, if I never came in that night, then all of this would have never happened, I'm so sorry Carol."

"Don't you dare go blaming yourself, what you said to Lloyd that night didn't give him any reason to get all riled up like that, and besides, after you left that night, Lloyd was in a good mood, so don't feel as if you are to blame, because you're not, you know Lloyd really likes you."

"Well we're less than a mile, what do you think, do you still feel like going home now, or would you rather go back to my place for another night?"

They both went really quiet, in deep thought.

"I think I'll go home now, hon, you know I wouldn't know what I'd do without you. I really appreciate everything that you do for me."

"You'd do the same for me too sugar, you've always where there for me when I needed you. Do you want me to come in with you to make sure everything is all right?"

"No...thanks anyways hon, but I think that it would be best if I just went in alone, I hope you understand."

"Don't worry about me, I understand. Now you remember, if there's the slightest bit of trouble, don't you hesitate, get out of there fast, and you can call me any time of the night okay?"

"I will, I promise." Carol gave him a kiss on the cheek, he watched her as she made her way to the front door. Carol waved as Garry pulled away, he waved back, then went on his way. Garry wondered if he did the right thing by letting her go back so soon. He knew that it was going to be a long sleepless night for him, thinking about his dear friend.

Carol shook like a leaf the minute she walked into the door, she knew there was no turning back now that she was inside. The only light on in the house was the lamp that was turned on in the living room. She could only see the outline of Lloyd's face, the silence was eerie, her mind was racing. She stepped back away from Lloyd.

"Lloyd, are you all right?" It was obvious that she was scared by her trembling voice.

Lloyd didn't say a word, he just slowly made his way to her, she was ready to scream, when Lloyd took her into his arms and held her so tightly like never before, he immediately broke down weeping so deeply that he was gasping for air. Now Carol could see why he had the lights off, and why he didn't say anything, he was just too overcome with emotion.

"It's okay hon, I'm here, don't cry, I know how hard every thing has been for you." She could feel his tears that fell onto her shoulder. Now Carol was the one who broke down. They just stood there holding onto each other. Carol lead Lloyd into the bedroom for the both of them could hold each other, and have a good cry and let all out.

Carol and Lloyd was now sitting on the edge of the bed talking things over in the dark.

"Carol, please tell me exactly what I did to you, because I just don't remember." Lloyd sound sincere. Carol tried so hard to believe him, but she didn't.

"Lloyd, it's over and done with now, there's no sense in bringing it all up again and getting us all upset again."

"You don't understand, I have to know what I did, just tell me?" He pleaded.

"Lloyd! I don't want to talk about it, okay? That night will be etched in my mind for the rest of my life and I'll be dammed if I'm going to replay it over for you. Carol was being assertive, almost to the point of aggression.

Let's worry about the future, not the past, that's what we should be talking about." Carol was dumbfounded at why he would want her to put herself through so much more torment than what she already had gone through.

"Okay, we'll just forget about it, I'm sorry." Lloyd said, feeling emotionally drained.

"I'm going to go take a shower, Lloyd, and freshen up, and try and pull myself together."

It was a long time since Carol called Lloyd by name, instead of calling him hon or sweetie, Carol didn't know what to think of that.

It was a real struggle for Lloyd to get himself up off the bed, he moaned in pain.

Carol jumped up and turned the light on. He was a total mess, his face looked twice as worse as it did when she had last seen him, his clothes looked as if he was dragged through the mud, with half of the buttons missing.

"What happened to you, who did this to you?" Carol asked with hysteria in her voice.

Lloyd sat back down on the bed.

When I got home the deputy was waiting for me, and he beat me. I laid there for hours until I was finally able to crawl over to the phone, and that's where I stayed, waiting and hoping that you would call, I prayed to God that you would."

"That son of a bitch deputy had no right doing this to you. Do you know his name?" Lloyd had never seen Carol so infuriated. It was a totally different side of her that he'd had never seen in her before.

"Yea, I know his name, why do you want to know that for?"

"Well I'll get us a lawyer, and we'll sue the ass off of that bastard, and he'll never work in law enforcement again."

"Carol, do you ever think that maybe I deserved it.?"

"What are you talking about you deserved it? No man deserves to get treated like that."

"Yes exactly darlin, but neither does a woman." Lloyd said with his head down.

Carol went completely quiet after what Lloyd had said, it really made her stop and think.

"Okay sweetie, lets get you all cleaned up."

Carol carefully removed his clothes, Lloyd was in excruciating pain. His ribs were completely black and blue.

"Sweetie, it looks pretty bad, we're going to have to go to the hospital."

To Carol's surprise, Lloyd agreed.

Carol had a hard time getting Lloyd into the car, she had to put him in the back seat for he would be more comfortable.

"You're pretty strong for a half pint." Lloyd snickered then moaned in agonizing pain.

"You never mind, half pint"

"And I don't want you to be flirting with any of those nurses there either... understood?" Carol was trying to lift his spirits.

"Yes hon, I won't. Please don't make me laugh, it hurts so much "

"I'm sorry sweetie, I won't make you laugh anymore."

They took Lloyd right in at Saint Joseph's Hospital. The x-rays showed that Lloyd had three cracked ribs and a separated shoulder. The doctor and a nurse put Lloyd's shoulder back in place. They taped his ribs and wrote him out a prescription for his pain.

CHAPTER TWENTY FIVE

Christmas went by very fast for Carol, she was very grateful for that. Carol and Lloyd spent Christmas day at her parents place, along with Garry, Everyone treated Lloyd with kid gloves. Even Jean kept her distance from Lloyd, she appeared to feel very uncomfortable being around him. Carol's parents as well as Garry could see a big change in Carol's personality, she just wasn't her usual lighthearted self and was very snappy with everyone, totally out of character. She showed absolutely no emotion opening her presents which really hurt Garry's and her parents feelings. This made for an awkward and not very festive Christmas for everyone.

Lloyd had completed his ten day anger management classes and although he never struck Carol since. He did fly off at the handle at the oddest times getting Carol all upset and more than a little nervous. He was so unpredictable, everything would be going smoothly and they were getting along fine, and for no apparent reason he would suddenly be filled with rage and he would end up smashing something or just storm out of the house. Carol still loved him so deeply, but she wondered how long she could go on never knowing when the next time he was going to go into one of his rampages and end up beating her up.

Everyone at the hospital seemed to lose all their respect towards Carol, everything was done in a professional manner when they were with her, they all just gave her the cold shoulder, she knew that they all looked down on her because she went back to Lloyd.

Carol fell into a deep depression, and looked so lethargic, but no one seemed to notice or even care.

"Carol, I want you to go clean up Mr. Sharp in room six, he needs an enema." Wanda seemed like she was demanding Carol to do it rather than asking her. Carol had just about had all that she could take of Wanda's callousness towards her, she tried her best not to let it get to her, but her feelings were so hurt every time she came in contact with Wanda. It really hurt her feelings because they were so close to each other at one time, and Carol missed that.

Carol just stood there, in a daze.

"Carol, I gave you an order and I expect you to do it!"

"Fine." Carol just stormed off and headed to room six."

"Hey beautiful, where's the fire, aren't you going to say hello to your old pal?"

"Oh hi Doctor Howell, how are you?

Carol thought for a moment wondering if she should say anything to Doctor Howell about the way that everyone was treating her.

" Dr. Howell why is everyone treating me like dirt in this damn place? I just about had all I can take. what did I do that was so bad to deserve all this?"

"Don't you worry sweetheart, how long do you have till the end of your shift?"

"About forty five minutes."

"Come here sweetheart." Dr. Howell showed Carol a lot of compassion. He felt so sorry for her. He put his hand on her shoulder. He knew what Carol went through. He walked up to

Wanda, Carol could see Dr. Howell really was giving Wanda a very stern talking to. He was pointing his finger right up to Wanda's face. When he walked away, Wanda gave Carol an evil stare.

Dr. Howell walked back to Carol, his face was beat red, he was very angry from the treatment that they were giving Carol. You go down to the cafeteria and have a coffee and relax, stay there until the end of your shift if you want, don't worry about anything up here, everyone else is just standing around with their fingers up their butts anyways. Oh, and I want to see you in my office sometime this week, okay sweetheart?"

"Okay, thanks Doctor Howell, what would I ever do with out you?" Carol gave him a kiss on the cheek, smiled, then made her way to the cafeteria. On her way she past Wanda.

"Carol, where do you think you"re going, you couldn't have finished already?" Wanda snarled. Carol just totally ignored her and just kept walking.

"Damn it Carol, I want to see you in the office" Wanda yelled out.

"What the hell is going on here Wanda?"

"Oh it's Carol, Doctor Howell. I told her to go and look after a patient in room four and she totally defied me. I don't know who in the hell she thinks she is anyway!"

"Well Wanda, who in the hell do you think you are?"

"Listen Doctor Howell, don't you be talking to me that way, I'm in charge of these nurses and they'll do exactly as I say."

"Wanda, do you have any idea what Carol is going through right now?"

"Yes I do, and if she would have left that son-of-a-bitch instead of going back to him then she wouldn't be going through so many problems and she would be able to do her job!"

"Well let me tell you something miss know it all. Right now, the biggest problem with Carol is with people like you. Who in the hell do you think you are? She's got enough problems with out you being on her back. What happened between you and Carol, you two use to be so close?"

"Yea we were until she went back to that ass hole. We all tried to help her out so much and what does she do in return, she goes back to him. Now if that isn't a slap in the face then I don't know what is."

"So you think Carol should have left him just because you helped her out? What is it, you think that she owes you something now just because you where there for her? Well where are you now when she needs you the most and how do you know what's going on between her and her husband? Damn it Wanda, is your ego bigger than your heart? Show her some compassion will you? And get some one else to do that in room six ... or better, why don't you do it yourself?" Dr. Howell stormed off.

Carol stopped off at a doughnut shop on her way home, she picked up a dozen doughnuts, thinking that it would be something nice for Lloyd to wake up to.

It was a long ride home for her after her long shift. She missed the times when everyone was like a close knit family at the hospital, but she knew now, that those days were gone. She just couldn't understand why everyone had turned against her. 'What did I do that was so wrong' was the question that she asked her self over and over again and never having an answer. The more she thought about it, the more depressed she became. She leaned forward and turned the radio on, hoping to take her mind off of everything and ease her troubled mind. Every station seemed to have a sentimental song which only made her feel more depressed or some loud mouthed talk show host. She turned off the radio and just let her emotions loose. She cried like she never cried before.

As she pulled into her driveway, she was pretty well all cried out.

She wiped away the tears from her pale face. She knew that Lloyd would still be sleeping and that she would be able to freshen herself up before he got up. She silently opened the front door, the first thing she noticed was that Lloyd had the set of her Norman Rockwell collectors plates on the wall that she received from Christmas. She just stood there with a proud grin on her face gazing at the wonderful job that Lloyd had done. She planned on taking a shower and getting all dressed up for Lloyd when he woke up and she wouldn't mention any of the troubles that she had at work.

She had a shower, then quietly crept into the bedroom and picked out the dress that Lloyd liked so much. She grabbed her makeup from her drawer. She stood there for a moment and watched Lloyd as he slept.

She wasted no time getting dressed. She went into the bathroom and put some lipstick and make up on.

She closed the door, and she blow dried her hair.

As she opened the door Lloyd was standing there, scaring her half to death.

Lloyd took one look at her and said: " Well look at you, don't you look pretty."

"Hi sweetie!" Carol felt absolutely electrified, the look on Lloyd's face said it all, for her, his smile and the way he noticed her put her in a state of bliss.

"Well come here, I got to give you a big hug and a kiss, you look so beautiful."

It was a magical moment for Carol, she was beaming. It felt so good to feel this way once again. They made their way to the bedroom where they made love. Every minute was like heaven for her, she didn't want it to ever end.

Afterwords they lay cuddled.

"I love you Lloyd" She said, with so much emotion.

"I love you too darlin' " Carol felt at peace, and there was no one there to take it away.

"Lloyd, why can't it be like this all the time?"

"What do you mean darlin?' I thought it was, why, don't you think that I love you?"

"I know that you love me, it's that I just wish things could be just like before, like walking through the park, being spontaneous ... you know, more romantic."

"Yea I know what you mean darlin', I just haven't been with it this past month, I don't know what it is, but don't you worry none darlin', how about if we go for a nice walk through the Lincoln Park Trail, remember that little kid that caught us doing it the last time we were there? Wasn't he adorable?"

"Ah, he was the sweetest little boy. Remember what he said to us? 'I know what you two guys are doing, I play it all the time, your piggy back riding.'" They both had a good laugh remembering that day.

"Carol, I think that it's time for us to have our own little Bobby or Krista."

"Really?" Carol was really taken back.

"You really mean it? Hun that would be so wonderful. It would be so good for the both of us."

"Yea, and you would make a wonderful mother darlin'."

They both just laid there thinking what it would be like to have a son or a daughter.

They spent the day at the Lincoln Nature Trails, the day went just as Carol had dreamed it would be, so romantic, so tranquil. She felt as if she didn't have a care in the world. They even made love at the same place where little Bobby had caught them before.

She assured Lloyd that they would have their own little Bobby or Krista soon, which made them both feel even closer to each other.

The drive to work was a lot more high spirited for her, she had the radio turned up and singing along, feeling on top of the world. Once she pulled into the hospitals parking lot, her spirits fell to a disheartening low.

She thought to herself, and made up her mind that she wasn't going to let anyone get her down, she was going to walk in the hospital with her head up and she was going to smile, and if anyone gave her a hard time, then that would be their problem and not hers.

She walked towards the nurses station, Wanda was standing there, watching her every step as she made her way towards her. She stared deeply into her eyes, without any expression, Carol stared right back at her.

"Hi Carol."

"Hi Wanda." They both could sense each others awkwardness.

"Carol, I'm sorry for being on your case lately, I guess that things would be a lot more easier around here if we both could get along."

There wasn't the slightest hint of sincerity in what Wanda had said, what made it even worse was nurse Debbie Bishop was standing behind Wanda with such a cocky smirk on her face.

"That's fine with me Wanda." Carol replied, then turned around and walked away, leaving Wanda and her new friend standing there. They were expecting for Carol to get all emotional, but Carol was wiser..

The night was a long one for Carol, she tried her best to keep her spirits up, but the way that everyone was still treating her, it made it hard.

She prayed that Lloyd would be in the same frame of mind as he was in when she had left for work that afternoon.

Carol unlocked the door, looked to see if the bedroom door was closed, it was, so she knew that Lloyd was still sleeping. She kicked off her shoes, one landed in front of the television, the other behind it. She sat down on the couch and placed her feet comfortably on the coffee table. It didn't take long before she fell into a deep sleep.

The sound of breaking glass jarred her awake. As she jumped to her feet she heard another terrorizing sound of something being smashed. Then she heard Lloyd, she knew there was going to be trouble, she shook like a leaf and a surge of panic rushed through her body.

"There you are you fuckin' bitch! You told me you were going to work and I know you where out with Garry, you lying whore!" He threw the glass coffee pot towards her, it shattered as it made contact with the wall right next to where she was standing, fragments of shattered glass covered her as she ducked out of the way.

"What are you talking about Lloyd, I worked all night?" Carol's whole body shook.

Lloyd stood there stunned. He looked so confused.

"Carol just stood there, staring at him.

"I'm so sorry Carol, I just don't know what came over me."

"Well sorry just doesn't cut it! I had enough of this bullshit Lloyd! I just don't know what to expect from you anymore!. I am sick of it! Why in the hell would you think that I was fooling around with Garry? Didn't we have a great time together today, what's wrong with you?" She screamed at the top of her lungs.

She suddenly realized that she was the one who was the aggressor now, she didn't like the way it made her feel, but, it got a lot of her anger and frustrations out. Lloyd looked shocked, he didn't know that she had it in her.

"I just don't know what came over me Carol, I'm so sorry."

"Well I'm going out for awhile ... damn it Lloyd, I'm too scared to even be around you anymore!"

"Please don't go darlin', I said I was sorry, please don't go...." Lloyd's tears began to fall, now Carol felt guilty from hollering at him and had second thoughts about leaving, but she just had to get away from Lloyd.

"I'm sorry Lloyd, I'm going out and I don't even know if I will be back.

"Okay darlin', you go out, but promise me that you'll be back, please don't leave me."

Carol didn't answer Lloyd. She brushed all the pieces of glass off of her, then stormed past Lloyd and walked out the door.

Lloyd stood at the door and said, with tears running down his face. "I love you Carol."

Carol turned around, looked up at him, thought for a moment then walked to her car.

As she pulled out of the driveway she turned her head in the direction where Lloyd was now standing on top of the stairs, he had his head hung down in shame.

Carol drove straight to Westwood, where she stopped off at a coffee shop. She had a couple of cups of coffee while she tried to figure out what she was going to do. It was after nine am, she decided to go and see her mom and dad. She knew that her dad would be worried about her.

Carol walked into her parents house, she could see her dad sitting at the kitchen table, in a deep thought, really thinking about something.

"Hi dad," she said softly for not to startle him.

Jason looked up, it took a moment for him to realize that it was Carol.

"Hi pumpkin, I was just thinking about you, come over here and give me a hug."

"Well I've been thinking of you too dad," she said as she gave him a hug.

"How is everything pumpkin, is everything okay at home?"

"Well Lloyd and I had a little falling out this morning, but nothing serious."

Carol didn't tell her father too much. She didn't want him to get all worked up.

"What in the sam hell is going on with that man? He better start smartening up."

"He has never had anyone that loved him before, and he's having a hard time dealing with his feelings right now. Can you imagine what it would be like to go through all your life without any love, especially as a child? So I don't blame him for feeling a little jealous and insecure."

"I'm sorry pumpkin, I didn't realize that life had been so cruel to him. I can relate with him pumpkin, I went through the same thing when I was a child, there was no love in our family and it carried on like that until I met your mother. She was the very first person that ever showed me any kind of love. It can feel pretty lonely when a person doesn't feel that there isn't anyone who really cares for them. You tell Lloyd that your mother and I love him very much. Will you do that for me pumpkin?" Jason's eyes teared up, Carol could see that he was feeling pretty low, talking about Lloyd brought out a lot of sad memories from his past.

"Lloyd and I love you very much too dad, don't you ever forget that." She got up from her chair and gave her dad a much needed hug. A tear rolled down his cheek, which he was quick to wipe away.

"Well how is mom doing dad, is she still doing her aerobics class?"

"Oh you'd never believe it pumpkin. Go go go, always on the go, she's still doing her aerobics class and she's showing no signs of slowing down. She wanted me to take her out dancing the other night, can you believe that?"

"Oh dad, you're a great dancer, it would be good for you to get out and go dancing, don't grow old before your time, you should go out and have some fun. What do you got to lose?"

"You know pumpkin, I'm am a damn good dancer, we just might go dancing. If your mother can do it, then so can I."

"That's the spirit dad, good for you!"

"Well I better go home and see how Lloyd is."

"Okay pumpkin, thanks for stopping by, I'll tell your mother that you said hi... that's if she ever gets her home."

"Okay dad, I love you." She gave her dad a hug and a kiss on his cheek, it was obvious that he was yearning for some affection, which made her feel a little guilty for not spending enough time with him.

"I love you too pumpkin.

Jason walked her out to her car and stood there smiling as she drove away.

She was starting to enjoy the long drive back and forth to Westwood and Cedar Rapids, enjoying the serenity and having some time to herself. Her mood quickly changed as she came with in a block of home, she just didn't know what to expect when she walked in the door. She knew things had to start changing with her and Lloyd. She couldn't keep living in fear.

Carol was now contemplating whether or not she was going to leave Lloyd. She decided that her and Lloyd needed a heart to heart about the way things are going. She prayed that Lloyd would change his ways.

As she pulled up into the driveway, she could see Lloyd sitting on the front steps. She gave him an apprehensive smile as their eyes made contact, he didn't smile back, which she knew that he was on the rampage once again. A jolt of fear went through her body. She stayed in the car contemplating weather to get out, or to restart the car and go back to her parents house. The car keys dropped from her trembling hand. She felt the keys hit her foot, she reached down to pick them up and when she got back up, Lloyd was standing at the side of the car with a look of evil in his eyes and in a frenzy. Carol knew that she was in for trouble once again. He violently swung the car door open as she attempted to lock it. He grabbed her by the arm and pulled her out of the car, pulling her so hard that she tumbled to the ground. He stood over her, he was staggering as if he had been drinking.

"You where with Garry again, weren't you bitch?" His words were slurred and his fists were clinched.

"I was not with Garry," she pleaded. "I was at my mom and dad's house, and you're drunk Lloyd." She held her arms out in defense.

"What the fuck are you talking about, I'm not drunk. Now get your fuckin' ass in the house." He bent over to take a hold of her arm and ended up falling on top of her.

"Get off of me, you're hurting me!"

He managed to get back to his feet and as he tried to grab her again, she slapped him across the face, which stunned him enough for her to be able to get back up and run into the house. She ran directly into the bedroom and locked the door behind her. She could hear him barging in to the house.

"Where the fuck are you bitch?"

She could hear him walking around, then things went silent. She put her ear to the door, but she didn't hear a sound. There was no way that she was going to take a chance and open the door. She suddenly heard his footsteps getting closer to the bedroom. She moved away from the door, just in case he tried to break it down. She climbed onto the bed and held one of the pillows tightly against her shaking body.

"Carol are you in there?" He asked.

"Yes I'm in here, just leave me alone." She cried out.

"Okay darlin', I'm going to go out for awhile, I'll be back later okay?"

"Okay." She replied, not knowing how to react to his sudden change in demeanor. He was even talking with out the slur that was so salient before.

"Are you mad at me darlin'?" He asked so shamelessly.

Carol thought for a moment, then said, "No I'm not mad at you, I'll see you when you get back." She just wanted him to leave.

"Okay darlin', I love you and I'll see you when I get back."

"Okay see you later."

Carol didn't understand about Lloyd's antics. He was like Jekyll and Hyde. She just didn't know what to make of it.

She heard the front door close. She waited until she heard the car drive away, then cautiously opened the bedroom door, then went to the window to make sure that he had really gone. She breathed a sigh of relieve to see that the car was no longer in the driveway. She sat on the top step, feeling more confused than anything else. She just couldn't come to terms about the way he just acted.

She still loved him, but she wondered to herself, how long could she go on living like this.

Was he going to get worse and become even more violent? Carol made the decision that she was going to leave Lloyd. It was going to be devastating the both of them, but she had no choice.

But where would she go? She knew that she could move back in with her parents, or even move in with Garry, at least until she could get an apartment of her own. She didn't know what would be worse, continuing to live with Lloyd and live like this, or move out and suffer the loneliness that she remembered so vividly before she had met Lloyd, and for her, it felt even worse than what she was feeling know. There was just too much for her to give up, a husband, a house, and a chance to have children that she had always dreamed about. For every answer she could come up with, only brought on different questions. The thought of moving out and leaving Lloyd made her feel even more depressed, and gave her a sick feeling in the pit of her stomach. She came to the decision that she would give it a little more time, and hoped that maybe Lloyd would see what he's doing to her and change his ways. She even thought about telling him that she planned on leaving him. She knew that it would break his heart, and maybe he would smarten up.

She got up off the step, grabbed hold of the railing to steady herself. She felt dizzy and suddenly weak. She knew that she hadn't been taking care of herself very well. She had hardly eaten anything in the past week and she was feeling the effects of it know. She stood there for a moment to let the dizziness pass.

She walked down the stairs, making sure that she had a good hold of the railings and walked to the back yard to see Sasha. She was so excited to see her. She was jumping up and down so much that she knocked Carol on the ground. She was so playful and excited, she kept licking Carol's face. Carol was laughing away. For a while Carol had forgotten all about her troubles until a car drove past the house, she was grateful that it had not been Lloyd. She didn't have the heart to tie Sasha back up out side, so she brought her into the house.

Over four hours had past since Lloyd had left. She envisioned him coming home in the same shape as he was in when he came home all drunk and beaten up. She was grateful to have Sasha with her, just in case he did come home in that kind of shape.

She had only a have an hour to get ready for work. She was becoming furious and more than a little worried that Lloyd had not come home yet. For all she knew, he could be laying in the back parking lot of the Cedar's Pub, drunk and all beaten up and left there to die. After she tied Sasha back up in the back yard and made sure that she had fresh water, she had only a few minutes to take a quick shower and get dressed for work. She rushed out the door, knowing that she was going to be late if she didn't speed all the way, she pulled out of the driveway, leaving a trail of dust behind her.

She slowed the car down as she came up to the Cedar's Pub. She switched on the left turning signal and pulled into the parking lot. Two drunken men spotted her right away and shouted obscenities at her, which she totally ignored.

Carol spotted Lloyd's car, so she knew that he was there.

As she slowly pulled the car around to the back, her heart felt as if it was going to come out of her chest everything felt like it was going in slow motion. At the side of the garbage bin, she could see the two legs of someone that seemed absolutely lifeless. She knew it had to be Lloyd. She was just too scared to get out of the car and go and see if it was him, but she knew that she had to.

As she got closer, she could see that the shoes looked the same as Lloyd's, this made her frantic, she rushed to his aid. "Lloyd!" She cried out. It wasn't Lloyd, she rushed back to her car.

"Damn you Lloyd! You rotten bastard!" She shouted as she pounded her fist on the dash board.

She drove out of the parking lot in a fury.

She pulled into the hospital parking lot, wiped the tears from her face, then looked at her watch, she was ten minutes late for her shift. She bolted out of the car and ran to the rear entrance of the hospital. As she walked towards the nurses station she was still whimpering.

CHAPTER TWENTY SIX

JANUARY 11, 1992

Carol laid on the floor in excruciating pain, every breath she took in felt like a knife was digging into her side. She barely managed to get back onto her feet. She knew every second counted, she had to get dressed and get out of the house before he came back out of the bedroom.

She cried out in agonizing pain as she put her nurses dress back on. She didn't even attempt to put her bra and underwear on, it was just to painful and it would take too long. She grabbed her keys off the table and staggered her way out the door. By the time she had made it to the bottom of the stairs, she was unable to stand up straight, she walked all bent over from the throbbing pain from her ribs.

She drove erratically as she tried so desperately to drive to her parents place, weaving all over the road. Infuriated drivers sounded their horns in disgust, presuming that she must be a drunk driver. She could barely see where she was going. As she pulled into her parents drive way, she held her shaking hand onto the horn. The horn blared loud enough to draw attention from the whole neighborhood. Jason jumped out of his chair and as soon as he seen it was Carol, he frantically came rushing out of the house to see what was wrong with his daughter.

"Carol, what's wrong?" He screamed out as he urgently opened the car door.

"Dad I can't move, I need help ... please help me!" She cried out.

Jason could see that she was in a bad way and she was in no condition to be moved.

"Don't you move sweet heart, I'll go call 911."

Her dad went running into the house and dialed 911.

"It's going to be okay pumpkin, I phoned 911 and an ambulance is on it's way. Did that son-of-a-bitch do this to you?"

"Yes he .... " She cried out in extreme pain.

Rescue One from the Westwood Fire Department was the first on the scene, they could hear the siren from the ambulance in the distance.

The attendants placed Carol onto a back board and put a neck brace on her. The ambulance sped off with it's siren blaring. The rescue squad called for another ambulance for Jason. He was so worked up that he was having chest pain, he was shaking like a leaf and had a hard time breathing.

The x rays showed that Carol had two fractured ribs, a dislocated shoulder, and a concussion. She would be staying in the hospital for at least a couple days.

She had all that she could take from Lloyd and from everyone else that upset her.

They gave Jason an electrocardiogram to check his heart, which came back normal. The doctor sedated him and he warned Jason not to drive.

Before he left, he went in to his daughters hospital room, she was sleeping, so he gave her a kiss on her forehead, whimpered, then walked out and called a cab.

The Sheriff and two deputies pulled up in front of Lloyd's and Carol's cottage. They were there to arrest Lloyd. Lloyd's car was in the driveway, so they knew that he was home. They had their guns drawn.

The Sheriff knocked on the door, there was no answer.

"Sheriff's Department open the door." He yelled out. Lloyd didn't come to the door. The six foot four deputy kicked in the door.

"Sheriff's Department." The Sheriff yelled out.

They went room to room. They seen that the bathroom door was closed. They warned Lloyd that they were coming in. The Sheriff cautiously opened the door, Lloyd was on the floor.

"Lloyd!" The Sheriff yelled out. Lloyd was unresponsive. The Sheriff radioed to dispatch for an ambulance.

Within eight minutes the ambulance arrived. Lloyd was still unconscious. The paramedics quickly took Lloyd's vitals, then rushed him to Westwood Hospital.

The doctors worked on Lloyd in the E.R. for a half hour, trying to bring him around. They rushed Lloyd to the intensive care ward.

Lloyd was in a coma. He had barely a pulse, and he needed to be incubated, he was not breathing.

They called in Dr, Murray, a specialist, who ordered a M.R.I.

Within fifteen minutes they determined that Lloyd had massive brain tumor which was inoperable. The doctor didn't expect Lloyd to last the night.

Te next morning nothing had changed, Lloyd was still in the coma, his vital signs weren't improving.

A nurse brought Carol into Lloyd's room in a wheelchair.. She was in a state of shock.

She took a hold of Lloyd's hand.

"I'm here sweetheart." Tears were running down Carol's face.

"Mrs Smith" the specialist walked up to Carol.

"I am Dr. Mitchel, your husbands specialist. I'm very sorry about your husband. The M.R.I. showed that your husband has a five centimeter tumor around his Medulla Oblongata, which is a part of the brain. He probably will not come out of his coma.

Mrs. Smith, has your husband been very aggressive in the past six months or so?"

"Yes he has been very aggressive and abusive in the past six months or so."

"I am very sorry, Mrs. Smith. He didn't know what he was doing. He wouldn't even realize what he did, or remember what he did when he went in to one of these episodes."

A rush of guilt went through Carol's mind. "It wasn't his fault...it wasn't his fault" She kept saying to herself.

"Is this fatal, doctor.?" Carol asked, terrified of the doctor's answer.

"Yes it is, Mrs. Smith. He most likely won't last through the night. I'm very sorry Mrs. Smith."

The doctor placed his hand on Carol's shoulder, then walked out of the room with his head hung down.

Carol got out of the wheelchair and walked over to Lloyd's bedside and hugged him, and said: "I love you Lloyd."

CHAPTER TWENTY SEVEN

Carol was standing in the hallway drinking a coffee. She had stayed with Lloyd all night. She phoned Garry and asked him to come. He was shocked by the news.

"Oh thank God you're here Garry."

"How is he, hon?" Garry sounded so concerned.

"He's critical, Garry. He went into cardiac arrest but they were able to bring him back. Dr. Murray should be in to see him soon."

"How are you holding up, sweetheart?" Garry asked as he caressed his hand along her pale lamented face.

Dr, Murray walked in to the room. He checked Lloyd's heart and his breathing. By the look on the young doctors face, things didn't look good.

"Mrs. Smith, it would be a good idea to bring in your family. I am so sorry, your husband could go any time now. All we can do at this point is keep him sedated and make him as comfortable as possible.

Is there anything at all that I can get for you? Would you like me to give you a mild sedative?"

"No thank you, Dr, Murray."

Carol stood beside Lloyd, holding his hand.

"I love you so much, Lloyd...please don't leave me."

Carol looked at the heart monitor, it read that his heart rate was down to forty one, it was getting lower.

Carol phoned her dad to tell him what had happened.

"Hello dad."

"Hi pumpkin, how yea doin' there kiddo?"

"Dad ... I got some bad news."

"What is it pumpkin, tell me?" Jason asked in a state of urgency.

"It's Lloyd, dad," Carol dropped the phone and broke down. She just couldn't do it.

"Hello Mr. Crawford, this is Garry ... "

"What the heck is going on there Garry?" Jason hollered.

"Mr. Crawford! Carol's quite upset. I don't want to get you all upset, but I think that it would best if you come down to the hospital as soon as you can. Lloyd was brought in by ambulance, and is in pretty bad shape."

"What happened, is he going to be okay?"

"Carol is in pretty rough shape, she needs you Mr. Crawford, she's very upset right now."

"Okay Garry, I'll be right there."

"Your dad's on his way sweetheart."

As they walked back to the room, it was too late, Lloyd had past away.

Carol leaned over and wrapped her arms around her lifeless husband.

"Why did you have to go...why?" She cried out hysterically.

CHAPTER TWENTY EIGHT

Garry tried to comfort Carol, she pounded her fists into his chest, Jason was also crying deeply. They could see Doctor Burns as he opened the door, he could see the three of them crying, he closed the door and let them grieve in private.

"What am I going to do with out him, what am I going to do?" Carol yelled out.

"It's my fault, it's my fault isn't it? I knew that he wasn't himself in the last little while. I should have brought him to the hospital as soon as I noticed he wasn't himself, instead, I ran away from him, it's my fault!"

"No Carol, it's not your fault. You couldn't have known what was happening to him. He had to have this tumor for over a year, possibly two years or even longer. This kind of tumor takes a long time before it gets to be this size. Please don't blame your self."

She felt little comfort from Garry's words, she still felt so guilty, she was convinced that there was something that she could have done to prevent all of this.

Jason sat quietly, his hands shaking, he was taking it very hard. Garry held his hand and compassionately rubbed his shoulder trying to ease his pain.

CHAPTER TWENTY NINE

A couple of hours had passed since Lloyd's passing. Jason, Jean, and Garry were sitting at the kitchen table, totally mesmerized and enlightened as they listened to Carol talk about all the good times that her and Lloyd had together. They smiled, but with tears in their eyes.

After Garry had left, and her mother had gone to bed, Jason lead his daughter into the living room where a beautiful bouquet of red roses sat on the coffee table with a heart shaped balloon in it that read 'I love you'.

"Pumpkin ... this was delivered just after you left here yesterday."

Carol held her breath, she just knew that it was from Lloyd. She pulled out the card, looked deeply into her fathers eyes, then opened it. It read: "I'm so sorry darling for what I have done. I love you so much and I never would want to lose you. I miss you so much, please forgive me and come home. Love Lloyd."

She held the card to her heart looked up and whispered, "I love you too sweetheart."

"You okay pumpkin?"

"Yes I fine dad," she replied, very choked up.

"Aren't they so beautiful dad?"

"Yes, they are beautiful, pumpkin, and so are you."

CHAPTER THIRTY

"I'm so sorry Carol." Wanda conveyed her sympathies as she hugged Carol. It was obvious that Wanda was uncomfortable, not being able to look Carol in her eyes.

"Thank you for coming Wanda."

About twenty people had attended the funeral, Carol was surprised about how many of her co-workers from the hospital had come to pay their respects. Matt Clark and a few unknown friends of Lloyd's had also attended.

Reverend Jacob Bishop made a very brief eulogy, then Jason took his place to say a few words.

"I would like to thank each and everyone of you for coming and paying your last respects to Lloyd Walter Smith. We had the pleasure of having Lloyd come into our lives, there wasn't too much love in his life. He wasn't much older than a child since he had last seen his parents. We really don't know much about his family, even if he still has any. But when Lloyd came into our lives, he brought so much love into all of our hearts. He not only was a wonderful son in law, but he was a dear friend. Lloyd was a person who wasn't afraid to show his affections and he always showed that he did care and love everyone who ever came into his life. In the last little while, Lloyd had been going through a very difficult time, which he had absolutely no control or recollection of." Jason took out his hankie and wiped the tears from his eyes. He took a couple of deep breaths to try and regain his composure. With his hands shaking, he continued:

"Why do we as people, once we see the bad in a person, we choose to forget all the good in them? "Lloyd was a wonderful loving man, but we all refused to see that side of him. Once we presumed to see him as a violent man we all stood in judgment him. Was he a vicious and violent man? No, he wasn't, but that's what we all perceived him to be, including ... myself, which I feel so ashamed.. I hope that each and everyone of us will learn from this, and I ask you all, when you think of Lloyd, remember him as the man he really was, a loving, kind and a very caring man. Lloyd and my wonderful daughter has suffered so much from all of our ignorance and our unjustified judgments.

So please ... remember Lloyd as the man he really was. Thank you. God bless you Lloyd, and may God bless you all."

CHAPTER THIRTY ONE

Carol sold the cottage, and moved back in to her parents house. She needed to be with her parents as much as they needed her.

Carol quit her job at the Westwood General Hospital and was hired at the Saint Joseph's Hospital just outside of Cedar Rapids. She was hired as a head nurse in the E.R.

Carol went to Dr. Howell's office for a complete physical. He put Carol on anxiety and anti depression medication. Dr. Howell sternly gave Carol a talk about her not accepting the diagnoses of her having bipolar disorder, also known as manic depression, a mood disorder. Once Carol started taking the medication and accepted the fact that she did have a mood disorder. It was a totally different life for her. She was so happy go lucky, and the best thing was...no more tears.

Her parents and Garry was so proud of her. She was just like a new woman, she had her zest for life back again.

Would you like to see your manuscript become a book?

If you are interested in becoming a PublishAmerica author, please submit your manuscript for possible publication to us at:

mybook@publishamerica.com

You may also mail in your manuscript to:

**PublishAmerica
PO Box 151
Frederick, MD 21705**

www.publishamerica.com